H... ...ng swallowtail ... ...ght silk evening breeches that between them left very little of the ... well-muscled form to ... imagination.

Julia glanced casually around the room and managed to register, in profile, tanned skin, an arrogant nose, a very decided chin and long dark lashes which were presently lowered either in deep thought or terminal boredom.

The knot of apprehension which had been lodged uncomfortably in the pit of her stomach all evening tightened. *I know you.* Which was impossible: she could not have forgotten this man. *I know you from my dreams.* He shifted, restless, as though he felt her scrutiny, and then, before she had the chance to move away, he turned his head and stared right into her face. And he was studying her with eyes that were the amber of a hunting cat's, the deep, peaty gold at the bottom of a brandy glass.

They were the eyes she had last seen burning with scarce-suppressed frustration in the face of a dying man. The eyes of her husband.

AUTHOR NOTE

Researching family history is a fascinating hobby, but it does give a sometimes shocking insight into how our ancestors lived. Following my ancestors' stories has often given me ideas for plots. The severity of punishments for crime and the often arbitrary court system in the Georgian period—a housemaid hanged for stealing a silver spoon that was later found to have fallen down the side of a chair, for example—made me wonder how an innocent person might react under threat of arrest, and was one strand in the making of this story.

The other strand was the poor level of medical knowledge at the time—doctors are thought to have killed more patients than they cured. And so I found I had a hero and a heroine who are both desperate, snatching at a marriage of convenience as a solution to their problems and never expecting it to last longer than one night.

But what if it did? What if Julia Prior and Will Hadfield found themselves very much alive and very much married—and effectively strangers? I hope you enjoy discovering the outcome as much as I did writing their story.

FROM RUIN
TO RICHES

Louise Allen

Published in Great Britain 2014
by Mills & Boon, an imprint of Harlequin (UK) Limited,
Eton House, 18-24 Paradise Road, Richmond, Surrey, TW9 1SR

© 2014 Melanie Hilton

ISBN: 978 0 263 90931 9

Harlequin (UK) Limited's policy is to use papers that are natural, renewable and recyclable products and made from wood grown in sustainable forests. The logging and manufacturing processes conform to the legal environmental regulations of the country of origin.

Printed and bound in Spain
by Blackprint CPI, Barcelona

Louise Allen has been immersing herself in history, real and fictional, for as long as she can remember. She finds landscapes and places evoke powerful images of the past—Venice, Burgundy and the Greek islands are favourite atmospheric destinations. Louise lives on the North Norfolk coast, where she shares the cottage they have renovated with her husband. She spends her spare time gardening, researching family history or travelling in the UK and abroad in search of inspiration. Please visit Louise's website—www.louiseallenregency.co.uk—for the latest news, or find her on Twitter @LouiseRegency and on Facebook.

Previous novels by the same author:

THE DANGEROUS MR RYDER*
THE OUTRAGEOUS LADY FELSHAM*
THE SHOCKING LORD STANDON*
THE DISGRACEFUL MR RAVENHURST*
THE NOTORIOUS MR HURST*
THE PIRATICAL MISS RAVENHURST*
PRACTICAL WIDOW TO PASSIONATE MISTRESS**
VICAR'S DAUGHTER TO VISCOUNT'S LADY**
INNOCENT COURTESAN TO ADVENTURER'S BRIDE**
RAVISHED BY THE RAKE†
SEDUCED BY THE SCOUNDREL†
MARRIED TO A STRANGER†
FORBIDDEN JEWEL OF INDIA††
TARNISHED AMONGST THE TON††

Those Scandalous Ravenhursts
**The Transformation of the Shelley Sisters*
†*Danger & Desire*
††*Linked by character*

and as a Mills & Boon® special release:

REGENCY RUMOURS

and in the *Silk & Scandal* mini-series:

THE LORD AND THE WAYWARD LADY
THE OFFICER AND THE PROPER LADY

and in Mills & Boon® Historical *Undone!* eBooks:

DISROBED AND DISHONOURED
AUCTIONED VIRGIN TO SEDUCED BRIDE**

Did you know that some of these novels are also available as eBooks? Visit www.millsandboon.co.uk

To Dr Joanna Cannon for her invaluable advice
and insights into Will's illness.

Louise Allen has been immersing herself in history, real and fictional, for as long as she can remember. She finds landscapes and places evoke powerful images of the past—Venice, Burgundy and the Greek islands are favourite atmospheric destinations. Louise lives on the North Norfolk coast, where she shares the cottage they have renovated with her husband. She spends her spare time gardening, researching family history or travelling in the UK and abroad in search of inspiration. Please visit Louise's website—www.louiseallenregency.co.uk—for the latest news, or find her on Twitter @LouiseRegency and on Facebook.

Previous novels by the same author:

THE DANGEROUS MR RYDER*
THE OUTRAGEOUS LADY FELSHAM*
THE SHOCKING LORD STANDON*
THE DISGRACEFUL MR RAVENHURST*
THE NOTORIOUS MR HURST*
THE PIRATICAL MISS RAVENHURST*
PRACTICAL WIDOW TO PASSIONATE MISTRESS**
VICAR'S DAUGHTER TO VISCOUNT'S LADY**
INNOCENT COURTESAN TO ADVENTURER'S BRIDE**
RAVISHED BY THE RAKE†
SEDUCED BY THE SCOUNDREL†
MARRIED TO A STRANGER†
FORBIDDEN JEWEL OF INDIA††
TARNISHED AMONGST THE TON††

Those Scandalous Ravenhursts
***The Transformation of the Shelley Sisters*
†*Danger & Desire*
††*Linked by character*

and as a Mills & Boon® special release:

REGENCY RUMOURS

and in the *Silk & Scandal* mini-series:

THE LORD AND THE WAYWARD LADY
THE OFFICER AND THE PROPER LADY

and in Mills & Boon® Historical *Undone!* eBooks:

DISROBED AND DISHONOURED
AUCTIONED VIRGIN TO SEDUCED BRIDE**

Did you know that some of these novels are also available as eBooks? Visit www.millsandboon.co.uk

To Dr Joanna Cannon for her invaluable advice
and insights into Will's illness.

Chapter One

16th June, 1814—Queen's Head Inn, Oxfordshire

He was all power and masculine arrogance with the candlelight dancing on those long, naked limbs as he stood and poured ruby-red wine into the glass and tossed it back in one long swallow.

To be in his arms, in this unfamiliar bed, had not been what she had imagined it would be. Less tender than she had hoped, more painful than she had expected. But then, she had been very ignorant and she would be more realistic next time. Julia snuggled back into the warm hollow his body had made.

'Jonathan?' He would come back now,

hold her in his arms, kiss her, talk more of their plans and all the uncertainties would vanish. On that headlong drive from Wiltshire he had ridden beside the chaise almost all the way and dinner in the public room below had not been the place to discuss their new life together.

'Julia?' He sounded abstracted. 'You can wash there.' He jerked his head towards the screen in the corner and poured himself another glass, his back still to her.

Unease trickled through the warmth. Was Jonathan disappointed in her? Perhaps he was simply tired, she certainly was. Julia slid from the tangled sheets, pulled one of them around her and padded over to the screen that concealed the washstand.

Making love was an embarrassingly sticky process, another small shock in an evening of revelations. That would teach her to think like a lovesick girl. It was about time she went back to being an adult woman making a rational decision to take control of her own life, she thought with a wry smile for her own romantic daydreams. This was real life and she was with the man she loved, the man who loved her enough to brave scandal and snatch her away from her relatives.

The screen overlapped one edge of the window and she reached to twitch the curtain completely over the panes of exposed glass before she dropped the sheet.

'London Flier!' There was the blare of a horn below, too dramatic to ignore. Julia looked through the gap as, wheels rumbling, the stagecoach pulled out of the arch from the stable yard and turned right. In a second it was gone. *Strange. Now why do I think that strange?*

She was too tired to puzzle over odd fancies. Julia washed, draped the sheet more becomingly and came out from behind the screen, unexpected butterflies dancing in her stomach. Jonathan was half-dressed now, seated staring into the empty grate, the stem of his wine glass twisting between his fingers. His shirt lay open, revealing the muscular flat planes of his chest, the dark arrow of hair that disappeared into his breeches... Her eyes followed it and she felt herself blush.

How cold it was away from the heat of his body. Julia poured wine and curled into the battered old armchair opposite his. Jonathan must be thinking of the next morning, of the long road north to the Scottish border and their marriage. Perhaps he feared pursuit, but she doubted Cousin Arthur would trouble himself with her whereabouts. Cousin Jane would screech and flap about and moan about the scandal, but she would be more concerned about the loss of her drudge than anything else.

The wine was poor stuff, tart and thin, but it helped bring things into focus of a kind. It was as though her brain had taken a holiday these past days and she had become nothing but an air-headed girl in love instead of the practical woman she really was.

You are *in love. And you've thrown your cap over the windmill with a vengeance*, the inner voice that was presumably her conscience informed her. *Yes, but that does not mean I have to be a useless ninny*, she argued back. *I must think how to be of help.*

The jolting, high-speed ride across country had been straightforward enough once Jonathan had explained why they were not going directly north to Gloucester and the road to the Border. Cutting north-east to Oxford and then going north would confuse pursuit and the road, once they got there, was better. They had turned on to the Maidenhead-Oxford turnpike about ten miles back, but apparently Oxford inns were wildly expensive, so this one, out of town, was the prudent option for their first night.

She would look after the money now, budget carefully, save Jonathan the worry of sorting out the bills, at least. *North to the border. To Gretna. How romantic.*

The north. That was what was wrong. The wine slopped from her glass staining the sheet like blood. The stage was going to London and it had turned right, the direction they had been heading when they arrived here.

'Jonathan.'

'Yes?' He looked up. Those long-lashed blue eyes that always made her heart flutter were as unreadable as ever.

'Why were we driving south for ten miles before we got here?'

His expression hardened. 'Because that's the way to London.' He put down the glass and stood up. 'Come back to bed.'

'But we are not going to London. We are going to Gretna, to be married.' She drew two painful breaths as he did not reply and the truth dawned. 'We were never going to Scotland, were we?'

Jonathan shrugged, but did not trouble

himself with denials. 'You wouldn't have come if you'd known otherwise, would you?'

How could the world change in one beat of the heart? She thought she had been chilled before, but it was nothing to this. It was impossible to misunderstand him. 'You do not love me and you do not intend to marry me.' There was nothing wrong with her thought processes now.

'Correct.' He smiled, his lovely slow, sleepy smile. 'You were such a nuisance to your relatives, clinging on, insisting on staying.'

'But the Grange is my home!'

'*Was* your home,' he corrected. 'Since your father died it belongs to your cousin. You're an expense and no one's fool enough to marry a managing, gawky, blue-stocking female like you with no dowry. So…'

'So Arthur thought a scandalous elopement with Jane's black sheep of a third cousin would take me off his hands for good.' Yes, it was very clear now. *And I have slept with you.*

'Exactly. I always thought you intelligent, Julia. You were just a trifle slow on the uptake this time.'

How could he look the same, sound the

same, and yet be so utterly different from the man she had thought she loved? 'And they made you seem a misunderstood outcast so that I felt nothing but sympathy for you.' The scheme was as plain as if it was plotted out on paper in front of her. 'I would never have credited Arthur with so much cunning.' The chill congealed into ice, deep in her stomach. 'And just what do you intend to do now?'

'With you, my love?' Yes, there it was, now she knew to look for it: just a glimpse of the wolf looking out from those blue eyes. Cruel, amused. 'You can come with me, I've no objection. You're not much good in bed, but I suppose I could teach you some tricks.'

'Become your mistress?' *Over my dead body.*

'For a month or two if you're good. We're going to London—you'll soon find something, or someone, there. Now come back to bed and show me you're worth keeping.' Jonathan stood up, reached for her hand and pulled her to her feet.

'No!' Julia dragged back. His fingers cut into her wrist, she could feel the thin bones bending.

'You're a slut now,' he said, 'so stop protesting. Come and make the best of it. You never know, you might learn to enjoy it.'

'I said *no*.' He was a liar, a deceiver, but surely he would not be violent?

It seemed she was wrong about that, too. 'You do what I say.' The pain in her wrist was sickening as she resisted.

Her feet skidded on the old polished boards, the hearth rug rucked up and she stumbled, off balance. There was an agonising jolt in her arm as she fell, then Jonathan's grip opened and she was free. Sobbing with pain and fear and anger Julia landed with a crash in the grate. The fire irons clattered around her, striking elbow and hand in a landslide of hard little blows.

'Get up, you clumsy bitch.' Jonathan reached out to seize her, caught her hair, twisted and pulled. It was impossible to roll away. Julia hit out wildly to slap at him and connected with a blow that jarred her arm back. With a gasp Jonathan released her. *Get up, run...* She rolled free, hit the foot of the bed, dragged herself up on to shaking legs.

Silence. Jonathan sprawled across the hearth, his head in a crimson pool. Her hand was wet. Julia looked down at her fingers, rigid around the poker. Blood stained her hand, dripped from the iron.

Blood. So much blood. She dropped the poker and it rolled to come to rest against his bare foot. *Not my dead body—his. Oh, God, what have I done?*

Chapter Two

Midsummer's Eve, 1814—
King's Acre Estate, Oxfordshire

The nightingale stopped her. How long had she been running? Four days…five? She had lost count… Her feet took her up the curve of the ornamental bridge, beyond pain now, the blisters just part of the general misery, and, as she reached the top the liquid beauty poured itself into the moonlight.

Peace. No people, no noise, no fear of pursuit. Simply the moon on the still water of the lake, the dark masses of woodland, the little brown bird creating magic on the warm night air.

Julia pulled off her bonnet and turned

slowly around. Where was she now? How far had she come? Too late now to regret not staying to face the music, to try to explain that it had been an accident, self-defence.

How had she escaped? She still wasn't sure. She remembered screaming, screaming as she backed away from the horror at her feet. When people burst into the room she'd retreated behind the screen to hide her near-nudity, hide from the blood. They didn't seem to notice her as they gathered round the body.

And there behind the screen were her clothes and water. She had washed her hands and dressed so that when she stepped out to face them she would be decent. Somehow, that had seemed important. She'd had no idea of trying to run away from what she had done so unwittingly.

Jonathan's pocketbook lay on top of his coat. It must have been blind instinct that made her stuff it into her reticule. Then, when she had made herself come out and face the inevitable, the room was packed and people were jostling in the doorway trying to see inside.

No one paid any regard to the young woman in the plain grey cloak and straw bonnet. Had anyone even glimpsed her when they burst in? Perhaps she had reached the screen before the door opened. Now she must have appeared to be just another onlooker, a guest attracted by the noise, white-faced and trembling because of what she had seen.

The instinct to flee, the cunning of the hunted animal, sent her down the back stairs, into the yard to hide amidst the sacks loaded on a farm cart. As dawn broke she had slipped unseen from the back of it into the midst of utterly unfamiliar countryside. And it felt as though she had been walking and hiding and stealing rides ever since.

If she could just sit for a while and absorb this peace, this blissful lack of people to lie to, to hide from. If she could just forget the fear for a few moments until she found a little strength to carry on.

The tall column of grey shimmered, moon-lit, in the centre of the narrow stone bridge. Long dark hair lifted and stirred in the night breeze: a woman. *Impossible.* Now he was seeing things.

Will strained every sense. Silence. And then the night was pierced again by the three long-held notes that signalled the start of the nightingale's torrent of languid music, so beautiful, so painful, that he closed his eyes.

When he opened them again he expected to find himself alone. But the figure was still there. A very persistent hallucination then. As he watched, it turned, its face a pale oval. *A ghost?* Ridiculous to feel that superstitious shudder when he was edging so close to the spirit world himself. *I do not believe in ghosts. I refuse to.* Things were bad enough without fearing that he would come back to haunt this place himself, forced to watch its disintegration in Henry's careless, spendthrift hands.

No, it was a real woman of course, a flesh-and-blood woman, the paleness of her face thrown into strong relief by the dark hair that crowned her uncovered head. Will moved into the deeper shadows that bordered the Lake Walk and eased closer. What was she doing, this trespasser far into the parkland that surrounded King's Acre? She must be almost a mile from the back road that led to the turnpike between Thame and Aylesbury.

Her long grey cloak swung back from her shoulders and he saw that she was tall. She leaned over the parapet of the bridge, staring down as though the dark waters beneath held some secret. Everything in the way she moved spoke of weariness, he thought, then stiffened as she shifted to hitch one hip on to the edge of the stonework.

'No!' Cursing his uncooperative, traitorous body, Will forced his legs to move, stumbled to the foot of the bridge and clutched the finial at the end of the balustrade. 'No... don't jump! Don't give up...whatever it is...' His legs gave way and he fell to his knees, coughing.

For a moment he thought he had so startled her that she would jump, then the ghost-woman slid down from the parapet and ran to kneel at his side.

'Sir, you are hurt!'

Her arm went around his shoulders and she caught him against herself in a firm embrace. Will closed his eyes for a moment. The temptation to surrender to the simple comfort of a human touch was almost too much.

'Not hurt. Sick. Not contagious,' he added as she gave a little gasp. 'Don't...worry.'

'I am not worried for myself,' she said with a briskness that bordered on impatience. She shifted her position so he fell back on her shoulder and then laid a cool palm on his forehead. Will bit back a sigh of pure pleasure. 'You have a fever.'

'Always do, this time of night.' He fought to control his breathing. 'I feared you were about to jump.'

'Oh, no.' He felt the vehement shake of her head. 'I cannot imagine ever being desperate enough to do that. Drowning must be such a terror. Besides, there is always some hope. Always.' Her voice was low and slightly husky, as if she had perhaps been weeping recently, but he sensed that it would always be mellow, despite its certainty. 'I was resting, looking at the moonlight on the water. It is beautiful and calm and the nightingale was singing so exquisitely. I felt some need for calm and beauty,' she added, with a brave attempt at a rueful laugh that cracked badly.

Something was wrong. He could feel the tension and the exhaustion coming off her in waves. If he was not careful, she would bolt. Or perhaps not, she seemed determined to look after him. As if he was dealing with a wounded animal he made himself relax and follow her lead. 'That is why I come down here when the moon is full,' he confessed. 'And Midsummer's Eve adds a certain enchantment. You could believe almost anything in the moonlight.' *Believe that I am whole again...* 'I thought you a ghost at first sight.'

'Oh, no,' she repeated, this time with a faint edge of genuine amusement that appeared to surprise her. 'I am far too solid for a ghost.'

Every fibre in his body, a body that he believed had given up its interest in the opposite sex long months ago, stirred in protest. She felt wonderful: soft and curved and yet firm where she still held him cradled against her shoulder. He managed not to grumble in protest as she released him and got to her feet.

'What am I thinking about, lingering here talking of ghosts and nightingales? I must get help for you. Which direction would be quickest?'

'No need. House is just—' His breath gave out and Will waved a hand in the general direction. 'If you can help me up.' It was humiliating to have to ask, but he had learned to hide the damage to his pride after long months discovering the hard way that fighting got him nowhere. She needed help, but he couldn't give it to her sprawled here.

'Stay there, then. I will go and get help.'

'No.' He could still command when he had to: she turned back to him with obvious reluctance, but she turned. Will held up his right hand. 'If you will just steady me.'

She wanted to argue, he could sense it, but she closed her lips tight—he fantasised that they were lush, framing a wide, generous mouth, although he could not be certain in that light—and took his hand in a capable grip.

'I suppose,' she said, as he got to his feet, 'that you would say you are old enough to know what is good for you, but I have to tell you plainly, sir, that wandering about in the moonlight when you have a fever is the height of foolishness. You will catch your death.'

'Do not concern yourself.' Will got a grip on the stone ledge and made himself stand steady and straight. She was tall, his ghost-lady, she only had to tilt her head back a little to look him in the face. Now he could see the frown on a countenance that the moonlight had bleached into ivory and shadow. He could not judge her age or see detail but, yes, her mouth was generous and curved, although just now it was pursed with disapproval. It seemed she liked being argued with as little as he did. 'I have caught my death already.'

He saw her take his meaning immediately and waited for the protests and the embarrassment that people invariably displayed when he told them the truth. But she simply said, 'I am so very sorry.' Of course, she would be able to see in the moonlight just what a wreck he was, so perhaps it was no surprise to her. It was a miracle that the appearance of a walking skeleton had not frightened her into the lake. 'I am trespassing on your land, I assume. I am sorry for that also.'

'You are welcome. Welcome to King's Acre. Will you accompany me back to the house and take some refreshment? Then I will have my coachman drive you onwards to wherever you are staying.' She bit her lip and her gaze slid away from his. It seemed he was not as harmless in her eyes as he felt. 'There will be whatever chaperonage you might require, I assure you. I have a most respectable housekeeper.'

His reassurances provoked a smile, as well they might, he supposed. He was deluding himself if he thought she had taken him for his regiment's most dangerous ladies' man, as his reputation had once been. Even the most nervous damsel would need only one glance to realise that the possibility of him ravishing them was slight.

'Sir, the question of chaperonage is the least of my concerns at the moment.' There was a bitter undertone to her voice that made no sense. 'But I cannot trouble you and your household at this time of night.'

His breathing had steadied and with it, Will realised, his wits. Respectable young ladies—and his companion was certainly a lady, if not a very young one—did not materialise in the moonlight *sans* baggage or escort without good reason.

'The hour is of no consequence—my staff are used to my penchant for late nights. But your luggage, ma'am? And your maid? I shall have someone fetch them to you.'

'I have neither, sir.' She turned her head away and the effort to steady her voice was palpable. 'I am…somewhat adrift.'

She could not tell him the truth, Julia knew that, although the temptation to simply burst into tears, throw herself into the arms of this elderly man and pour out her story was shockingly strong. He was probably a magistrate and, even if he was not, he would be duty-bound to hand her over to the law. But she had been tramping across country, hiding in barns, spending a few coppers here and there on bread and cheese and thin ale, and she was exhausted, lost and desperate. Something of the truth would have to suffice and she must take the risk that she would prove to be a good liar.

'I will be frank with you, sir,' Julia said, grateful for the protection of the shadows. She wished she could see his eyes. 'I ran away from home. Several days ago.'

'May I ask why?' His voice, strangely young for one advanced in years, was as studiously non-judgemental as his haggard face.

'My cousin, on whom I am totally dependent, schemed to give me to a man who wanted only my...undoing. Running seemed the only way out, although I am just as effectively ruined as a result, I realise that now. I am sure you would not wish to entertain me under the circumstances. Your wife—'

'I do not have one,' he said, his voice cool. 'And I have no objection, only a regret on your behalf, ma'am, that you find yourself in such a predicament.'

He should not be talking. Julia had no doubt that he meant exactly what he said about his health: the man was desperately ill. His body when she had supported it had felt like bones and sinew contained in skin and expensive superfine. He was tall, over six foot, and in his youth must have been well muscled and powerful. Now his breathing was ragged and his forehead under her palm had been damp with fever.

He had come to her aid when he thought she was going to cast herself into the lake and he had not insulted her when she told him a little of her disastrous misjudgement. Now the very least she could do was to assist him home and risk the slight chance that the description of a wanted murderess had reached them here. Surely she was safe for a night? The authorities could not know her name and Jonathan's card case was with his pocketbook in her reticule—the local constable would have a nameless body to deal with, as well as a nameless fugitive.

This was no time to be scrupulous about accepting help. 'Come, sir. If you will not allow me to go for assistance, at least take my arm. I am certain you should not be out here tiring yourself.'

'You sound remarkably like Jervis, my valet,' the man said with an edge of asperity. For a moment she thought stubborn pride would win out over common sense, but then he let her put her forearm under his and take a little of his weight.

'This way, I think you said, sir?' She made her sore feet move, trying not to limp in case he noticed and refused her help.

'My name is William Hadfield,' he said after a few steps. 'Just so you know whom you are rescuing. Baron Dereham.'

She did not know the name, but then she was adrift more than a hundred miles from home and her family, although gentry, did not mix with titled society. 'My name is—'

'There is no need to tell me.' He was breathing hard. Julia slowed her pace a little, glad of the excuse to do so. She was tired and sore and almost more exhausted by fear than from physical exertion.

'It is no matter, my lord. I am Julia Prior. *Miss,*' she added bleakly. Live or die, she was never going to be anything else now. And then she realised that she had given her real name. *Foolish,* she chided herself. But it was too late now and it was common enough.

'Left here, Miss Prior.' Obedient, she took the path he indicated. To her consternation the ground began to slope upwards. How was

Lord Dereham going to manage this with only her feeble help? As if he read her mind he said, 'Here is the cavalry, you need not carry me any further.'

Julia opened her mouth to protest that she was merely steadying him, then shut it again. There was enough edge in his voice for her to know the baron was not resigned to his condition and would bitterly resent any attempt to jolly him along. He must have been arrogant and self-assured in his prime, she concluded, to resent his decline so fiercely now.

'My lord!' Two men hurried down the slope from where a gig stood waiting. One, when he got closer, could have been identified as a valet at a glance: neat, dapper and immaculate, he was making clucking sounds under his breath. The other, in boots and frieze coat, was just as obviously a groom.

'Jervis, help this lady into the gig.' Her arm was released and Julia found herself being ushered into the humble vehicle as if she was a duchess and it a state coach. Behind, she could hear a low-voiced exchange that ended abruptly with a snapped command from the baron as he took the seat opposite her.

The groom went to the horse's head and

led it on, the valet followed on foot. After a few minutes passed in silence they emerged on to a great sweep of lawn and then crunched across a gravelled drive.

'But it is a castle!' Startled out of her circling thoughts, Julia blinked up at crenellations, a turret, arrow slits, all preposterously Gothic and romantic in the silvery light.

'A very small one, I assure you. And disappointingly modern inside to anyone of a romantic nature. The moat is dry, the cellars full of wine bottles. The portcullis has long since rusted through and we rarely pour boiling oil on to anyone these days.' He sounded as though he regretted that.

'Fetch Mrs Morley to Miss Prior,' Lord Dereham ordered as the groom helped her to descend. Her legs, she discovered as she stumbled, were almost too tired to support her. 'Tell her to place the Chinese bedchamber at Miss Prior's disposal and then have Cook send up a hot supper to the library.'

'But, my lord, it must be midnight at least—' He should not be worrying about feeding her at this hour, let alone housing her.

'I will not have you wandering about the countryside or going to bed hungry, Miss

Prior,' he said as he climbed down, leaning on the groom in his turn. Here under the bulk of the building it was almost dark and she could not see his face at all, only judge his mood by the autocratic orders. 'You will oblige me by spending the night and tomorrow we can see what may be done.'

He will not have it, indeed! A forceful old gentleman, the baron, whatever his health, Julia decided. *But it is rather beyond his powers to find a solution to this problem. A new dawn will not make matters any better.*

'Thank you, my lord. I should not trouble you, I know, but I will not deny that your offer is most welcome.' She had thought she could never trust another man, not after Jonathan. But the baron was advanced in years and could be no threat to her. Or her to him, provided he had no idea who he was sheltering.

'I will see you in the library then, Miss Prior, when you are ready,' he said behind her as she followed the valet into the hall.

'Just down the main stairs and the door to the left, Miss Prior.' The housekeeper stood aside as Julia murmured a word of thanks and left the warmth and comfort of the bed-chamber for the shadowy panelled corridor.

The woman had shown no surprise at the state of her travel-worn clothes, although she had tutted in sympathy over the state of Julia's feet and had produced copious hot water, linen for dressings and salves. Now, clad in some borrowed undergarments beneath her brushed and sponged walking dress, Julia felt a new surge of courage. She had heard that prisoners were more easily broken if they were kept dirty and unkempt and now she could well believe it. She had felt her strength and will ebb along with her self-respect.

The house had been decorated a few years ago, she judged as she negotiated the broad sweep of an old oak staircase. All was in good repair with an intriguing glimpse of ancient baronial castle here and there beneath the modern comfort. Yet there was an impersonal air about it as though efficient staff kept it running, but the driving force behind it, the spirit that made it a home, had vanished.

It had happened at the Grange after her father had died and she had not had the strength to simply carry on as before. It had only lasted a few weeks, then she had made herself take up the reins again. Pride, and the refusal to let her cousin and his wife find the slightest thing to criticise when they came to claim their inheritance, had dried her tears and stiffened her will. Here, with the master dying, the staff were obviously doing the best they could, which argued loyalty and efficiency.

The heavy panelled door swung open on to a room that was all warmth: a fire in the grate despite the season, crimson damask curtains at the windows, the soft glow of old waxed bookshelves. The man in the chair beside the hearth began to get to his feet as she came in and the hound at his feet sprang up, her teeth bared as she ranged herself in front of her master.

'Down, Bess! Friend.'

'My lord, please—there is no need to stand.' Julia took three hasty steps across the carpet, dodged around the dog and caught the baron's arm to press him back into the seat. She found herself breast to breast with him, the light from the fire and the candelabra on the side table full on his face.

This was the man from the lakeside? The man she had held in her arms, the one she thought elderly and harmless? 'Oh!' She found herself transfixed by amber eyes, the eyes of a predator, and blurted out the first thing that came into her head. 'How old are you?'

Chapter Three

Lord Dereham sat down as she released his arm. His breathless laugh was wicked. 'I am twenty-seven, Miss Prior.'

'I cannot apologise enough.' Cheeks burning with mortification, Julia took a hasty step backwards, tripped over the dog and found herself sprawling into the chair opposite his. 'I am so sorry, I have no idea why I should blurt out such a impertinent question, only—'

'Only you thought I was an old man?' Lord Dereham did not appear offended. Perhaps in his currently restricted life the sight of a lady—*female*, she reminded herself—behaving with such appalling gaucheness and lack of elegance was entertainment enough to distract him from her outrageous lack of manners.

'Yes,' she confessed and found she could not look him in the face. *Those eyes.* And he might be thin and ill, but he was unmistakably, disturbingly, male for all that. She bent to offer an apologetic caress to the elderly hound who was sitting virtually on her feet, staring at her with a reproachful brown gaze.

'Miss Prior.' She made herself lift her eyes. 'You are quite safe with me, you know.'

Her head agreed with him. Every feminine instinct she possessed, did not. 'Of course, I realise that. Absolutely,' Julia said, in haste to reassure herself. Her voice trailed away as she heard her own tactless words and saw his face tighten.

He had been a handsome man once. He was striking still, but now the skin was stretched over bones that were the only strong thing left to him, except his will-power. And that, she sensed, was prodigious. His hair was dark, dulled with ill health, but not yet touched with grey. He had high cheekbones, a strong jaw, broad forehead. But his eyes were what held her, full of life and passionate, furious anger at the fate that had reduced him to this. Were they brandy-coloured or was it dark amber?

Julia could feel she was blushing as they narrowed, focused on her face. 'I mean, I know I am safe because you are a gentleman.' Safe from another assault, not safe from the long arm of the law. Not safe from the gallows.

She sat up straight, took a steadying breath and looked fixedly at his left ear. Such a nice, safe part of the male anatomy. 'You are being remarkably patient with me, my lord. I am not usually so…inept.'

'I imagine you are not usually exhausted, distressed and fearful, nor suffering the emotional effects of betrayal by those who should have protected you, Miss Prior. I hope you will feel a little better when you have had something to eat.' He reached out a thin white hand and tugged the bell pull. The door opened almost immediately to admit a pair of footmen. Small tables were placed in front of them, laden trays set down, wine was poured, napkins shaken out and draped and then, as rapidly as they had entered, the men left.

'You have a very efficient staff, my lord.' The aroma of chicken broth curled up to caress her nostrils. Ambrosia. Julia picked up her spoon and made herself sip delicately at it instead of lifting the bowl and draining it as her empty stomach demanded.

'Indeed.' He had not touched the cutlery in front of him.

She finished the soup along with the warm buttered roll and the delicate slices of chicken that had been poached in the broth. When she looked at Lord Dereham he had broken his roll and was eating, perhaps a quarter of it, before he pushed the plate away.

'And a very good cook.'

He answered her concern, not her words. 'I have no appetite.'

'How long?' she ventured. 'How long have you been sick like this?'

'Seven—no, it is eight months now,' he answered her quite readily, those remarkable amber eyes turned to watch the leaping flames. Perhaps it was a relief to talk to someone who spoke frankly and did not hedge about pretending there was nothing wrong with him. 'There was a blizzard at night and Bess here was lost in it. One of the young underkeepers thought it was his fault and went out to look for her. By the time we realised he was missing and I found them both we were all three in a pretty poor state.'

He grimaced, dismissing what she guessed

must have been an appalling search. And he had gone out himself, she noted, not left it to his keepers and grooms to risk themselves for a youth and a dog. 'After four years in the army I thought I was immune to cold and wet, but I came down with what seemed simply pneumonia. I started to cough blood. Then, although the infection seemed to go, I was still exhausted. It became worse. Now I can't sleep, my strength is failing. I have no appetite, and there are night-fevers. The doctors say it is phthisis and that there is no cure.'

'That is consumption, is it not?' As he had said, a death sentence. 'I expect the doctors think saying it in Greek makes them seem more knowledgeable. Or perhaps it justifies a higher bill.'

'You have no great love of the medical profession?'

How elegant his hands were with the long bones and tendons. The heavy signet on his left ring finger was so loose that the seal had slipped round. 'No,' Julia admitted. 'I have not. No great faith, would perhaps be truer.' The doctors had done little enough for Papa, for all their certainties.

'You seem to understand that speaking

about problems is a relief after everyone pretending there is nothing wrong.' He looked
away from the fire and into her eyes and for
a moment she thought the flames still danced
in that intent gaze.

Jonathan's beautiful blue gaze was always
impenetrable, as though it was stained glass
she was looking at. This man's eyes were
windows into his soul and a very unpleasant place it seemed to be, she thought with
a shiver at her Gothic imaginings.

'Would it help to confide your story in a
total stranger? One who will take it to—'
He broke off. 'One who will respect your
confidence.'

Take it to the grave. He was no priest
bound to silence, she could hardly confess
to her actions and expect him to keep the
secret, but perhaps talking would help her
find some solution to the problem of what
she could possibly do now.

'My father was a gentleman farmer,' Julia
began. She sat back in the chair and found
she could at least begin as though she was
telling a story from a book. The hound circled on the hearth rug, sighed and lay down
with her head on her master's foot as if she,
too, was settling to listen to the tale. 'My

mother died when I was fifteen and I have no brothers or sisters, so I became my father's companion: I think he forgot most of the time that I was a girl. I learned everything he could teach me about the estate, the farm, even purchasing stock and selling produce.

'Then, four years ago, he suffered a stroke. At first there was talk of employing a steward, but Papa realised that I could do the job just as well—and that I loved the place in a way that an employee never would. So I took over. I thought there was no reason why we could not go on like that for years, but last spring he died, quite suddenly in his sleep, and my Cousin Arthur inherited.'

She would not cry, she had got past that. Just as long as the baron did not try to sympathise: she could not cope with sympathy. Instead he said, 'And there was no young man to carry you off?'

'I had been too busy being a farmer to flirt with young men.' He had seen, and heard, enough of her now to understand the other reasons no-one had come courting. She was hardly a beauty. She was too tall. And too assertive, too outspoken. *Unladylike hoyden*,

Cousin Jane called her. *A managing, gawky blue-stocking female with no dowry,* that was what Jonathan had flung at her. He was obviously correct about her lack of attraction—it was quite clear in retrospect that she had been a complete failure in his bed.

'My cousins allowed me to stay because I had nowhere else to go, but it was unsuitable for me to take any interest in the estate, they said, and besides, they made it very clear that it was no longer any of my business. Cousin Jane found me useful as a companion,' she added, hearing the flatness in her own voice. *A drudge, a dogsbody, the poor relation kept under their roof to make them appear charitable.*

'But then it changed?'

'They must have grown tired of supporting me, I suppose. Of the cost, however modest, and tired too of my interference in estate matters. There was a man—I think they intended to make it worth his while to take me off their hands. He did not offer marriage.'

A squalid story, Will thought as Miss Prior ran out of words. Those lips, made for smiles, were tight, and she had coloured painfully. It was unwise of her to flee her home, but the alternative seemed appalling and few unprotected young women would have had the resolution to act as she had done. 'You ran away, eventually found yourself in my parkland and the rest we know,' he finished for her.

'Yes.' She sat up straight in the chair as if perfect deportment could somehow restore her to respectability.

'What is their name? Someone needs to deal with your cousin. Even if he had not been in a position of trust, his behaviour was outrageous.'

'No! Not violence…' He saw her bite her lip at the muttered curse that escaped him. She had gone quite pale.

'No, of course not. You need have no fear that I might call him out. I forget sometimes that my fighting days are over.' *Damn.* And he hadn't meant to say that, either. Self-pity was the devil. 'I am not without influence. It would be my pleasure to make his life hell in other ways than by threatening him at swordpoint. Is his name Prior? Where is your home?'

She shook her head in silent refusal to confide. Will studied the composed, withdrawn, face in the firelight. He had never met a woman like her. Even in this state she seemed to have the self-possession of someone older, an established matron, not a girl of perhaps twenty-two or three.

In the candlelight her skin was not fashionably pale, but lightly coloured by the sun. Her hands, clasped loosely in her lap, were like her whole body—strong and graceful with the physical confidence that came from fitness and exercise. She moved, her cuff pulled back and he saw bruises on her wrist, black and purple and ugly. That a woman should be under his protection and yet he could not avenge such treatment was shameful. No, she must not go back to that, he could do that for her at least.

'I hope your father did not know that his heir would wilfully ignore the expertise you could have shared with him,' he said at last when a log broke in the grate, sending up a shower of sparks and jerking him back from his bitter reverie. 'I know all too well the character of my own heir, my cousin Henry. He'll squander away the lifeblood of the estate within a year or two—that's all it took him to lose what was not tied down of his own inheritance.'

'You are estranged from him?' Miss Prior's face was expressive when she allowed it to be. Now the little frown between the strongly marked dark brows showed concern. She was too tall, no beauty. One would almost say she was plain, except for the regularity of her features and the clarity of her gaze. And the generous curve of lips that hinted at a sensuality she was probably unaware of.

Will felt a *frisson* of awareness run through him, just as he had when she had held him in her arms on the bridge, and cursed mentally. He did not need something else to torture him and certainly not for his body to decide it was interested in women again. If he could not make love with the stamina and finesse that had caused his name to be whispered admiringly amongst certain ladies, then he was not going to settle for second best.

A wife, he had realised, was out of the question. He had known he must release Caroline from their betrothal, but it had shocked him, a little, how eagerly she had snatched at the offer amidst tearful protestations that she was not strong enough to witness his suffering. She was a mass of sensibility and high-strung nerves and he had found her delicate beauty, her total reliance on his masculine strength, charming enough to have talked himself half into love with her. To have expected strength of will, and the courage to face a husband's lingering death, was to have expected too much.

Miss Prior was waiting patiently for him to answer her question, he realised. Will jerked his wandering thoughts back. 'Estranged? No, Henry's all right deep down. He's not vicious, just very immature and spoilt rotten by his mama. If he wasn't about to inherit this estate I'd watch his antics with interested amusement. As it is, I'd do just about anything to stop him getting his hands on it for a few years until he grows up and learns to take some responsibility.'

'But you cannot afford to do that, of course.' Miss Prior had relaxed back into the deep wing chair. Another five minutes and she would be yawning. He was selfish to keep her here talking when she should be asleep, but the comfort of company and the release of talking to this total stranger was too much to resist.

'No. I cannot.' *I cannot save the only thing*

left to me that I can love, the only thing that needs me. My entire world. There must be a way. In the army before he had inherited, and in the time he had been master of King's Acre, he had relied both on physical prowess and his intellect to deal with problems. Now he had only his brain. Will tugged the bell pull. 'Go to bed, Miss Prior. Things will look better in the morning.'

'Will they?' She got to her feet as the footman came in.

'Sometimes they do.' It was important to believe that. Important to believe that he would think of something to get King's Acre out of this coil, important to hope that the doctors were wrong and that he had more time. If he could only *make* time, stretch it…

'Goodnight, my lord.' She did not respond to his assertion and he rather thought there was pity in those grey eyes as she smiled and followed James out of the room.

The ghost of an idea stirred as he watched the straight back, heard the pleasant, assured manner with which she spoke to the footman before the door closed. A competent, intelligent, brave lady. Will let his head fall back, closed his eyes and followed the

vague thought. Stretch time? Perhaps there
was a way after all. Unless he was simply
giving himself false hope.

Do things look better in the morning light?
Julia sat up in the big bed, curled her arms
around her raised knees and watched the
sunlight on the tree tops through the bay
window that dominated the bedchamber.

Perhaps she should count her blessings.
*One: I am warm, dry and comfortable in a
safe place and not waking up in another dis-
reputable inn or under a hedge. Two: I am
not in a prison cell awaiting my trial for mur-
dering a man.* Because Jonathan was dead,
he had to be. There was so much blood. So
much... And when people had come, pouring into the room as her screams had faded
into sobs, that was what they were all shouting. *Murder!*

And now she was a fugitive, her guilt
surely confirmed by her flight. Julia scrubbed
her hands over her face as if that would rub
out the memories *Be positive. If you give up,
you are lost...* Was there anything else to be
thankful for?

Try as she might, there were no other
blessings she could come up with. It was

dangerous to try to think more than a few days into the future because that was when the panic started again. She had spent an entire morning huddled in a barn because the fear had been so strong that she could not think.

One step at a time. She must leave here, so that was the next thing to deal with. Perhaps Lord Dereham's housekeeper could recommend a nearby house where she might seek work. She could sew and clean, manage a stillroom and a dairy—perhaps things were not so very bad after all, if she could find respectable employment and hide in plain sight. No one noticed servants.

The baron came into the breakfast room as she was addressing a plate laden with fragrant bacon and the freshest of eggs. Her appetite had not suffered, another blessing perhaps, for she would need strength of body as well as of mind. *A mercy that I possess both.*

'My lord, good morning.' Lord Dereham looked thin and pale in the bright daylight and yet there was something different from last night. The frustration in the shadowed amber eyes was gone, replaced with something very like excitement. Now she could imagine him as he had been, a ruthless physical force to be reckoned with. A man and not an invalid.

'Miss Prior.' He sat and the footman placed a plate in front of him and poured coffee. 'Did you sleep well?'

'Very well, thank you, my lord.' Julia buttered her toast and watched him from under her lashes. He was actually eating some of the scrambled eggs set before him, although with the air of a man forced to swallow unpleasant medicine for his own good.

'Excellent. I will be driving around the estate this morning. You would care to accompany me, I believe.'

It sounded remarkably like a very polite order. He was, in a quiet way, an extremely forceful man. Julia decided she was in no position to take exception to that, not when she needed his help, but she could not spare the time for a tour. 'Thank you, I am sure that would be most interesting, but I cannot presume further on your hospitality. I was wondering if your housekeeper could suggest any household or inn where I might find employment.'

'I am certain we can find you eligible

employment, Miss Prior. We will discuss it
when we get back.'

'I am most grateful, of course, my lord,
but—'

'Is your Home Farm largely arable?' he
asked as if she had not spoken. 'Or do you
keep livestock?'

What? But years of training in polite conversation made her answer. 'Both, although
cattle were a particular interest of my father.
We have a good longhorn herd, but when
he died we had just bought a shorthorn bull
from the Comet line, which cost us dear. He
has been worth it, or, at least he would be if
my cousin only chose the best lines to breed
to him.' Why on earth did Lord Dereham
want to discuss animal husbandry over the
coffee pots? 'May I pass you the toast?'

'Thank you, no. I am thinking of planting
elms on my field boundaries. Do you have a
view on that, Miss Prior?'

Miss Prior certainly had a view on the
subject and had left a promising nursery of
elm saplings behind her, but she was beginning to wonder if the absence of a Lady
Dereham was due to his lordship's obsession
with agriculture and an inability to converse
on any other topic. 'I believe them to be very

suitable for that purpose. Marmalade and a scone, my lord?'

He shook his head as he tossed his napkin on to the table and gestured to the footman to pull back his chair. 'If you have finished your breakfast we can begin.'

Can we indeed! Was the man unhinged in some way? Had his illness produced an agricultural mania? And yet he had shown no sign of it last night. As she emerged into the hall she saw the maid who had helped her dress that morning was at the foot of the stairs, holding her cloak, and a phaeton waited at the front steps with a pair of matched bays in the shafts. Her consent had been taken for granted, it seemed.

Julia closed her lips tight on a protest. Without Lord Dereham's help she was back where she had been the night before. With it, she had some hope of safety and of earning her living respectably. It seemed she had no choice but to humour him and to ignore the small voice in her head that was telling her she was losing control and walking into something she did not understand.

'I am at your disposal, my lord,' she said politely as she tied her bonnet ribbons.

'I do hope so, Miss Prior,' Lord Dereham

said with a smile that was so charming that for a moment she did not notice just how strange his choice of words was.

Chapter Four

Were his words strange, or sinister? Or quite harmless and she was simply losing her nerve and her sense of proportion? Lord Dereham handed her up to her seat in the phaeton and then walked round and took the reins. The groom stepped back and the baron turned the pair down the long drive. They looked both high-bred and fresh. A more immediate worry overtook her concerns about his motives. Could he control them?

After a few minutes of tense observation it appeared that skill was what mattered. As Julia watched the thin hands, light and confident on the reins, she released her surreptitious grip on the side of the seat and managed not to exhale too loudly.

'The day I cannot manage to drive a phaeton and pair I shall take to my bed and not bother to rise again, Miss Prior,' he remarked, his voice dry.

How embarrassing, he must have sensed her tension and probably showing a lack of confidence in a man's ability to drive was almost as bad as casting aspersions on his virility. And, safe as he was in his weakened condition, she had a strong suspicion that Lord Dereham's prowess in the bedroom had probably been at least equal to his ability as a whip. The thought sent a little arrow of awareness through her, a warning that Lord Dereham was still a charismatic man and she was in danger of becoming too reliant on his help.

She repressed a shudder at the direction of her thoughts: she was never going to have to endure a man's attentions in bed again. *Another blessing.*

'Cleveland bays?' she asked. Best not to apologise. Or to speculate on the man beside her as anything but a gentleman offering her aid. Or think about that inn bedroom, not if she wanted to stay calm and in control.

'Yes, they are. They were bred here. Now, Miss Prior, what do you think I should do about this row of tenants' cottages?' He reined in just before they reached a range of shabby thatched cottages. 'Repair them or rebuild over there where the ground is more level, but there is less room for their gardens?'

'Why not ask the tenants?' Julia enquired tartly, her temper fraying along with the dream-like quality their conversation was beginning to assume. 'They have to live in them.' Really, she was extremely grateful to Lord Dereham for rescuing her, but anyone would think she was being interviewed for the post of estate manager!

He gave a grunt of agreement that sounded suspiciously like a chuckle. Julia bristled as he drove past the cottages with a wave of the whip to the women hanging out sheets and feeding chickens. Was he making fun of her because she claimed to have run her family estate? He had been polite enough about it last night, but most men would find her interest in the subject laughable, if not downright unfeminine.

'I also have views on poultry, the management of dairies, sawmills and crop rotation,' she said with false sweetness. 'I know a little about sheep, but more about pigeons, pigs and the modern design of farm buildings, if those are of any interest to you, my lord.'

Again that scarcely repressed chuckle. 'They are, but I think I had better explain myself before you lose all patience with me, Miss Prior. Would you care to look at the view from the temple over there?'

They had been climbing a low hill and the temple was revealed as a small folly in the classical style overlooking the lake. Julia closed her eyes and took a steadying breath. If she was not so tense and, under the surface, so scared, she would be able to cope with this perfectly adequately. Perhaps he was simply gauche and had no idea how to make conversation, although there had been no sign of that last night.

She mentally smoothed her ruffled feathers and replied with dinner-party graciousness, 'I am sure it will be a delightful prospect, my lord. And you have no need to explain yourself to me. I must apologise if my nerves are a little…'

'Frayed?' he enquired as he brought the pair to a standstill and climbed down. Julia sat tactfully still while he tied the reins to a post and came round to hand her from her seat. 'Well, I hope I may ravel them up again, a little. I have a proposition for you, Miss Prior.'

Proposition. That was a word with connotations and not all of them good. She closed her teeth on her lower lip to control the questions that wanted to tumble out, took his arm and allowed herself to be guided towards the curved marble seat at the front of the folly. She could at least behave like a lady for today—this was surely the last time a gentleman would offer her his arm. And if he proved not to be a gentleman?

When they were seated side by side Lord Dereham crossed one leg over the other, leaned back and contemplated the view with maddening calm.

Julia attempted ladylike repose at his side, but all that relaxation did was to allow the waking nightmares back into her head. 'My lord? You said you had a proposition? You have thought of some post I might apply for, perhaps?'

'Oh no, not…exactly. You, I believe, are in need of some time to recover from your precipitate flight, to rest physically and to collect yourself mentally.'

'Yes,' she agreed, wary. 'That would be an agreeable luxury, I must admit.'

'And I would appreciate the company of someone who is knowledgeable about estate management. I have ideas I would like to talk through. If you would accept my hospitality for, let us say, a week, it would give you breathing space and allow me to think of some respectable employment I might suggest.'

The baron did not look at her as he spoke and she studied his profile as she considered, trying to imagine him with the weight back that he had lost, with colour in that lean, hard face and a gloss on that thick hair. He had been a very attractive man and his character still was. He might have autocratic tendencies, but he seemed understanding, intelligent and his actions, right from the start, had been gentlemanly and protective.

She would be in no danger from this man, she knew. But was it safe to stay, even for a few days? *Safer than wandering around with no plan and no money*, Julia told herself. 'Thank you, my lord. I would appreciate that and I will do my utmost to assist you.'

'Excellent. Shall we begin by being on rather less formal terms? My name is Will, I would like you to use it. May I call you Julia?'

In for a penny, in for a pound... 'Yes,' she said. 'I would like that. Can you not discuss your thoughts with your...I mean, the man who will...' Goodness, it was hard to think of a tactful way of saying, *The man who will take over when you die.*

'My heir, you mean?' His lips curled into a sardonic smile. 'Cousin Henry Hadfield. He has no interest in the land. He wasted his inheritance from his father on enjoying himself in town until his mother finally reined him in. Not a bad youth at heart—but if I were to talk to him about elm tress and field boundaries he would think me all about in the head.'

'Most people would, frankly, if they aren't practical landowners.' Julia got up and strolled a little way so she could look down on the lake lying below to her right and the edge of the park with the ploughlands beyond to the left. 'You have some long boundaries there. From all I have read elm grows fast and the roots go straight down and do not steal goodness from the crops or interfere with the plough. You raise a timber crop and waste no land. I have... I had started a nursery of cuttings from a neighbour's trees.'

'There's some land that might do for that,' Will said. 'Shall we drive on and have a look?'

They spent all morning driving around the estate and Julia gradually relaxed in Will's company. They did not agree about everything, but that, she supposed, was only to be expected and the mood was amiable as they finally returned to the house.

'I will take luncheon in my chamber, if you will excuse me. Then I have paperwork to see to in the library.' Will surrendered his coat and hat to the butler. 'Please feel free to explore the house as you wish. Or the pleasure grounds.'

It was a little like a fairy tale, Julia decided as she strolled through a rose garden. She had fled from evil and found herself in some enchanted place where the outside world did not intrude and everything conspired to make her comfortable and safe.

A gardener materialised at her side with knife and basket and asked which blooms she would like cutting for her chamber.

'Oh, I had better not,' she demurred.

'Lord Dereham sent me.' The man glanced

towards the house and Julia saw the silhouette of a man watching her from one of the long windows. The baron in his study, she assumed.

'Then thank you,' she said and buried her face in the trusses of soft fragrance.

At dinner she mentioned the roses, but Will waved away her thanks with a gesture of his long fingers. 'They are there to be enjoyed. What do you think of the gardens?'

'They are lovely. And the vegetable gardens are quite the most wonderful I have ever seen. You even have a pinery—I confess to quite indecent envy!'

The mobile mouth twitched a little at that, but Will only said, 'I haven't succeeded in getting a single edible pineapple out of it yet.'

'More muck,' Julia said. 'I was reading all about it and you need a huge, steaming pile of manure, far more than you would think.' She caught the eye of the footman who was bringing in the roast and he looked so scandalised for a second that she stopped with a gasp. 'I am so sorry, of all the things to be discussing at the dinner table!'

But Will was laughing. It was the first time she had heard more than a chuckle from him—an infectious, deep, wholehearted laugh—and she found herself laughing, too, until he began to cough and had to sip water until he recovered.

The next day was overcast with a cool wind so they had gone to the stables in the morning and walked slowly from box to box, admiring the mares and then smiling over the yearlings and the foals in the paddocks. Will had let her take his arm as though he felt at ease enough not to hide the fact that anything more than a stroll was tiring.

Julia explored the house in the afternoon. She found an upstairs sitting room with bookshelves and a deep window seat and curled up with a pile of journals and some novels, but after a while she realised that she was simply staring out of the window.

This place was still a fairy tale, a sanctuary from the dark that she had left behind, a place out of time with its prince, struck down by a wicked enchanter, but still strong enough to defend its walls and keep her safe.

The whimsy made her smile until the chill of reality ran down her spine. It could not last and she should not delude herself. Soon she would have to leave here and find employment and never, ever, be herself again. She had a week, and two days of that were gone already.

At dinner Will was quiet, almost brooding. *Tired, perhaps,* she thought and did not attempt to make conversation. When the footman cleared the plates and set the decanter at his elbow she rose, but he gestured her back to her seat.

'Will you keep me company a little longer, Miss Prior?' Before the servants he was always meticulous in observing the proprieties, she noticed. 'Thank you.' He nodded to the footman. 'I will ring if we need anything further.'

When they were alone Will said, without preamble, 'I have a proposal, Julia.'

'Another one?' Her heart sank for all her light words. He had changed his mind about the week's respite, found her some position as a housemaid...

'That was a proposition. This is literally a proposal.' He poured two glasses of port and pushed one across the table to her.

Bemused, she ignored the wine and studied his face instead. From the intensity in his expression she realised his calm was not quite as complete as she had thought. His voice, however, was quite steady as he said, 'Will you do me the honour of becoming my wife?'

Julia found she was on her feet, although she could not remember getting up. 'Your *wife*? Lord Dereham, I can only assume you are mocking me, or that your fever has become much worse.'

She walked away from the table on legs that shook and struggled for composure. It was safer for her self-control not to be looking at him. One could not be rude to an invalid as sick as he was, but how could he not realise how hurtful his teasing was?

'Miss Prior, I cannot talk to you if you stalk around the room,' Will drawled. The weak desire to cry turned into an itch in her palm and a disgraceful urge to slap his face. 'Please will you come back here so I can explain? I am not delirious and I have no intention of offering you insult.'

'Very well.' It was ungracious and she could not bring herself to return to the table, but she turned and looked at him, swallowing hurt pride along with the unshed tears. 'Please explain, if you can. I find my sense of humour has suffered somewhat recently.'

But he was not smiling. The haggard face was as serious as if he truly was making a proposal of marriage, but his words were strangely far from the point. 'You know what I have told you about Henry. For the good of this estate and its people I need to prevent my cousin from inheriting until he is older, has matured and learned to control his spendthrift ways.'

'You believe he can?' Julia asked, diverted by scepticism for a moment.

'I think so. Henry is neither wicked nor weak, simply spoiled and indulged. Even if he does not improve, the longer I can keep him from inheriting, the better. I need time, Julia.'

'And you do not have that.' Intrigued, despite herself, she sat again.

'Do you know the law about inheritance when someone disappears?' She shook her head. 'If the missing person does not reappear within seven years of their disappearance, the heir may apply to the courts for them to be presumed dead and for the inheritance to proceed.'

She began to understand. 'And you intend to disappear?'

'I intend to travel. I have always wanted

to go to North Africa, Egypt, the Middle East. I hope I can make it that far, because once there, away from British authorities, I can vanish without trace when…when the time comes.'

Julia doubted he would make it across the Channel, never mind southern Europe, but if this daydream was keeping him going, who was she to disillusion him? She understood the power of dreams, the need for them. 'But what has that got to do with me?'

'I must leave King's Acre in good hands. I could employ an estate manager, but they would not have the commitment, the involvement, that a wife would have. I could not guarantee continuity and, if they left, who would appoint their replacement? And by marrying before I go I would remove the suspicion that my disappearance is a stratagem.'

Julia stared at the thin, intelligent face. His eyes burned with intensity, not with fever or madness. For a moment she thought she saw what Will Hadfield had looked like before this cruel illness had taken him in its claws and something inside her stirred in response. 'It matters this much to you?'

'It is all I have. Our family has held this land since the fourteenth century when it

was given to Sir Ralph Hadfield as a reward
for services to the crown—hence the name.
I am not going to be the one who lets King's
Acre fall apart.'

'And there is no woman you *want* to
marry?'

The baron closed his eyes, not to shut out
the world, but to hide his feelings, she was
certain. 'I was betrothed. I released her, of
course, and she was relieved, I think, to be
freed from the burden of being tied to a
dying man.'

Will opened his eyes and there was no
emotion to be seen on his face. Then he
smiled, an ironic twist of the lips. 'Besides,
she has no views on elm trees or cattle breed-
ing.'

'So you only thought up this insane
scheme when I stumbled into your life?' It
might be insane, but, Heaven help her, she
was beginning to contemplate it, look for the
problems and the advantages. *Stop it!* Julia
told herself. *It is an outrageous idea. I would
be heaping deception upon deception.*

'That first night, after you had retired, I sat
thinking that I needed a way to stretch time.
Then I realised I might have had the answer
sitting in front of me at my own fireside.'

The past days had been a test to see if she really knew as much as she said, to see if she had an attraction to this place. *And I have.* Then common sense surfaced. Fate would not rescue her so simply from the consequences of her own folly. 'Your relatives will never accept it.'

Besides, with the wedding her name would be known to all and sundry… *But Prior is quite common and Julia is not my first name. Lord Dereham seems to live fairly retired, this would not be a major society wedding to be mentioned in the newssheets. If I can ask him not to place an announcement, there is no reason to think it would ever be noticed in Wiltshire.*

'My relatives will have no choice but to accept it. I am of age, no one can suggest I am not in my right mind. They will be present at the wedding—along with my man of law and any number of respectable witnesses. You will not be dependent upon them in any way. Only the land is entailed, so the income will be yours to spend as you wish until my death is finally pronounced. Then you will have the use of the Dower House for life and a very generous annuity in my will.'

'You would give me all this? I am ruined,

an outcast from the only relatives I have. I have no material resources to bring to the marriage—not a penny in dowry.'

Arthur and Jane will not seek for me, they will simply be glad I am gone, she told herself. Would they even hear of Jonathan's death? He was a distant relative, she had left no identification in the inn. Perhaps they would think he had simply disappeared along with the money they had no doubt paid him to remove her.

'I am not *giving* you anything.' The amber eyes were predatory as they narrowed on her face. He knew she was weakening as a hunter knew when the prey began to falter. Again the sense of his power swept over her, the feeling that she could not resist him. 'I am purchasing your expertise and your silence.'

'People will talk, wonder where on earth I have come from. What will we tell them?'

'Nothing.' He had heard the capitulation in her voice, she realised, and he was right: she would do this if she could, snatch at this miracle. All that remained were the practicalities. Julia took an unthinking gulp of wine. 'Think of some story—or let them speculate to their hearts' content on where we met.

'There is little time to waste. I had asked you to stay a week, but I have seen enough, I know you will be perfect for this. Fortunately the Archbishop of Canterbury is in the vicinity—he is staying with his godson, the Marquess of Tranton. I can obtain a special licence with no trouble and we will be married the day after tomorrow.' He stood up. 'Say yes and I will drive over tomorrow and see the vicar on the way back.'

Say yes, *say* yes *and accept this miracle.* What should she do?

Chapter Five

'Will!' Julia came round the table and caught at his sleeve. 'It is impossible, I cannot marry you at such short notice.'

'Why ever not?' He put his hand over hers and she looked up into his eyes. There was only that mesmerising amber gaze full of passion and intensity, only the warmth of his hand, those long fingers closing over hers. Julia felt hot and cold and as disconcerted as the first time Jonathan had kissed her. This was a man, a young man, a man of passion, and something deep inside her responded to him.

She felt her lips part, her heartbeat stutter, then the grip of his fingers lifted and the illusion of intimacy fled.

'Had you some other plans for the day after tomorrow?' Will persisted.

Safe, protective irritation took the place of whatever insane emotions she had just been experiencing. *The man is completely focused on what he wants without a thought for me. It is a very good thing he is going away,* Julia thought, *otherwise we would be falling out for certain.*

'I haven't said *yes* yet,' she protested. He just looked at her. 'Oh, very well! Yes! But I do not have a thing to wear.' His eyebrows shot up. 'Except this.' She swept a hand down to encompass her skirts. 'I can hardly marry a baron in a creased, stained walking dress and old cloak.'

'Then go shopping tomorrow. I will give you money. There are no shops of very great fashion in Aylesbury, not even for ready to wear, but you will find something adequate and you can always go up to London shortly. Just hire a town house, if you wish, Julia.'

She had a sudden, welcome, thought. 'Everyone calls me Julia, but for the licence you must have my first name. Augusta.' She saw his face and almost laughed. 'I know. It was the name of my mother's godmother and they were in hopes of some generous present from her. No one ever uses it—in fact, I doubt anyone recalls it now.' Even if they saw any mention of the marriage in some newssheet, no one would think that Augusta Prior, making an excellent match to a baron in Buckinghamshire, might be Julia Prior of Wiltshire, fugitive.

'But what of your cousin?' she worried. 'I cannot help but feel we are cheating him.'

'If I had married as planned, I could have an heir due shortly and Henry's nose would be permanently out of joint. Or if I had not been caught in that blizzard I might be in excellent health now. What we are doing is ensuring that when he does inherit he will have an estate in fine heart and, I trust, the maturity to appreciate it.'

Julia prodded herself with the thing that was troubling her conscience, deep down below the worry and the fear. 'And I am being rewarded for sin,' she muttered as she sat down again. She had eloped with a man, slept with him out of wedlock and then, however unintentionally, killed him. She could not absolve herself from blame—if she had not done that first shocking thing, then Jonathan would still be alive.

'Sin?' Will Hadfield must have ears like

a bat. 'Running away to save your virtue? And fleeing from physical abuse—I saw your wrist.'

Her fingers closed protectively around the yellowing bruises. *Eyes like a hawk as well.* 'It was poor judgement,' she argued. 'I had no plan other than escape. Goodness knows how I would have found a respectable way of supporting myself.' She had to remember the story she had told him, act in character. 'I should have thought of something else, something less shocking.'

After a moment she added, 'All you know of me is what I told you. I wonder that you trust me with this scheme of yours.'

'But *my* judgement, my dear Miss Prior, is excellent. I have watched you and listened to you. I have seen how you look at the land, how you talk to the people. I have heard how you think things through and deal with problems. I have every confidence in you—after all, once you are safely married to me, you will not be a target for predatory young men.'

He blithely ignored her sharp intake of breath and continued before she could reply. 'Will you go shopping tomorrow? I will send a maid with you and a footman for your parcels, and Thomas the coachman will deliver you to the Rose and Crown where you will find a private parlour and reasonable refreshments.'

'Thank you, I shall do as you advise. It seems you have thought of everything,' she added, managing with an effort not to allow her ungrateful resentment at his masterful organisation to show in her voice. It would serve him right if the archbishop refused to give him a licence and he found himself saddled with a fallen woman with a price on her head and a very large pile of bills.

And then her conscience pricked her. Will Hadfield was doing this because he was driven to it, he had been kind to her and now he was helping her out of danger in a way that was little short of a miracle. She wished she had known him before he had become ill, wished she could know him better now.

Or perhaps not. Even ill he was dangerously attractive. She did not want to grow to like him, to be hurt when he left, to agonise more than she would over the fate of any chance-met stranger.

'You have known my nephew for how long, exactly? I do not think I quite caught what dear William said.' Mrs Delia Hadfield had doubtless heard perfectly well everything that had been said to her and her façade of vague sweetness did not deceive Julia for a moment. The widow, she was certain, was aghast that her husband's nephew had married and was consumed with a desire to discover everything she could about the circumstances.

Julia saw that Will was seated on the far side of the room, deep in conversation with the vicar. She could hardly expect him to rush to her side to rescue her. 'It seems only days,' Julia parried with an equally sweet smile and sipped her champagne. 'But it was something we simply felt compelled to do.'

'And we had thought him so happy in his engagement to Caroline Fletcher. Of course that could never be once he was so ill, but I had no idea dear William would prove so fickle. Such a *suitable* girl. So beautiful.' The widow's smile hardened and her eyes narrowed. *She thinks she is sliding her rapier under my guard.*

People were watching them, Julia could feel their curious stares like a touch. The salon was a long room, but even with the windows open wide on to the terrace overlooking the dry moat it was crowded with the wedding guests that Will had managed to assemble at such very short notice. She dared not let any of her true feelings show, but the recollection of the last time she had been in a press of people was making her heart beat faster and her skin feel clammy.

She made herself breathe slowly and shallowly. These people laughing and talking were nothing like that avid crowd and no one looking at her would guess that the new Lady Dereham in her pretty gown and elegantly coiffed hair was a fugitive with a deadly secret.

'I thought I loved another, you see...' Julia let her voice trail off artistically. 'And then...' *Really, where did I get this ability to play-act! I have been reading too many novels. Desperation, I suppose.* 'Then we found each other again, when Will's betrothal had been ended and I had realised that there was no one else for me but him,' she finished. 'So romantic, is it not?'

'So William knew you some time ago?' Mrs Hadfield was intent on pursuing this mystery.

'I would rather not talk about the past,' Julia murmured, improvising frantically. Will had assured her no one would ask awkward questions. He might have been correct so far as he was concerned, for she was sure he could depress vulgar curiosity with one look, but she had been an idiot to take his word for it and not prepare a careful story.

'I was sadly disillusioned in the man I thought I loved and that made me see Lord Dereham's qualities in a different light.' Set against a scheming, mercenary rake who tried to force her, she was certain even Will's undoubted faults would be preferable.

'Lady Dereham—or may I call you Cousin Augusta?' With an inward sigh of relief she turned to Henry Hadfield, Will's cousin and heir. She could see the relationship in the height and the straight, dark brows and something about the way his mouth curved when he smiled, but there was no strength of character in the handsome, immature, face. She tried to imagine those features super-imposed on Will's strong bones and experi-enced a slight shock of…what? Attraction? Not desire, surely, not after what she had experienced.

The momentary feeling passed and she was able to concentrate again. It would not do to let her guard down with either of the Hadfields. Henry had not quite worked out what a threat to him she represented, but his mama would soon enlighten him.

'Why, Cousin, certainly. But Julia, please. I never use my first name.' She smiled. He was young and it was up to her to get to know Henry and to influence him if she could, instil in him a love for an estate she did not know and remain on good terms through seven long years of uncertainty.

The setting sun slanted in through the long windows, setting the silverware gleaming and painting a pink glow over the faces of the guests. Not that they needed much colouring, Julia thought. Will had not spared the champagne and cheeks were flushed and conversation still lively, although it was almost half past seven and the party had gathered to eat after the church service at noon.

'Friends.' Everyone turned. Will was standing in front of the cold hearth, a glass in his hand. Did everyone see how his knuckles whitened where his left hand gripped the mantelshelf, or was it only she who realised how tightly he was controlling himself?

The image of the statue of the dying Gaul that she had seen once as an engraving caught at her imagination. Will was still on his feet but only because of that same indomitable refusal to give up and die. What was it? she wondered. Pride? Anger partly, she was certain. Courage. He was fighting Death as though it was a person who had attacked his honour.

Her eyes blurred and she swallowed hard. If she had met him before he became sick… *He would have been betrothed to Caroline Fletcher,* she told herself with a sharp return to reality. And he would probably have been as dictatorial and single-minded as he was now.

'Firstly my wife and I must thank you for your support today at such short notice. Secondly, I must ask you for further support for Lady Dereham as I will be travelling abroad for some months and must leave immediately on the morrow.'

A babble of questions broke out and then the tall man who had come down from London to stand as groomsman, the friend from Will's army days, Major Frazer, said, *'Abroad?'*

'I intend to develop the stud here and I wish to purchase Andalusians from Spain and Arabians from North Africa.' The major said something in an undertone, but Will answered him in the same clear voice. 'My health? I am feeling much stronger. It is best that I go now while the weather holds. And finally, my friends, I must ask your indulgence if we retire so I can rest before the start of my journey.' He raised his glass, 'To my wife, Julia.'

'To Lady Dereham!'

Blushing, Julia made her way through the scarcely repressed whispers and speculation to Will's side. 'That has put the cat amongst the pigeons with a vengeance, my lord,' she murmured. 'I had no idea you intended to leave so abruptly.'

She saw with a pang of anxiety that the lines of strain around his eyes and mouth were even more pronounced than before. 'There is not a great deal of time to waste, is there?' he said with a wry smile. 'Come, let us go up.'

He was so determined. She felt sick at the thought of what he was going through, but there was nothing she could do to help him except what, for such selfish reasons, she was doing now.

People were considerate and did not detain them with more than a few words of good wishes. Julia made her way into the deserted hallway before she slid her hand from resting on Will's arm to a steadying pressure under his elbow. 'I will ring for your valet,' she said when they paused at the second turn.

'Jervis will be already waiting with your maid in our bedchamber.'

'*Our* chamber?'

'Certainly.' Julia looked up sharply and thought she caught just the faintest hint of a smile. 'In my state of health you surely do not expect me to be negotiating draughty corridors in the middle of the night in order to visit you?'

'Are you saying that you expect me to share your *bed* tonight?' It had never occurred to her for a moment that this marriage would be anything but one in name only. Surely a man in his state of health could not…could he? She stumbled on the next step with images, sensations, shuddering through her memory.

'Shh,' Will murmured as a door below opened and the noise of the dispersing guests filled the space. 'This is not the place to be discussing such matters.'

Julia swallowed, nodded and somehow managed the rest of the stairs without blurting out the protests that were on the tip of her tongue. When Will opened the door to the master bedchamber Nancy, the chambermaid, was waiting there, chatting to Jervis, filmy white garments draped over her arm and a wide smile on her lips. This was no place for that discussion, either. The servants had to believe this marriage was real as much as anyone.

'There you are, my lady! I've had hot water brought up to the dressing room for your bath and Mr Jervis will see to his lordship in here.' She swept Julia in front of her through another door into a small panelled room with a steaming tub standing ready.

'I've sprinkled that lovely nightgown with rosewater,' she went on chattily as Julia stood like a block to be undressed. She had indulged herself with a pretty summer nightgown and robe when she had shopped for her wedding clothes and the other wardrobe essentials in Aylesbury. What she had not expected was that anyone but herself and her maid would ever see them.

'Excellent,' she managed as she climbed into the bath and began to soap herself. From the other room came the sounds of conversation, the bang of a cupboard door closing, the rattle of curtain rings. Next door was a man, a virtual stranger, getting ready to go to bed and expecting her to join him. The last man with those expectations had played on every one of her love-filled fantasies, taken her virtue and then betrayed her.

This one, she reflected as she climbed out of the bath and was swathed in towels, had at least married her. But could a man in Will's state of health consummate a marriage? She had no idea how the mechanics of male desire actually worked, but the performance was certainly physically demanding. What if Will expected *her* to do something…? With Jonathan she had simply lain there, held him and tried to do what he wanted of her. It seemed from his words that she had not been very good at it. Julia pressed her hand to her midriff as if that would calm the rising panic.

Jervis bowed himself out. A moment later Nancy bustled from the dressing room with her arms full of towels, bobbed a curtsy in the direction of the bed and hurried after the valet. The outer door closed with a heavy thud, the inner one stood open on to an apparently empty room.

Will lay back against the heaped pillows and got his breathing under some sort of control. He was bone-weary, aching and the night fever was beginning to sweep through him, but he had to stay in sufficient control to cope with Julia who, it seemed, had not thought beyond the marriage ceremony. *She is a virgin,* he reminded himself.

'Are you still in there?' he enquired. 'Or have you climbed down the ivy to escape me?' There was a pause, then she appeared in the doorway in a gown of floating white lawn, her hair loose on her shoulders, her hands knotted before her. His breathing hitched. 'You are a white ghost tonight, not a grey one.' She was certainly pale enough to be a spirit.

Julia took one step into the chamber. Her feet were bare. For some reason that was both touching and disturbing. 'I had not realised that you would expect me to share your bed,' she said. Her chin was up.

'I am sharing my title, my home and my fortune with you,' Will pointed out, goaded by her obvious reluctance into tormenting her a little.

She went, if anything, paler. 'Of course. I have no wish to be difficult. It is simply that we had not discussed it.'

'True. I have to confess that I have no experience of virgins.'

'I am glad to hear it,' Julia said, with so much feeling that Will blinked. 'I mean, one would hope that a gentleman does not go around seducing virgins.' She bit her lip, then put back her shoulders, tossed her robe on to a chair and walked over to the bedside.

Will was powerfully reminded of pictures of Christian martyrs bravely facing the lions and felt a pang of conscience. For all her maturity and poise and her scandalous circumstances, Julia was an innocent and his own frustrations at his weakness were no reason to scare the poor girl. 'Perhaps I should make it clear that I do not expect you to do anything but sleep in this bed.'

'Oh.' Julia froze, one hand lifting the covers to turn them back. The colour seemed to ebb and flow under her skin and he wondered if she was about to faint. 'Truly?'

Her relief was palpable. Will told himself that he was a coxcomb to expect anything else: she scarcely knew him, he looked like a skeleton, he could hardly stand up half the time—why on earth would the poor woman *want* to make love with him? The very fact that she feared he might attempt it showed how innocent she was.

'Get into bed, I promise you are quite safe.'

Julia pushed back the covers, climbed in and sat upright against the pillows. A good eight inches of space and the thickness of his nightshirt and her gown separated their shoulders: it must be imagination that he could feel the heat of her skin against his. She smelled of roses and Castile soap and warm woman and her tension vibrated between them like a plucked harp string.

'It is important that no one can challenge this marriage,' he explained, more to keep talking until she relaxed than anything else. 'We have a licence from the Archbishop, we were married by the local vicar in the face of the largest congregation I could bring together and now both our houseguests and our servants will vouch for the fact that we spent the night in this room. If and when my aunt decides she is going to challenge your control of the estate, she will not be able to shake the legitimacy of this marriage or contest your position as my wife.'

'I see. Yes, I understand why it is necessary.'

It sounded as though Julia was having difficulty controlling her breathing. She was not the only one, Will thought with an inward grimace. The spirit was very willing indeed as far as he was concerned—but the flesh was certainly too weak to do anything to upset the composure of the warm, fragrant, softly rounded and very desirable female so close to him. She was not a beauty, but she was, he was uncomfortably aware, an attractive, vibrant woman.

'Go to sleep,' he suggested and reached out to snuff the candles.

'Goodnight,' she murmured and burrowed down under the covers.

Will willed himself to stillness as gradually her breathing slowed and he waited for sleep to take her. Then a small hand crept into his. He froze. After a moment Julia shifted, murmured something and, before he could react, she snuggled right up to his side, her cheek on the thin cotton of his nightshirt over his heart.

'Julia?' His heart pounded in his chest until he felt dizzy. Or perhaps it was simply the scent and the feel of her. Somehow Will managed not to put his arms around her and drag her tight against him

'I am sorry,' she said. 'I should have known I would be quite safe with you, that you are a gentleman. I do not want you to think I was unwilling because you are ill.' She wriggled and came up on her elbow. Before he realised what she was doing she bent her head. The kiss would have landed on his cheek—instead, as he turned his head, their lips met.

Soft warmth, the yielding curve of that lovely mouth he had been trying to ignore for days. The whisper of her breath between slightly parted lips, the hint of the taste of her—champagne, strawberries, woman.

Hell. The torture of this was going to kill him. He couldn't breathe, his heart would surely give out. He wanted to touch her, caress her, because he was suddenly acutely aware that this trusting sensuality *could* overcome his body's weakness.

But he had just given her his word. He pressed his lips lightly to hers and then murmured, 'Goodnight, Julia. Better that you sleep on your side of the bed or you will find me a very hot companion with this fever.'

'Is there anything I can do for you?' she asked. He could almost feel her blushes as she lay down a safe distance from him.

Yes, kiss me, touch me, let me make love to you. 'No, thank you.' Will closed his eyes and made himself lie still. It would be a long night.

* * *

Julia woke in the dawn light. Exhausted by fears and emotion and the strain of the wedding, she had slept as though drugged and Will had let her. 'Will?' Silence. As she turned something crackled on the empty bed beside her. The note when she unfolded it said simply,

Goodbye. I will write when I can. All the information and addresses you need are in my desk in the study. I have taken Bess with me. Good luck. Will.

A key slid out of the folds and fell into the creased hollow where he had lain beside her all night. She was alone. A widow in all but name.

Her fingers closed around the key as they had around his hand last night. Will Hadfield had given her her life back, as his was ending. He had not realised what a gift he was making her, what he had saved her from, but he had shown trust and confidence in her and that was balm to her bruised soul. She had tried, in sheer self-preservation, to feel nothing for him but a polite, remote concern, but she was aware that somehow the essence of the man had touched her heart.

'Oh, Will.' Julia curled up on his side of

the bed and buried her face in his pillow. Was it imagination, or did it still hold a faint warmth, a trace of the scent of his skin?

Chapter Six

Three years later, 21st June, 1817—
Assembly Rooms, Aylesbury,
Buckinghamshire

'Do try and look as if you are enjoying yourself, Julia!' Mrs Hadfield scolded in a whisper. 'Do you have a headache?'

'A little. I really do not think I should have agreed to come to this dance, Aunt Delia.' Julia eyed the noisy throng around them with misgiving as they made their way into the market town's Assembly Rooms. She tried to avoid any kind of large public gathering where she did not know everyone present. Even after three years she had nightmares of someone pointing an accusing finger at her, shouting *Murderess! Arrest her!* She made herself breathe slowly, shallowly, and focused on negotiating the steps up to the front doors. Usually the panic could be kept under control by such tactics.

It was a long time since she had attended a dance of any kind, let alone a public assembly, and she should have known she would regret not standing up to Aunt Delia's bossiness. She cast around for an explanation for her subdued spirits. 'Under the circumstances—'

The older woman bridled. 'The circumstances are that my nephew took off in a most ill-considered manner three years ago. The fact that you have not heard anything from him for almost eighteen months does not mean you should be behaving like a widow.' The words *not yet* hung unspoken between them

On the surface Mrs Hadfield had mellowed since her first resentment over Will's marriage, disappearance and the events that followed. After nine months, when she finally appeared to accept that Henry's position was unassailable and that Julia was not doing anything to damage his inheritance, she unbent towards the younger woman, although her tendency to patronise and to attempt to organise her niece by marriage grated on Julia's nerves.

But she suppressed her own forceful nature and worked hard to foster good relations between the households. She suspected that the other woman, foolish though she was in the way she indulged her son, was both a realist and also potentially a danger.

Julia knew that Delia had demanded that the vicar show her the licence and Nancy had confided indignantly that Mrs Hadfield had questioned her about where her mistress had slept on her wedding night.

'And did you tell her?' Julia asked.

'I did that! She asked me about the sheets, would you believe? I put her straight, interfering old besom,' the maid said darkly.

So, Julia reflected, the pain of jabbing a large sewing needle into her thumb and sacrificing a few drops of blood had been worthwhile.

Mrs Hadfield might have accepted the marriage, but she had a clear eye on the calendar, and had no doubt consulted her lawyer over the necessary action to take in 1821 in the absence of proof of Will's fate. She was intelligent enough to know that they must wait, even if she was probably crossing off the days in her almanac, and the fact that Julia made a point of consulting Henry upon every decision relating to the estate at least appeared to mollify her.

'I do not behave like a widow,' Julia protested now as they inched their way to the foot of the stairs, Henry protectively at their backs. 'I do not wear mourning.' She glanced down with some complacency at the skirt of her highly fashionable shell-pink evening gown with its daring glimpse of ankle and then the months when she had worn black, when her heart had seemed frozen with grief, came back to reproach her for her mild vanity.

She pushed away the memory of those months, of the child she had lost, and made herself focus on the present. 'I will not give up on Will until I absolutely have to.' And somehow that was true. A whimsical part of her mind had a fantasy of Will well and happy and living an exotic life as an eastern pasha although the letters, the straightforward letters sent via his lawyer saying where he was, had long since ceased. She had never written back for he made it quite plain he was constantly on the move and had nowhere to send the letters.

The fantasy Will was strong and handsome and responsible for some rather disturbing dreams about things that, in the cold light of day, she preferred not to contemplate.

'I go to dinner parties and hold them,' she went on, calmer now they were climbing the stairs and she had something to concentrate on. 'I attend picnics and soirées and musical evenings. It is just that this seems rather… boisterous.'

And exposed. And full of people she did not know, people from outside the small, safe circle of friends and acquaintances around King's Acre. Improbable though it was after three years that anyone would recognise a half-naked, distraught murderess in the fashionably gowned, utterly respectable, Lady Dereham.

'Boisterous? The young people may romp. I shall not regard it,' Mrs Hadfield observed. 'For myself I am just thankful to be out of the house now that wretched summer cold has left me. I confess I am starved of gossip and fashions, even provincial ones.'

A faint headache, irrational fears and a growing, inexplicable, sense of foreboding were no excuse to be churlish, Julia told herself. And the Assembly Room, when they finally managed to enter it, was certainly a fine sight with the chandeliers blazing and the ladies' gowns and jewels like a field of flowers in sunlight. She relaxed a trifle as Henry, on his best behaviour, found seats for the ladies and melted away into the crowd to find them lemonade.

'He wants me to agree to him going off to the Wilshires' house party next week,' his doting mama said. 'Which probably means there is a young lady he has his eye upon amongst the other guests.'

More likely some congenial company his own age and a tempting array of sporting pursuits, Julia thought cynically as one of Mrs Hadfield's bosom friends greeted her with delighted cries and bore down upon their alcove. Henry was maturing, but he was still not much in the petticoat line and far more likely to flee than flirt if confronted by a pretty girl.

'I will take a turn around the room, if you will excuse me, Aunt.' Mrs Hadfield, already embarked upon some prime character assassination, merely nodded.

Everyone was having a very good time.

So why could she not simply settle down and enjoy watching? Or even dance, if anyone asked her? The familiar crowd-induced panic was gone, but there was still this odd feeling of apprehension, of tension. Perhaps she was coming down with something. Not Aunt Delia's cold, she sincerely hoped.

Julia stopped by a pillar halfway down the room and fanned herself, amused by the chatter of a group of very young ladies who could only just have come out that Season.

'I do not know who he is, I have never seen him before,' one said as she peeped through the fronds of a palm. 'But have you ever seen such wonderful shoulders?'

'So manly,' another agreed with a sigh. 'And his hair—so romantic!'

Julia looked to see the paragon who had attracted their wide-eyed admiration. *Goodness.* There was no mistaking which man it was as he stood surveying the room with his back to them. Silly chits they might be, but they could recognise a fine figure of a man when they saw one. *That certainly is a magnificent pair of shoulders.* And his glossy brown hair was indeed romantically long.

The young ladies were far too bashful and shy to do more than giggle and swoon at a distance. Julia told herself that she was a matron and therefore perfectly at liberty to wander closer to inspect this threat to female susceptibilities.

She was not given to admiring gentlemen. She was a respectable lady with a reputation to maintain and the loss of her virginity had taught her that yearning after a handsome face was one thing—the reality of amorous men, quite another. Her body might disagree sometimes, her dreams conjure up fantasies, but, waking, she knew better. A solitary bed at night was a positive benefit of life as a grass widow, as she frequently reminded herself.

Even so, this man intrigued her for no reason she could put a finger on. She paused a few feet away from him, swept her fan languidly to and fro and studied him from the corner of her eye. This was easier when the heroine of a romantic tale did it, she realised, eyes watering. What she could tell, without blatantly staring, was that his valet and tailor had between them contrived to send him forth outfitted to constitute a menace to any woman who set eyes upon him.

He was clad in a close-fitting swallow-tail coat and skin-tight silk evening breeches that between them left very little of the gentleman's well-muscled form to the imagination. Julia glanced casually around the room and managed to register, in profile, tanned skin, an arrogant nose, a very decided chin and long dark lashes which were presently lowered in either deep thought or terminal boredom.

The knot of apprehension that had been lodged uncomfortably in the pit of her stomach all evening tightened. *I know you.* Which was impossible: she could not have forgotten this man. *I know you from my dreams.* He shifted, restless, as though he felt her scrutiny and then, before she had the chance to move away, he turned his head and stared right into her face. And he was not bored or thoughtful now for he was studying her with eyes that were the amber of a hunting cat's, the deep peaty gold at the bottom of a brandy glass.

They were the eyes she had last seen burning with scarce-suppressed frustration in the face of a dying man. The eyes of her husband.

Julia had always imagined that fainting was a sudden and complete loss of consciousness: blackness falling like a curtain.

But now the margins of her sight began to narrow down until all she could see was the face of the tanned man, those extraordinary eyes locked with hers. *Will.* Then the only noise was the buzzing in her head and the blackness came and on a sigh she escaped into it without a struggle.

He could hold one tall, curvaceous woman without trouble. Will registered the fact with the faint surprise that still struck him when his body obeyed without faltering, when his sinews and muscles flexed and responded with their old confidence and power.

'The lady has fainted. There is nothing to be concerned about.' The cluster of helpful matrons surrounding him were still thrusting smelling bottles forwards, waving fans, calling for sal volatile. 'If someone could please direct me to a quiet retiring room with a couch?'

Several led the way, bustling around and offering advice until he secured peace by the simple expedient of shouldering the door shut behind him and leaving them on the other side. Julia slid limply from his arms on to the rather battered leather *chaise* and he shot the bolt to give them privacy.

They appeared to be in a storeroom, now doing service as a makeshift retiring room with a cheval glass propped against the wall, a few chairs and a screen. Not the place he would have chosen to be reunited with his wife, but it had the virtue of privacy at least.

It was not the time of his choosing either, which should be a lesson to him not to yield to sudden impulses. He should have stayed in his bedchamber and ignored the lights and music from the Assembly Rooms opposite and then, as he had planned, arrived at King's Acre in the morning. So close now to his dream, so close to coming home.

He had been thinking of the morrow when something had made him look up, glance to the side. He had recognised her at once, although this was no longer the anxious, tired woman he had married, but a poised and elegant young matron. Her eyelids flickered as he watched her now.

'Will?' The whisper from the *chaise* was incredulous. He spun a chair round and sat beside her. No time for dreaming yet. This was not going to be easy for he had no idea of what his own feelings were, let alone hers. Julia lay still, her face white, but she was thinking, calculating, he could tell. She might have fainted, but she was not in a daze any longer. 'I thought you were a ghost,' she murmured.

'That was my line when we first met, if I recall. I am perfectly real, Julia.' He remembered the courage and the pallor and the height. He recalled his body's surprising arousal and, looking at her now, he was no longer so amazed that Julia had sent tremors of desire through a dying man.

'I am very glad. And you are perfectly well by the look of you, which is wonderful,' she said slowly, as though she could still not believe in him. 'But, Will, what happened? You were so ill, and there has been no letter from you for eighteen months at least. I am delighted to see you again, of course, but it is such a shock!'

The colour was beginning to come back to her cheeks. Three years had indeed wrought changes in her. The clinging silks of her evening gown revealed lush curves, smooth skin. Her hair was fashionably dressed, glossy with health. Julia was not a fashionable beauty, but she was undeniably attractive. She caught her lower lip between her teeth, drawing his eyes to the fullness and sending a bolt of desire through him. This was his wife. The emotions that produced were confusing and not all welcome, not yet. She was real now and he was going to have to deal with that reality.

'Yes, I am completely well.' He might as well explain now and get it over with. 'I was very ill in Seville and the doctor that Jervis found, quite by accident, was one who practised Jewish and Moorish medicine. He gave me some drugs, but mainly he made me rest, out in the sunshine. He took over my diet and gradually the coughing stopped and the night sweats got less frequent. I began to sleep and gain strength.

'Then he sent me south to the coast and from there over to North Africa to a doctor he knew.' Will shrugged. 'There is more to it than that, of course. Exercise, massage, swimming to build up my muscles again, days when I feared I would never get back to how I was before.

'But the miracle happened, although for months I could not believe I was really cured. Every time I picked up the pen to write I did not know what to say. If I said I was getting better and it was just a false hope… I have been fully well for over six months but it is hard to believe it sometimes.'

It was no easier speaking of it than it had been to try to write. Eventually he would learn to accept that he was going to have a future. A life. 'I thought it would be better simply to come home.'

Julia sat up and swung her feet on to the ground. Pink satin slippers and a provocative amount of ankle showed beneath her hem. His wife had obviously decided it was far too early to go into mourning for him, or perhaps she had simply found it easier to forget him.

She is still damnably self-possessed, he added mentally as she studied him, her face almost expressionless. And yet, there was something beneath that cool scrutiny. *What is she thinking?* He did not like secrets. Probably she was still recovering from the shock of seeing him and that was all it was.

'Why are you here?' she asked. 'At this dance, I mean.'

'I intended to come to King's Acre in the morning rather than turn up on the doorstep when you were about to sit down to dinner. And then I saw the lights and heard the music and decided to dip my toe into English life once more. It never occurred to me that you might be here.'

'Aunt Delia persuaded me to come. I am

not much given to large public assemblies.'
Julia studied him. 'And you have had no
news of home, of course.'

Something *was* wrong, he could sense it.
'I have had no news at all. I collect that you
and Aunt Delia are on good terms?'

'We have learned to rub along together,'
she said drily. 'And I have learned to bite my
tongue even if she still sees no need to hold
hers. But I should not be disrespectful, I have
found her kind on many occasions. This is
going to be a considerable shock to her; she
has quite decided that you…that Henry is
definitely going to inherit.'

'Did you travel with her this evening?'
Time enough tomorrow to face Delia and
Henry and shatter their hopes.

'No. I used my own carriage. It is out of
their way to collect me and I prefer to be in-
dependent.'

'Then we will go back together, you and I.'
Now this meeting had happened there was no
going back, no retreat into the neutral ground
of a solitary inn bedchamber for the night.
'If Delia has not seen me there is no need to
tell her I have returned, not until tomorrow.
Are you well enough to find her and let her
know you are returning home?' Julia nod-

ded. 'Then I will go and settle my account, pay off the postilions and collect my baggage. Jervis and I will meet you in the yard of the Stag's Head opposite.'

Something flared in her eyes, but it was gone before he could analyse it. Julia pressed her lips together as if on a retort and nodded again. This was not the place to talk. Will got to his feet and let himself out, wary now that Delia or Henry might see him. A confrontation in a crowded ballroom would set the district on its ears for weeks. That was the only reason for the knot in his gut, surely? He would be home within the hour. His life could begin again—on his terms now.

Julia stared blankly at the battered door panels as the catch clicked shut. She was not a widow. She was not even the pretend-wife of a man who had vanished as though he had been a dream. Her husband was alive and fit and, as far as she could tell, in the very best of health. Which meant he would find out exactly what had happened at King's Acre in his absence.

She had no idea what Will imagined he was coming home to, but she rather suspected that he had not thought through the implications of surviving his hasty marriage. Finally she would find out exactly what manner of man she was tied to, for this was all going to shake him off balance enough to reveal his true character. The baby. Her mind shied away from how she was going to break that to him.

Think of something else. My goodness, but he is attractive. Julia jabbed loose hairpins in securely and told herself that physical attractiveness was no guide to inner character. And if Will Hadfield thought he was coming home to her bed tonight he must think again. There was far too much to be said, to work out, before things became that intimate. She swallowed. If they ever did. She was not at all certain what she wanted, although that was probably academic. Her desires were not going to affect Will's reactions. For all she knew he might try to repudiate her now he no longer needed her. He certainly might when he learned what had happened in his absence.

But that was something to worry about when she was alone. Now she must leave without arousing Delia's suspicions. Julia opened the door and almost bumped into Henry. She slid her arm into his and produced a faint smile. 'Cousin Henry! Just the person I need. I have such a headache—would you be a dear and let your mama know I am returning home now?'

'Of course. Shall I go and call your carriage?'

He was a nice young man, Julia thought, watching him weave through the crowd to the front door. Still self-centred and inclined to believe that things would fall into his lap by right, but he would learn. Yet however little he wished his cousin ill, the discovery that he was not going to inherit King's Acre in a few years would be a blow that would set his world on its ear.

When her carriage pulled into the inn yard the footman jumped down from the box to open the door and let the steps down and almost fell over his feet when he saw the two men waiting. 'Mr Jervis! And—oh, my Heavens, it's his lordship! Thomas, look, it's his lordship just like he used to be!'

'Praise be!' Thomas the coachman must have jabbed the horses' mouths in his excitement. The carriage rocked back and forth and she saw Will grin in the lamplight. It was the first time she had ever seen him smile like that. How had she ever thought him old, even when he had been so sick? This was a man in his prime.

'Praise be, indeed, Thomas. Good to see you again, Charles. Now, load up the bags and let us be going. We can't keep her ladyship sitting around like this.' He climbed in, the valet on his heels.

'Good evening, your ladyship.' The valet sat down with his back to the horses, his hat held precisely on his knees.

'Good evening, Jervis. Welcome home. I am delighted to see you after all this time.' And thankful that his presence in the carriage would bar any but the most commonplace conversation. Shock was beginning to give way to apprehension. It was no more than that, she assured herself. There was nothing really to actually be *afraid* of. Was there? Only some very unpleasant revelations to deal with.

'You have bought a new team,' Will observed. Perhaps he too was glad of their involuntary chaperon. 'There will be more horses arriving in a few weeks. I bought an Andalusian stallion and two mares and a dozen Arabians.'

'Fifteen horses?' Julia felt a surge of excitement sweep back the fears into their usual dark corner. 'We will need new stabling. And to extend the paddocks,' she added. 'Thank goodness the feed stocks are so good and the hay crop should be excellent if the weather holds. We may need to hire new grooms.' Mind racing, she started to make lists in her head. 'I will get Harris the builder up tomorrow to discuss plans. Jobbins will have ideas about any likely local lads to hire, of course, but we will need someone used to stud work—'

'I have it all in hand,' Will said. 'You have no need to trouble yourself with such things now that I am home.'

'It will be no trouble,' Julia retorted. She knew exactly what state the grass was in, how much new fencing was needed, where an extended stable block would go and the strengths and weaknesses of the current stable staff. There was going to be a territorial battle, she could tell, because she was not prepared to let three years of hard work go and retire to her sitting room and her embroidery. But that was something else that could wait until the morning.

'We can have supper while they make up the bed in the master suite,' she said into the silence that had fallen. 'And make sure your room is aired, of course, Jervis.' In the gloom of the carriage she could sense the sudden sharpening of Will's attention. He was hardly going to discuss their sleeping arrangements now. When the time came to go upstairs she would just have to be very clear that she wished to be alone.

No doubt that would be another subject on which Lord Dereham had very firm opinions. And then there was the secret tragedy that, somehow, she was going to find a way to confess before anyone told him of it.

Chapter Seven

W‌ill rolled over on to his back and opened his eyes. Above him, lit by the early morning light, was the familiar dark blue of the bed canopy. He blinked the sleep out of his eyes and focused on the stars embroidered in silver thread by some long-ago ancestress. Home. He really was home.

Without turning his head he stretched out a hand as he had every morning since he had finally accepted that he was not about to die. Beside him the bed was empty, the covers flat, the pillow smooth and cool. No one was there, of course.

Julia had not been very communicative last night, not after the brief verbal tussle over where he was sleeping. Which she had won, he reflected. For one night, at any rate. He was hard, aroused, but then he was every morning since he had recovered.

Will threw back the covers with an impatient hand and let the cool air of dawn flow over his naked, heated body. He had made his bed and now, he supposed, he must lie on it. Not that it would be such a hardship to lie with Julia. His mouth curved at the memory of her in that pink silk last night. He had thought about her these past years, but the memories had been of her spirit and her intelligence, not of her looks.

But marrying Julia had been a brilliant piece of improvisation by a dying man. A marriage of convenience that he had expected to last mere months. For a man with the prospect of a long life ahead of him it was a sentence to a loveless but solid and respectable future.

Or, given the hideous example of his own parents' *convenient* marriage, loveless and cold, although, if he had anything to do with it, not spectacularly scandalous. He winced at the remembrance of the raised voices, the banging doors, the sniggers at school and the oh-so-careful reports in the scandal sheets—*It is said that a certain Lady D—...*

It is the talk of the town that Lord D—'s latest companion...

All those lies, all the pretence. His father pretending he was not unfaithful, his mother pretending her heart was not broken, both of them lying to him, fobbing him off, whenever he asked if anything was wrong, when Papa would be home, why Mama was weeping again. It had felt as though they simply did not care enough about him to talk to him, to explain, to comfort the confused small boy. Looking back, he saw no reason to modify that explanation.

Thousands married without love and managed to live perfectly affectionate, civilised, faithful lives, he knew that. But, for a man who had once dreamed of something more for himself, it was a damnably unpleasant place to be. He had lived with a vision of bringing love back to Knight's Acre and he had to accept that now he never would. He could sense that Julia would find it difficult to have him home and he could understand her feelings.

The night before he had told Jervis to leave the curtain drawn back. Now the sun flooded in through the window and he gazed down the long avenue of oaks towards the glimmer of the lake in the distance while he found his equilibrium again. He had managed to survive a death sentence, the loss of his betrothed and exile from the place he loved with a bone-deep passion. He had taken a gamble to save King's Acre and if he had not, and had stayed, he would be dead by now and Henry in his place.

You're an ungrateful devil, he told himself. He was alive, well and had an intelligent, attractive wife. King's Acre had been in good hands, he felt confident of that. Of course Julia had been cool and had wanted to sleep alone last night. After all, she was a virgin and was probably shaken to the core to have her virtually unknown husband turn up without notice. That would change and he would be careful with her. And she would realise this morning that the master of the house had returned and she could place all the business affairs in his hands and, no doubt, be glad to shed the responsibility.

But for now the house was quiet in the dawn light. Down in the kitchens a yawning scullery maid would be riddling the grate and making up the range to heat water for the other servants. Up here all would be undisturbed for at least an hour.

King's Acre lay open and waiting for him, like a mistress awaiting her lover's return, and he would savour it, rediscover it and his hoarded, happy memories. Will pulled on a brocade robe and, without bothering to find his slippers, opened the door on to his dressing room.

He wandered from room to room, looked out of windows, touched furniture, picked up trinkets. Under his fingers the house came to life again in a myriad of textures: polished wood and rough tapestry; smooth porcelain, cold metal; cut glass and ornate ormolu. His eyes lingered on favourite paintings, achingly remembered views, familiar spaces. In his nostrils was the smell of lavender and beeswax, wood smoke and, unsettlingly unfamiliar, a hint of the perfume he remembered from Julia's skin as he had carried her into the retiring room the evening before.

On this upper floor every door opened to him. At the other end of the main passageway lay the oak panels leading to the bedchamber Julia was using and he passed that by. Today she would move her things into the suite next to his and that would put an end to this nonsense of sleeping apart.

The final door, the one beyond her dressing room, did not open. Will twisted the handle, pushed, expecting it to have stuck. But it stayed firm. Beyond, he recalled, was a small room with a pretty curve to the wall where it fitted into one of the old turrets. There was no reason for it to be locked. Thwarted, he frowned. It could wait, of course. He would get the key… But the rest of the rooms had opened to him as if welcoming him back, giving themselves up again to their master. It jarred that this one remained blankly inaccessible.

Frustrated, Will hit the panels with his clenched fist. The sound echoed down the quiet corridor like a hammer blow.

A sharp intake of breath was all the warning he got that he was not alone. When he turned Julia was standing in the doorway of her room, her eyes wide, one hand clenched in the ruffles of her robe.

Will should not look so much bigger in a robe with bare feet and yet he seemed to fill the space. His eyes ran over her as she stood there in the flimsy summer robe until she felt naked and exposed.

'I am sorry, I did not mean to wake you. I was surprised to find the door locked.'

'There are just some things stored in there,' she said vaguely. 'Did you need the room? I will have it cleared.' *Oh, I am such a fool! Why didn't I do it before? I don't need an empty nursery to remind me of the child I lost. Can I tell him now? No.* All night she had tossed and turned, trying to think how she would break the news of what she had discovered after he had left.

'No, I don't care about the room,' Will said. 'But may I come into yours?'

'My bedchamber? But, why?'

'Why?' One dark brow rose and his smile became sensual. That look had been in Jonathan's eyes that night in the inn. Her pulse spiked. 'I am your husband,' Will pointed out.

'But our marriage was only a sham, a device. You cannot expect to…to come to my bed just like that, without any discussion, without giving me any time—I hardly know you!'

'Then I suggest we make up for lost time.' His expression softened. 'I find you very attractive, Julia. Do I…frighten you? Is that it?'

He was so close she could see the individual stubble of his night-beard, see the crisp curl of hair in the vee of his robe. *He is naked under it, just as I am beneath mine.* He was a virile, attractive man. Head and heart and body seemed to be at war in her. Her feminine reactions to him were primal, she could not help them, she knew that. Even before, when he had been so ill, she had felt that flicker of heat, that attraction. And it was her duty to lie with him, she had taken everything he offered her and been grateful for it.

'No,' she admitted and saw the tension leave him.

But… She swallowed as he came closer still. She only had to close her eyes and she thought of Jonathan, his hands impatient, the painful thrusting into her body, his sneers, the betrayal. And he had left her with child.

Will reached out and pulled her against him and then there was nothing but those amber eyes holding hers as he lowered his head and kissed her. One hand slid up to hold her head and his fingers sifted into the mass of hair, loosened from its night-time plait. With the other arm he encircled her shoulders. She felt herself become stiff, un-yielding, as reactions and instincts warred within her.

Will was overwhelming. Overwhelmingly big, overwhelmingly male. His mouth, as it crushed down on hers, was unlike anything she had experienced or imagined.

His tongue slid along the tight seam of her lips, seeking entrance, and she tasted him, felt his heat. *This is not Jonathan.* Suddenly her body was fluid, curving against his, only thin muslin and thick silk separating their bare flesh.

Jonathan had not seemed to want to kiss her much. There had been romantic, respectful kisses when he was courting her. Fleeting caresses that she now knew to be hypocritical ploys. When he had taken her to his bed she had ached for kisses, had wanted their reassurance, but he had been urgent, focused on sheathing himself in her body and, she realised now, reaching his own satisfaction.

She tensed at the memory, transferring those feelings to Will, wanting to reject him, but her body was sending her clamouring messages of need, of surrender. Of desire. He felt so strong against her. The thrust of his erection pressed against her belly. His skin smelt of musk and, faintly, of last evening's shaving soap. His morning beard was rough against her cheeks.

Her body wanted to be seduced. Her common sense, squeaking faintly to be heard against the clamour of emotion, told her that he was her husband, that she should simply allow herself to be swept off to his bed.

No. Will's tongue probed along her lips, seeking entrance. Some instinct that she did not dare to quite trust murmured that he would not force her. *But he will make my body force me,* she argued back. *He thinks he holds every card, the arrogant devil.*

Then take control, don't let him dominate you so. As she thought it she felt her body melting, answering him, demanding with as much urgency as his was. He used his strength and she could not match it, but she could use it against him as a wrestler uses his opponent's weight to overbalance him.

Damn you, Will Hadfield, Julia thought as she opened her lips, felt the triumphant surge of his tongue. *You will be my husband, not my master.* Rather than yield she would give as good as she got. Her own tongue met his, boldly, and then she lost track of time, of coherent thought and, certainly, of speech.

Will kissed as though this meeting of mouths was the sex act in itself: hot, demanding, intimate. She had no idea what she was doing as her tongue tangled and duelled with his, as the taste of him filled her and her ears were deafened by the sound of his breathing and her thundering heart.

His robe was too thick. *Touch him.* Julia pushed it back and found naked skin, hot and smooth over shifting, hard muscle. She wanted to bite, to kiss…

His hands came down, over her back, down to her waist and he pulled her against him and she felt the hard ridge of arousal pressed against her stomach and the memory of the pain came back, sweeping away the passion in a cold flood.

Will released her, stepped back his expression rueful. 'I *have* frightened you. For a moment I forgot you were a virgin, Julia. It will be all right, I promise you.'

'Yes, of course.' From somewhere she found a smile.

'Those few days we were together before we married—we are still those people. I have not changed so very much and I doubt you have either. We trusted each other. There was liking, I think. We can build on that. And attraction as we have just proved.'

Attraction, yes. She nodded, it was impossible to pretend otherwise. *Trust. But I lied*

*to you. You married a woman who killed a
man. I was a fugitive. And now I have to tell
you I bore, and lost, that man's child and I
have to beg you to acknowledge it as yours.
If I let you lie with me then the marriage is
consummated and I will have trapped you.*

'I'll let you get dressed,' Will said. 'We'll
meet at breakfast and talk afterwards. You
can move into the chamber next to mine and
this will all be all right, you'll see, Julia.'

'Thank you.' Her smile was slipping, but
it was only a few steps to her chamber. Julia
closed the door behind her with care. She
was shaking, but she made herself walk to
the armchair at the window, not collapse on
the bed. She would be in control, she would
not panic.

Before she slept with him she had to tell
him the truth. Not all of it, not that she was
responsible for Jonathan's death, but about
the elopement and about the baby. She owed
it to him to be honest about that before he
made love to her.

He would be angry, and shaken, but she
had to hope he would understand and forgive
her the deception because there was only so
much weight her conscience could bear.

Once she had thought that the guilt and

fear over Jonathan's death would lessen, that she could forget. But it did not go away. It was always there and so was the pain and loss of her child, the two things twisting and tangling into a mesh of emotions that were always there waiting to trip her, snare her, when she was least expecting it. And now Will was home there was the added guilt of keeping her crime from him. But it was not a personal shame like her elopement or the pregnancy. This was a matter of law and she could not ask him to conceal what she had done.

The sensitive skin of her upper arms where Will had held her still prickled with the awareness of his touch. Her mouth was swollen and sensitive and the ache between her thighs was humiliatingly insistent.

He was her husband. She owed him as much truth as she could give him and, unfair though it might be, she wanted something in return. *I want a real marriage.*

Papa had taught her to negotiate. *Know what your basic demands are, the point you will not shift beyond,* he had told her. *Know what you can afford to yield, what you can give to get what you want.* He had been talking about buying land and selling wheat, but the principles were surely the same.

Julia lay back in the chair, closed her eyes against the view of the garden coming to life in the strengthening sunlight, and tried to think without emotion. She could not risk the marriage: that was her sticking point. She wanted her husband's respect, and equality in making decisions about their lives and that included the estate and the farm. She wanted him to desire her for herself, not just as a passive body in his bed to breed his sons. *Sons.* The emotion broke through the calculation. Could she bear that pain again? Could she carry another child, knowing what it would be like to lose it before it had even drawn a breath?

Yes. Because if I am not willing to do that, then the marriage cannot stand. I made a bargain and I cannot break it. She felt one tear running down her cheek, but she did not lift her hand to wipe it away.

Chapter Eight

$\mathcal{OSSSSO}$

At length Nancy, her maid, arrived. Julia bathed, dressed and, still deep in thought, walked to the head of the stairs to be greeted by loud wailing rising from the breakfast room. When she ran down and along the passageway she was confronted by a view of the door jammed with all three of their strapping footmen, craning to see what was going on inside. Julia tapped the nearest liveried shoulder and they jumped apart, mumbling shamefaced apologies.

The wailing female was revealed as Cook, her apron to her face, sobbing with joy on Will's shoulder. 'I never thought to see the day… Oh, look at 'im… Oh, my lord…just like when he was a young man!'

Will had the usual expression of a man confronted by a weeping female, one of helpless alarm, as he stood patting Cook ineffectually on the back.

'Mrs Pocock, do calm down!' The relief of having some ordinary crisis to take control of almost made Julia laugh out loud. 'Gatcombe, will you please find someone to take Cook downstairs and make her a nice cup of tea and the rest of you, get on and fetch his lordship's breakfast. He will think he has come home to a madhouse.'

'My lady, I must apologise.' The butler glared at the footmen until one of them helped Mrs Pocock from the room, then waved the others in with the chafing-dishes. 'Cook had retired to her room when you returned last night and the kitchen maids did not inform her until this morning of his lordship's presence and his good health.'

'Of course.' Julia took her place at the foot of the small oval table as Will straightened his rumpled neckcloth and collapsed into his chair. 'I had forgotten that Cook has known Lord Dereham for many years.' Gatcombe went out, closing the door on the sounds from the corridor and leaving them alone.

'Coffee, my lord?' Will looked decidedly

off balance. Whatever he had been doing for the past three years, he had certainly not been gaining experience in dealing with difficult females. But then, since he had recovered his health, they had probably been all willing complaisance. Julia tried hard not to imagine just how her husband would have celebrated his returning health and vigour.

'Thank you.' The heavy-lidded look had shivers travelling up and down her spine, but all Will said was, 'You appear to have rather more control over the domestic staff than I have, my lady. Mrs Pocock would not stop wailing.'

'It is only to be expected,' Julia said as she racked her brains to recall whether her husband took cream and sugar with his coffee. He could say if it was wrong, she decided with a mental shrug and simply passed the cup. 'They are all delighted at your recovery and as for control, I have been dealing with them daily for three years, after all.'

'I trust there will be no more weeping females today.' Will sipped his coffee without a grimace, so she had that right at least. None of the servants knew the true story behind this marriage, or even where they had first met—the more familiar she seemed with Will's habits, the better it would be.

'I doubt any more of the female staff will shed tears at the sight of you.' Julia studied him over the rim of her chocolate cup as Charles came in and began to serve Will breakfast.

As was her habit, Julia started her day with only chocolate, bread and butter and preserves, but it seemed someone had warned the kitchen and Cook had managed to at least put a decent breakfast for a hungry man in train before her emotions overcame her.

Bacon, eggs, a slice of sirloin, mushrooms. Will nodded thanks to Charles when his breakfast plate was finally filled to his satisfaction. The contrast with the emaciated invalid picking at a spoonful of scrambled egg during their first breakfast together could not have been greater.

'What are you thinking?' Will asked as he reached for the toast.

'Thank you, Charles, that will be all.' Julia waited until he footman had closed the door behind her. 'I was reflecting that I would not have recognised the man I married if it were not for your eyes.'

'And that recognition was enough to make you faint?'

'You must know perfectly well how distinctive a feature your eyes are. I had thought you must be dead, although I never once admitted it to anyone else. To tell the truth, I was surprised to receive the letters for as long as you sent them. When you left I had not expected you would make it across the Channel. So the shock of seeing you again with no warning was…intense.'

Will pushed the empty plate away with sudden impatience. 'I will not beat about the bush. What is the matter, Julia? You know I am the same man you married, but you have changed. You are wary now and it is not simply the shock of seeing me. What else are you hiding from me?'

Hiding? For a moment Julia froze. Had Will the powers to read her mind? *Of course I am wary! A ghost appears, kisses me until I am dizzy with desire…and whatever happens I must reveal one secret that may break our marriage into pieces and hide another for my very life.*

Julia spread honey on a roll to give herself time to collect her thoughts, then answered as though the situation was as uncomplicated as everyone else believed it to be. 'Of course I have changed. I have been alone for three years and I have just had a severe, but very welcome, shock.' That was not entirely a lie. 'You try hiding so much as an extravagant piece of shopping with Aunt Delia's beady eye on you.' Will gave a snort of laughter and she added, 'Any woman would be wary if her lord and master had been away for so long and then returned unexpectedly.'

He paused, one hand outstretched to the fruit bowl. 'Is that how you see me now you have had time to think it over? Your lord and master?'

'Certainly not,' she answered with as much composure as she could summon and was pleased to see the amusement vanish from his face. 'It is how society views you. I regard you as an unknown and very uncertain factor in my life.'

He was peeling an apple, his eyes clashing with hers as the peel ran slowly over his fingers. The chocolate threatened to slop over the cup. Julia put it down carefully before he noticed the effect he had on her. 'I have no idea if I will be happy married to you. Or you to me. But I will do my level best.' She braced herself for an explosion of wrath.

'Happiness? You aim high. I was hoping for mere contentment as a starting point. An absence of scandal would be desirable.' There was an edge to that, she noticed, puzzled. He could have no idea what she was hiding, so why the reference to scandal? 'Well, we will see. My experience of marriage is as brief as yours, but I have no doubt you will point out to me where I am going wrong.'

All very calm and polite, Julia thought, but under the civilised words was more emotion that he was keeping hidden from her. Which was fair enough, she supposed. She had no intention of making her own emotions any more transparent than most of them undoubtedly were just now, not yet.

'Your own childhood memories will guide you, I imagine,' she replied with equal calmness.

'Do you? If you mean I should seek for a model of the ideal husband in my own parent I am afraid you would not be very happy with the result. He gave me these eyes and he left me the only thing I love: King's Acre. I suspect you would want something more from me in the way of conjugal virtues.' He drained the coffee and tossed his napkin onto the table. 'Have you finished, Julia?

'Certainly.' In the face of that matter-of-fact bitterness there were no words of comfort to offer to a virtual stranger. She waited as he came round to pull her chair back. 'What do you wish to do first?'

'Any number of things, but please do not let me interfere with your morning. I will go and speak to my steward.'

'Mr Wilkins will wait on us at eleven o'clock. Mr Howard from the Home Farm will be here after luncheon. I have sent for Mr Burrows, the solicitor, but I would not expect him until tomorrow.'

'You have been very busy, my dear.' The blandly amiable expression had ebbed from Will's face. Those strong bones she had been so aware of when he was ill were apparent still, the stubborn line of his jaw most of all.

'I habitually rise early,' Julia said. 'And not just because unexpected noises outside my room waken me.' Although not, normally, as early as she had got up that morning to pen letters to all the men of business who must wait on the returning baron. She had just sealed the last letter when the sound of his fist on the nursery door had brought

her into the corridor. 'But before you do anything else we must call on the Hadfields.'

'Must we, indeed?' There was more than a
hint of gritted teeth about his polite response.

Julia swept out of the breakfast room,
along the corridor and into the library. 'If
you are going to shout, please do it in here
and not in front of the servants,' she said over
her shoulder.

'Was I shouting?' Will closed the door behind him and leaned back on the panels. 'I
do not think I raised my voice.'

'You were about to. We need to call because it will appear very strange if we do
not, and as soon as possible.'

'You will find, Julia, that I very rarely
shout except in emergencies. I do not have
to.' He crossed his arms and studied her as
she moved restlessly about the room. 'You
are very busy organising me. I am neither an
invalid nor Cousin Henry.'

'You have been away for three years.' She
made herself stand still and appear calm. 'I
am in a position to bring you up to date with
everything. I am only trying to—'

'Organise me. I do not require it, Julia. I
am perfectly fit and able. You have done very
well, but I am back now.'

'Indeed you are, you patronising man!' The words escaped her before she could bite them back. 'I apologise, I should not have said that, but—'

At his back the door opened an inch and slammed back as it met resistance. Will turned and pulled it wide. 'Gatcombe?'

'I beg your pardon, my lord. Mrs Hadfield and Mr Henry have arrived and are asking to speak to you, my lady. I was not certain whether, under the circumstances, you are At Home.'

'Yes, we are receiving, Gatcombe.' Her stomach contracted with nerves. This encounter was not going to be pleasant, especially if Will continued in this mood. And if she could not keep Delia from blurting out something about the baby it might well be disastrous.

The butler lowered his voice. 'Mrs Hadfield is complaining about a stupid hoax and rumours running around the neighbourhood. I did not know quite how to answer her, my lady. I did not feel it my place to apprise her of his lordship's happy return.'

'I quite understand. You did quite right, Gatcombe. Where have you put them?'

'In the Green Salon, my lady. Refreshments are being sent up.'

'Thank you, Gatcombe. Please tell Mrs Hadfield we will be with her directly.'

'Will we?' Will enquired as the butler retreated. 'This is an uncivilised hour to be calling.'

'She is not going to believe it until she sees you with her own eyes,' Julia said with a firmness she was far from feeling.

'And she is not going to want to believe it, even then.' Will opened the door for her. He sounded merely sardonically amused, but she wondered what his feelings might be behind the façade he was maintaining. Her husband had come back from the dead and it must seem to him that the only people who were unreservedly pleased to see him were the servants.

She listened to his firm tread behind her and told herself that soon enough he would make contact with his friends and acquaintances and resume his old life. But he had come home to a sorry excuse for a family: an aunt and cousin who would be happier if he were dead and a wife who had fainted at the sight of him and who was very shortly about to release a bombshell.

'Good morning, Aunt Delia, Cousin Henry.' She tried to sound as happy as a wife with a returned husband should be.

'Have you heard this ridiculous rumour?' Mrs Hadfield demanded before Julia could get into the room. She was pacing, the ribbons of her bonnet flapping. 'It is all over the village! I had Mrs Armstrong on my doorstep before breakfast demanding to know if it true, of all the impertinence!'

'And what rumour is that?' Will enquired from the shadows behind Julia.

'Why, that my nephew Dereham is alive and well and here—' She broke off with a gasp as Will stepped into the room. 'What is this? Who are you, sir?'

'Oh, come, Aunt.' Will strolled past Julia and stopped in front of Mrs Hadfield. Her jaw dropped unflatteringly as her face turned from pale to red in moments as she stared up at him. 'Do you not recognise your own nephew? Is this going to be like those sensation novels where the lost heir returns only to be spurned by the family? Well, if you require physical proof, Mama always said you dandled me on your knee when I was an infant. I still have that birthmark shaped like a star.'

He put one hand in the small of his back, where only Julia could see, and tapped his left buttock with his index finger. Mrs Hadfield was beginning to bluster and from behind his mother Henry was trying to say something and failing to get a word in edgeways. Julia decided it was time to support her husband.

'You mean the birthmark on your, er, *left posterior*, my lord?' she enquired. 'This is hardly the conversation for a lady's drawing room, but I can assure you, Aunt Delia, the birthmark is most assuredly where you will remember it.'

'Mama,' Henry managed finally. 'Of course it is Will—look at his eyes!'

'Oooh!' With a wail Mrs Hadfield collapsed onto the sofa and buried her face in her handkerchief.

'Aunt Delia, please do not weep, I realise what a shock it must be—we were going to send a note and then come and call on you later today.' Julia sat down and put her arms around the older woman. The main thing, she thought rather desperately, was to stop Delia saying something that must cause an irrevocable rift and to prevent her leaving and creating a stir in the neighbourhood before she had time to consider the situation rationally.

The men, as she might have expected, were absolutely no help whatsoever. They stood side by side, Henry looking hideously embarrassed, her husband, wooden. *'Will.'* He looked at her, his dark brows raised. 'You remember I was telling you how kind Aunt Delia has been to me and how helpful Cousin Henry has been with the estate.'

Henry, who, to do him justice, was no hypocrite, blushed at the generous praise. 'Dash it all, I only did what I could. You helped me far more with my lands than I could ever repay here, Cousin Julia.'

'You were very supportive to me. But indeed, Will, Cousin Henry has been making improvements on his own estate. Why do you not both go to the study and talk about it—and have a glass of brandy or something?'

Will looked from her to the clock, his brows rising still further. Admittedly half past nine in the morning did seem a little early for spirits, but she needed to be alone with Delia. Giving up on subtlety, Julia jerked her head towards the door and, to her relief,

Will took his cousin by the arm and guided him out.

'Now then, Aunt Delia, you must stop this or you will make yourself ill. Yes, I know it is a shock and you could quite reasonably have believed that Henry would inherit the title and King's Acre. But Will is home, hale and hearty and quite cured by a very clever doctor in Spain, so you must accept it, for otherwise you will attract the most unwelcome and impertinent comments from the vulgarly curious. And you do not want our friends and neighbours to pity you, do you?'

Will's aunt emerged from her handkerchief, blotched and red eyed. 'But Henry—'

'Henry is a perfectly intelligent, personable young man who has started to retrieve the mistakes he made with his own inheritance, if you will forgive me for plain speaking,' she added hastily as Delia bristled. 'If he finds a sensible, well-dowered young lady to marry in a year or two all will be well.'

'But the title,' Delia muttered and then bit her lip.

'If Will had married before he fell ill then he would probably have his own son by now and you and Henry would never have had your hopes raised,' Julia said. There was no point beating about the bush. But Delia had been kind to her when she was pregnant, she reminded herself. She owed it to the older woman to help her through this and not condemn her for her ambitions for her son. 'You do not truly wish Will dead, do you?' she asked.

'No.' It was almost convincing. 'Of course not.' That was better. 'It was just the unexpectedness of it.'

'I know. I fainted dead away when I saw him. It is such a comfort to me to have a female friend at a time like this,' Julia said, crossing her fingers in her skirts. 'And, please, can I ask you and Henry to say nothing about the baby? I have got to break the news to Will and it will be a shock.'

The other woman nodded. 'Of course, you can rely on me.'

Thank Heavens! If she could only do this right, then Delia would leave the house convinced she had supported Julia in her shock, had greeted Will with open-hearted warmth and was a paragon of selflessness. It might help quell the rumour-mongers.

An hour later the Hadfields left and Julia followed Will back to the study. There were, indeed, glasses and a decanter standing on the desk and she felt like pouring herself a stiff drink, despite the hour and her dislike of spirits.

'He has improved,' Will remarked. He stood beside the big chair, the one she always used, courteously waiting for her to sit. Julia took the chair opposite—she was going to have to find herself a desk, they could hardly share this one. 'How much of that is due to your influence?'

Julia found herself studying the long, elegant figure, thinking how right he looked in the ornate chair. He sat with his fingers curling instinctively around the great carved lion heads at the ends of the chair arms. Her own hands were too small to do that.

'To me? The improvements in his character I can claim no credit for. I believe he is maturing as you had guessed he would once he began to escape from his mother's apron strings. He does not enjoy being made to think hard, or to face unwelcome truths, but he is learning.' She felt her mouth curving into a smile at the memory of some of their tussles. 'I do believe I would make a good governess after the way I have had to cajole, lecture and bully poor Henry.'

Will did not speak. A ploy to make her gabble on, no doubt. It was, unfortunately, working. The relief of having the dreaded encounter with Delia over with was having its effect. 'If he can just find a nice girl to marry, I think it will be the making of him, although he is still very shy of girls.'

'You think you can recommend marriage from your own experience, do you?' Julia glanced up sharply to find Will doodling patterns up the margins of the sheet on which she had been calculating wheat yields.

She would not let him fluster her. 'Hardly,' she said with a smile, making a joke of it. If he wanted plain speaking, he would get it. 'A husband who vanishes less than twenty-four hours after the ceremony and returns three years later with no warning is hardly a model of ideal matrimony.'

Will raised a quizzical eyebrow, prepared, it seemed to be amused. He steepled his fingers and regarded her over the top of them. 'You dealt with Delia very effectively. I must thank you for your support. The tone in which you said *left posterior* was exactly right, although it was a miracle I kept my countenance.'

'It was fortunate that it was you who raised

the subject of birthmarks—if Mrs Hadfield had asked I would not have had the slightest idea what to say.'

The left side of Will's mouth quirked into a half-smile that produced, improbably in that strong face, a dimple. Julia stared at it, distracted by how it lightened his whole expression. 'I wouldn't worry about that kind of slip,' he said. 'She is perfectly well aware that for a couple married three years we have had only two nights when it was theoretically possible to see each other's…shall we say, *distinguishing marks*.' The smile slipped easily from amused to wicked. 'So far. And, for all my aunt knows, we might be a most prudish couple who retire to bed in our nightgowns and blow out all the candles.'

Julia's mood moved just as easily as that smile, from almost relaxed to exceedingly flustered. If Will was not regarding her so watchfully from those heavy-lidded predator's eyes she would think him flirting. Perhaps he was, or perhaps he was trying to unsettle her—and succeeding very effectively, she had to admit. The thought of being naked with him, in a well-lit room, brought back all the memories of losing her virginity and added an all-too-tangible layer of apprehension and embarrassment to the mix of emotions that were unsettling her breakfast.

'I will show you the books now to save time when Mr Wilkins arrives.' Accounts, rents and the problems of the unsatisfactory tenant of Lower Acre Farm should divert her thoughts from the bedroom most effectively. The clock struck the half-hour, reminding her that distractions only served to bring bedtime closer and she still had no idea how she was going to react when Will came to her chamber door. Or how she was going to tell him what she must.

'That can wait.' He stood up, long and lean and as disturbing as a panther in the civilised room. Julia sat quite still in her chair as he walked past her. If he was going out, it would give her a soothing half-hour with the books…

'You were very kind to Aunt Delia, although she cannot have been easy to get on with, these past three years,' he said. Right behind her.

'We have learned to rub along. Your return was a shock and I feel sorry for her—she knows Henry is slipping out of her control and she has invested all her energies in him. It can only get worse when he begins to take an interest in courting. She will be a lonely woman soon.'

'And you were not only supportive to my aunt.' Will must be standing immediately behind her. Julia imagined she could feel the heat of his body. The upholstered chair back moved slightly and she realised he had closed his hand over it, just beside her shoulder. 'You have been loyal to me. *Wifely.*' He seemed to find the word amusing: she could hear the smile in his voice.

'Naturally. I am your wife, after all. It is important to keep up appearances.' She was *not* smiling. In fact, even to herself, she sounded miserably priggish.

'You are anxious to make this marriage work, then?' A featherlight touch on her shoulder, barely discernible through the light muslin scarf that filled the neckline of her morning gown. *Imagination. No, real.* Now the finger was stroking across the muslin, touching the bare skin of her neck, lingering to explore the sensitive skin just behind her right ear.

When she swallowed he must have felt it. She hated to betray her agitation, even by a little involuntary movement. 'Of course I am.'

'What is this?' Will's breath stirred the fine wisps along her hairline. He must have bent close. If she turned, they would be face to face, their lips might meet...

Chapter Nine

She felt as though she was made of tinder
and Will was holding a flame so close, so
very close. Julia kept still with an effort and
said lightly, 'The scar? I was chased by a
bull and had to throw myself into a hedge.
I emerged rather the worse for wear.' It was
only a little scar, just a quarter of an inch
long. She could feel it under her fingers when
she washed or dabbed scent behind her ear.
'I had not thought it showed. Is it very red?'

'Not at all. I only noticed it because I
was looking very closely.' The warm breath
moved, trailed its caress right round to the
other side of her neck. Julia rolled her eyes
uncomfortably to the left, rigid with the effort not to shiver. Will loomed beside her.

After a moment, to her intense relief, he straightened up and strolled back to hitch one hip on the edge of the desk. 'Farming appears to be a dangerous operation when you undertake it. I never found it necessary to traipse around fields looking at bulls, let alone provoke them into chasing me.'

'Which explains why the one you had was an inferior specimen with an unreliable temper. Unlike my...*our* current bull.' From the way he narrowed his eyes at her Julia could only assume that criticising a man's bull was like criticising his own virility.

'It will not be necessary for you to get your hands dirty, or your shoes muddy, or to endanger yourself in any way connected with the estate from now on. Let alone indulge in such occupations as judging stud animals. Hardly a ladylike thing to be doing in any case.'

That was the attitude she had feared he would adopt. 'But I am good at it. And I enjoy it. All of it. It is, after all, why you married me.' She kept her tone free from any hint of pleading, or of aggression.

'But the situation has changed. And there are many things in life that we enjoy that it is not acceptable that we indulge ourselves in.'

Julia swallowed the very rude retort that sprang to her lips, although the impulse to demonstrate just how unacceptable her behaviour could be by going upstairs, changing into her divided skirt and boots and riding astride round the estate was almost overwhelming. She folded her hands neatly in her lap and remarked, 'That is the sort of remark that gentlemen make when they intend it to apply to wives and daughters, never to themselves.'

'Are you suggesting that I behave in a manner not befitting a gentleman?' The lazy amusement had quite vanished although Will still lounged there, apparently at ease.

Julia shrugged. 'Gentlemanly behaviour appears to encompass gaming, whoring and drinking. All wives can do about it, so I understand, is to hope that the mistresses are not too expensive, that the gaming is for low stakes and that the drinking does not lead to imprudent expenditure on the other two entertainments.'

'I see.' Will got off the desk and went back to his chair. All inclination to flirt, or tease her by caressing her neck, had obviously vanished. 'It is a little late to be enquiring about my character, don't you think?'

'If it was vicious, or your activities scandalous, I would doubtless have heard about it by now.' Julia got up and went to the pile of ledgers stacked on a side table. She knew where she was with those. They did not answer back, play with words or look at her with eyes that tried to strip her to the soul. She wanted to tell him that of course she knew his character was good, but she could not find the words.

'You may rest assured, my dear, that I dislike over-indulgence in drink, I gamble well within my means and I am not in the habit of whoring.' When she did not reply Will added, 'I assume you also wish to know whether I have a mistress in keeping, but do not like to ask directly?'

She had not meant this to go so far, or even to mention the subject. Her back to him, Julia shrugged, pretending an indifference she found she certainly did not feel. What she felt was a surge of uncivilised jealousy at the very thought. 'I presume that you have.'

'No.'

The heavy cover of the ledger for the Home Farm slipped from her fingers and banged shut as she turned. 'But you have been gone three years.'

'Until I began to get better again I had neither the inclination nor the strength for… dalliance.' Will was doodling again so she could not see his face, but his voice was stiff. 'Since I regained both I have reminded myself that I am a married man who made certain vows.'

Oh. She believed him. It was not easy for a man to admit that his virility had suffered in any way, she suspected. But that meant her husband was not simply feeling normally amorous. He had been celibate for months, so the restraint he had shown with her so far was nothing short of amazing.

Will had made vows and so had she. She had no intention of keeping him from her bed, however frightened that made her. But she was *damned* if she was going to allow him to seduce her into being simply a meek little wife—in bed or out of it.

'Then I imagine I should be looking forward to tonight?' she asked. It came out sounding more flippant, or perhaps provocative, than she intended and she saw from the flare of heat in his eyes that she had both aroused and shocked Will.

'Julia,' he said, his voice husky, getting to

his feet, 'you may be certain of a most appreciative reception.'

'Mr Wilkins, my la…my lord, I should say.' Gatcombe sounded unusually flustered. Julia could only hope it was as a result of getting in a tangle over who he should be addressing and not because he had heard anything of their conversation when he opened the door.

The steward was a wiry Midlander with a cautious attitude and a depth of knowledge that Julia admired. It had taken her several weeks to break down his reserve when he discovered he was expected to take orders from a woman, but the realisation that she knew what she was talking about, and was quite tough enough to hold her own in an argument, soon swayed him.

Now, she could tell, Wilkins was uneasy because he was uncertain who was in control. 'I'm right glad to see you back with us, my lord,' he said, when greetings had been exchanged. 'I've no doubt her ladyship's been telling you all we've been about while you've been away.'

'Nothing, beyond the fact that you have been most effective, Wilkins.' Will gestured to a chair. 'Come and brief me.' He stood up and smiled at Julia. 'Thank you, my dear.'

It was a polite dismissal she had no intention of accepting. Julia smiled sweetly back and feigned not to understand him. 'It was my pleasure,' she said, settling back into her own chair. 'Mr Wilkins, perhaps you could bring those ledgers over.'

For a long moment it seemed likely that Will was going to order her from the room, witness or no witness, then he smiled wryly and sat down again. 'Let us begin with the livestock, Wilkins. I understand we have a new bull.'

Julia had done a good job, Will had to acknowledge—it far exceeded his hopes when he had thought up this scheme in the first place. She had gone beyond offering Wilkins informed support, she had taken the lead and steered the rather cautious steward into projects and changes he would never have dreamt of on his own initiative.

But now she was not going to hand back control without a fight. Will let them both talk, interjected a question now and again and realised it was going to take a while to break Wilkins of the habit of looking to his wife for approval with every comment. He did not want to be unkind to her, or unappreciative, but damn it all, he was master here and he was going to make that clear. In the estate, on the farm, in the bedchamber.

'I have horses arriving in a few weeks,' Will said when they had talked themselves to a standstill.

'Fifteen, Wilkins,' Julia said. 'We are going to need new paddocks, stabling. More staff…'

'I have men coming with them,' Will overrode her smoothly. 'And plans for the stables. Where would you suggest for the paddocks, Wilkins?'

'To the west of the existing ones,' Julia answered before the steward could. 'I have been considering it. We can move the beef cattle down to Mayday Field and Croft Acre and—'

'We do not have fields with those names.'

'We do now. I bought Hodgson's farm when old Jem Hodgson died last year,' Julia said, as if purchasing a large farm was as simple a matter as buying a new bonnet. 'His son has gone into the building business and needed the capital urgently so we settled on a keen price. I had the house done up and I lease it and ten acres to make a small park to a cit called Maurice Loveday. It brings a good income and we've gained another mile of water meadows into the bargain.'

He had had his eye on that farm for years and old Hodgson had refused to sell. Now his wife had calmly snapped it up, at a bargain price, and secured the income from the house—which had never occurred to him as an asset—while she was at it.

Will trod firmly on what felt uncomfortably like jealousy and smiled at Julia. 'You must have had hardly a moment to yourself, taking so much responsibility. Now I am back you can relax and get back to all your normal pursuits.'

'Oh, but these are my normal pursuits,' she responded with an equally false smile. 'This is what I enjoy doing.' *And try to take it away from me if you can,* those grey eyes said, meeting his with flint-hard resolve.

One thing had kept him going in those years of exile. His love for King's Acre was real and solid and his control of it was not negotiable.

What his wife needed was something else to keep her occupied. Womanly things. A man in her bed, babies in the nursery. Both of those, he realised with some surprise, would be an absolute pleasure to provide.

Will had not been pleased with her contribution to the meeting with the steward. Nor with the free expression of her thoughts when Mr Howard from Home Farm arrived after luncheon. It was obvious that the deference those gentlemen showed to her opinions was also an irritation. There was no need for her to attend when he met tomorrow with Mr Burrows the solicitor, Will had informed Julia with a smile that had not reached his eyes.

The words did not pass his lips, but it was plain to her that he considered her continuing interest meddling and interfering. Her proper place, in his opinion, was in the bedchamber and the drawing room and the only servants she should need to concern herself with were the domestic staff.

I have been the regent while the king was in exile, she thought with a grim attempt at humour that evening. *The state has been well governed but now the queen must go back to woman's work and leave the serious business to the men.*

But kingdoms required heirs—that was

what husbands wanted, whether they were King of England or Joe Bloggs at the village forge. She stared blankly into the mirror on her dressing table until her maid put down the evening gown she had been shaking out and said, 'Excuse me, my lady, but are you all right?'

'What? Oh, yes, perfectly, thank you, Nancy.' Julia went back to dabbing Warren's Milk of Roses on to her face. She was persevering with this infallible remedy for freckles and the effects of the sun on the complexion more in the hope than the expectation of a fashionably pale skin. The true remedy, of course, was to wear a broad-brimmed hat at all times, or, better still, as Aunt Delia so often told her with a sigh, to stay inside as a lady should.

If Will had his way, she would be as pale as a lily in no time. And drooping like one too, from sheer boredom. Her mind was still skittering away from contemplating the prospect of becoming pregnant again. It seemed very likely to happen quickly once her husband came to her bed: after all, she had lain just the once with Jonathan.

Her fingers fumbled as she tried to replace the top of the bottle and Nancy fell to her knees and started to search under the skirts of the dressing table for the dropped stopper. Julia had dammed it up so long—the shock when she had realised that the changes in her body were not the result of terror and distress, then the joy at the realisation that she was carrying a child and the appalled comprehension of what she must do if it proved to be a boy.

But, even with that hanging over her, the overwhelming emotion had been delight and love. If the child was a daughter, then she would not have to tell anyone, for a girl would be no threat to Henry's rights. And even if it was a boy, she would work something out to give him a future and happiness.

It never occurred to her, with all her worries and plans, that she might lose the baby. Now she wondered about future pregnancies. What if there was something wrong with her? What if she was not capable of safely birthing a child? She had not even considered it before, because she had expected to stay a widow for the rest of her days, contentedly farming King's Acre and then, when Henry inherited, buying her own land. But now she was no longer a widow.

'That lotion is working a treat, my lady.'

Nancy sat back on her heels with the stopper in her hand and regarded Julia with satisfaction. 'I swear you're a shade paler for using it.'

'I fear it is simply that I have a slight headache, Nancy.' Julia attempted a smile. 'I will be better for a glass of wine and my dinner, I am sure.'

By the time her stays had been tightened and the gown was on and her hair dressed there was some colour back in her cheeks and at least the freckles were not standing out like dots on white paper.

It was a warm evening, almost sultry. Julia draped her lightest shawl over her elbows, chose a large fan and went down to the drawing room. Her first proper evening as a married lady, she realised as the butler opened the door for her and she saw Will standing by the long window that was open to the ground to let in the evening air.

He was dressed with as much careful formality as she. Julia admired the effect of silk evening breeches, striped stockings, a swallowtail coat that must have been bought in London on his way home and a waistcoat of amber silk that brought out the colour of his eyes and matched the stone in the stickpin in his neckcloth. Regarded dispassionately, she thought, her husband was a fine figure of a man. Discovering *how* to be dispassionate about him was going to be the problem. *A lost cause, in fact,* she told herself.

'Good evening, Lady Dereham.' He gestured towards the decanters set out on a tray. 'A glass of sherry wine?'

'Good evening, my lord.' She sat precisely in the centre of the sofa and spread her almond-green skirts on either side as though concerned about wrinkles. They covered virtually all the available seat and left no room for anyone to sit beside her. She did not think she could cope with any sly caresses just now. 'Thank you. A glass of sherry would be delightful.'

Will poured a glass for both of them, placed hers on the table beside her and went back to the window and his contemplation of the view, which allowed her the perfect opportunity to admire his profile. Dispassionately, of course.

'Did your meeting with Mr Burrows go well?' Julia asked after a few minutes' silence. She took a sip of her wine while her husband pondered his reply.

'It was most satisfactory, thank you,' he said politely and tasted his own drink.

If this continues, I may well scream, simply for the diversion of seeing the footmen all rush in, Julia decided. 'I have always found him extremely helpful.'

'He tells me you have not asked for any of the jewellery from his strong room.'

'I did not consider it mine to wear.' For some reason decking herself out in the family jewels had seemed mercenary in a way that taking all the other benefits of their arrangement did not. Jewellery was so personal. 'Besides,' she added in an effort to lighten the cool formality, 'think what a wrench to have to hand it all over after seven years when Henry inherited.'

'There was no need for such scruples. But you will wear it from now on, I hope.' She suspected that was an order. 'Burrows brought it with him.' Will gestured towards a side table and she noticed the stack of leather boxes on it for the first time. 'There is a safe in your dressing room. If there are any pieces you dislike they can be reset, or go back to the vault.'

There seemed a lot of boxes. Small ring boxes, flat cases with curving edges that must contain necklaces, complicated shapes that presumably enclosed complete parures including tiaras. Did Will expect her to pounce on them with cries of delight?

He thought she had only married him for purely mercenary reasons and to protect her good name, of course, so he must find her lack of interest in this treasure trove puzzling. She could hardly tell him that she did not want his money or his gems, only sanctuary from the law.

'Thank you. But I have not found a safe. Is it behind some concealed panel?'

'Behind a panel, yes, but in the baroness's dressing room. Nancy is moving your things there now.'

Somehow Julia kept her lips closed on the instinctive protest. Will was high-handed, insensitive, but, of course, he was in the right and she had agreed he would come to her bed.

He might not want her, of course, when she told him about Jonathan and about the child.

She pushed that thought and its implications deep into her mind. There were practical reasons also. Her place should be in the suite that was the mirror image of his:

anything else would cause gossip and wild speculation amongst the servants. She knew, however loyal they were, gossip always leaked out to the staff in surrounding houses, then to the tradesmen and in no time at all the entire neighbourhood would know.

'Thank you,' she said with a genuine smile and was rewarded by the faint surprise on Will's face. He had expected a fight, but she was going to keep her opposition for the issues that were important to her. Jewels did not matter one way or the other, except that now she must make the effort to care for them and to select suitable ones for each occasion.

Julia exerted herself over dinner to make conversation and bring Will up to date with the local news. He would be riding round to visit their neighbours over the next few days, so she must set the scene for him. It also meant she could steer well clear of any personal matters. There was plenty to tell him about with a new curate, several marriages, some deaths, the strange case of sheep-stealing last year, Sir William Curruther's new wife's frightful taste in interior decoration and, of course, numerous births to the gentry community. She hurried over those and started enumerating the changes to their own staff while he had been away.

'Thank you,' he said drily when she reached the new scullery maid and the gardener's boy as the dessert plates were cleared. 'I will endeavour to recall all that tomorrow.'

Julia bit her lip—he made it sound as though she had been prattling on and not allowing him to get a word in edgeways. She had kept pausing, hoping Will would pick up his side of the conversation and tell her about his three years away. But he showed no sign of wanting to confide in her. 'I have got all the news I was saving for you off my chest,' she said. 'Tomorrow you can tell me yours.'

'I have told you most of what there is to know.' His long lashes hid his eyes as he looked down, apparently interested in the piece of walnut shell that lay beside his plate. 'I have no wish to revisit the past.'

'But your travels must be fascinating. I would so like to hear about them.' A neutral subject of conversation on an engrossing subject seemed like a godsend.

'I lost almost four years of my life to that illness,' Will said and looked up to catch her staring at him. 'I just want to forget about it and get on with living.'

She could hear the anger and the loss under the flat tone, see the heat in his eyes.

'Very well.' She had no wish to invite any further snubs. 'I will leave you to your port.' One of the footmen came to pull back her chair, another to open the door for her. Like all the staff, they were normally efficient and attentive, but somehow she sensed they were making a special effort to look after her at the moment, just as they had when she lost the baby. She could only hope that Will did not notice and feel they were being disloyal to him.

If she could just focus her mind on those sort of worries and not what was going to happen when the bedchamber door closed behind them, then she could, perhaps, remain her normal practical self. As she walked across the hall to the salon she could feel the brooding presence in the room behind her like heat from a fire. Common sense seemed as much use as a fireguard made of straw.

Chapter Ten

Will did not leave her alone in the salon for long. Julia had hardly picked up her embroidery, sorted her wools and begun on one of the roses that formed a garland on the chair seat she was working when he walked in, still carrying his wine glass, Charles on his heels with the decanter.

'What are you making?' He sank into the wing chair opposite her, stretched out long legs and sipped his port. Charles put the decanter down and took himself off. They were alone at last, with no servants present to keep the conversation on neutral lines.

'A new set of seat covers for the breakfast room.' She tilted the frame to show him.

'The existing ones are sadly worn and the moth has got into them.'

'My paternal grandmother made those.'

'I was not going to throw them away,' Julia hastened to reassure him. 'I will try to save as much of her embroidery as I can and perhaps incorporate it into window seat covers or something of the sort.'

'It is a lot of work for you.' Will was twisting the stem of the glass between his fingers, watching the red wine swirl in the glass.

'I do not mind. I dislike being idle.'

'Hmm.' It seemed her husband did not wish to make conversation. Perhaps he wanted her to retire. *Well, my lord, I have no intention of going to bed at half past nine so you can exercise your conjugal rights!* Nor was she looking forward to the conversation that she knew she must have with him first. She could not talk about it down here and risk being interrupted.

Julia executed a complex area of shading and worked on in silence attempting, with what success she had no idea, to exude an air of placid domesticity. At nine forty-five she rang for tea and contemplated her husband over the rim of her cup.

If she did not know better she would think

him not *nervous*, exactly, but certainly edgy. Which was nonsensical—women were the ones supposed to be anxious about this sort of situation, not adult males with, she had no doubt, years of sexual experience behind them.

Now she had made herself nervous. Julia set down her cup with a rattle. 'I shall retire, if you will excuse me.'

Will stood up with punctilious courtesy and went to open the door for her. She had thought that she had got used to his presence, but the sense that he was too big and too male swept over her again and it was an effort not to scuttle into the hall like a nervous mouse. *Calm, seductive,* she reminded herself. *Make him want* you, *not just any wife.* But perhaps, when she had told him as much as she dare about Jonathan, he would not want her at all.

Nancy was waiting to help her undress when she made her way to her new suite. 'I've moved all your things, my lady. Such a nice spacious dressing room: there's plenty of room for your new gowns. And Mr Gatcombe brought all the jewellery boxes up and has put them in the safe. Shall we check the inventory tomorrow, my lady? I don't like to be responsible when we haven't got a list of what's there.'

'Yes,' Julia agreed, studying the room as if she had not seen it before. It was large with a deep Venetian window, a marble fireplace and a handsome bed in the classical style with pale-green curtains. The pictures were dull, she thought, attempting to divert her thoughts from the bed. There were others in the house that would look better here—that was something to do tomorrow. And there was the jewellery to look at. And she must think about new gowns for the entertaining Will was sure to want to do.

If she was not careful her day would become filled with all the trivial domestic duties her husband thought she should be engaging in.

'Such a pity we didn't know his lordship was coming home,' Nancy said as she picked up the hairbrush and began to take down Julia's hair. 'You could have bought some pretty new nightgowns, my lady.'

Now the butterflies really were churning in her stomach. She was about to sleep with a man for only the second time in her life. No, third, she supposed, although sharing a bed with Will on their wedding night had been sleeping only in the literal sense.

She was not in love with him and he was certainly not in love with her. She did not have a pretty new nightgown, and, rather more importantly to her confidence, she had carried a child to term, which doubtless would make her body less desirable to him.

When he learned that she was not a virgin perhaps he would expect considerably more sensual expertise than she could possibly muster. She was not at all sure what sexual expertise consisted of for a woman. Her resolve to make him desire her just as much as she desired him was beginning to look much like wishful thinking.

But sitting up in bed ten minutes later she did feel rather more seductive. If, that is, one could feel seductive and terrified simultaneously. Her nightgown might not be new, but the lace trim was pretty, her hair was brushed out smoothly about her shoulders and she could smell the scent of rosewater rising from a number of places that Nancy assured her were strategic pulse points.

All she needed now, Julia thought as Nancy left the room with a cheerful, 'Good-night, my lady', was a gentleman to seduce.

She kept her eyes on the door panels and tried to conjure up the image of Will to practise on. Smiling was too obvious. She tried to achieve a sultry smoulder. The nightgown was too prim. She unlaced the ribbon at the neck and pushed it down over her shoulders a little. Even without the help of stays her bosom, she decided, was acceptably firm and high. Men liked bosoms, she knew that much.

Now, all she had to do was to maintain that look and manage not to be sick out of sheer nerves until the door opened. Then she realised that she had her confession to make first and that to attempt seduction and *then* to reveal the unpleasant truths would seem as if she was trying to manipulate him. Julia threw back the covers to climb out of bed.

'Very nice.' The husky voice came from inside the room to her left.

Julia gave a small scream and twisted round to find her husband lounging against the frame of an open jib door she had quite forgotten about. Of course, she realised as she fought for some poise, it led to his dressing room, but it was so cunningly set into the panels it was almost invisible when closed. 'You made me jump.'

'And that was very nice, too.' He strolled into the room and closed the door behind him. His eyes were on her body and when she looked down she realised that her involuntary start combined with the loosened ribbon had revealed more of the swell of her bosom than she ever intended.

Will was still wearing the thin evening breeches and his shirt, but everything else had gone, the shirt was open at the neck and the cuffs turned back. The casual disarray seemed even more intimate than the silk robe he had been wearing that morning and the part of her brain that was not either panicking, or thinking shamefully wanton thoughts, wondered if that was deliberate.

'May I join you, my lady?' His hands were on the open edges of his shirt.

'I... Of course. But not in bed. Not yet. I have to talk to you.'

'Talk? We have been sitting downstairs for some time this evening. I would have thought that the time for talking was past.'

Julia took a shuddering breath. 'This is not something I wanted to discuss downstairs. This is in the nature of a confession.'

The amusement, and the sensuality, were

quite gone from Will's face now. 'Confession?'

Julia took a key from the bedside table. 'We need to go back to my old room.'

'Very well.' His eyes were narrowed in calculation, or perhaps suspicion, but he waited while she tied her robe and led the way along the passageways until they were outside the door next to her room. She unlocked it and stood aside, feeling sick. With a sharp glance at her face Will pushed it open and went in.

What the devil was going on? Will had expected to be making love to his wife by now, not looking at spare rooms. He glanced around. When he had left this had been a sitting room, a little boudoir for lady guests using the bedchambers at this end of the house. Now there was a cradle draped in white lawn, a low nursing chair, a pretty dresser.

The nursery was up on the floor above. It still had, he recalled, his old crib, his childhood bed, his toys. What was this room doing furnished as a nursery? This *unoccupied* room? Behind him Julia was silent. Will opened a drawer in the dresser. It was full of tiny garments, a lacy shawl, little caps. One pile was weighted down with a rattle, silver and coral that jingled as he lifted it.

He dropped the rattle back into the drawer with a faint tinkle of bells, the realisation of what this meant stealing through his consciousness. He felt sick.

'Where is the child?' he asked as he turned back to the door.

His voice was perfectly calm, but Julia flinched as though he had shouted, struck at her. 'He was born dead.'

Will stayed precisely where he was until he got the flare of anger under control. If it *was* anger, that sharp nauseating pain under his breastbone. He had never lifted a finger to a woman in his life and he was not going to now. He was not his father: civilised men dealt with these things in a civilised manner. But he had not expected to be cuckolded, which, he supposed, showed a lack of imagination on his part, given the family history.

'Well,' he drawled, 'I have heard of some interesting accidents of birth, but I hope you are not going to tell me fairy stories. Whose child was he?'

'Yours,' Julia said flatly. 'In law. He was born nine months after I married and was bedded by my husband. By you. The law accepts any child born in wedlock as legitimate unless the husband refuses to acknowledge it. If you deny him, then you can only do it by revealing our marriage for the sham that it was.'

It took him a moment to find his voice. 'That little speech sounded rehearsed. Have you been lying awake all night fretting over how you were going to talk yourself out of this predicament? No wonder the door was locked. How long did you expect to keep me in ignorance?'

Julia pushed herself away from the door, walked across to the table set in the window alcove and began to shift things around with jerky, nervous movements. 'This is not how I meant to tell you. I could not find the words and now it has all gone wrong. But predicament? Is that what you call it? A child died. It was a tragedy.'

She started to turn away, but Will caught her wrist, the narrow bones delicate in his grip. She went white, but pulled against him with surprising strength. He stopped himself from tightening his hold, but he did not let her go.

'Whose child was he? Henry's?'

'Henry's?' Her expression was one of total shock. 'Of course not! How could you think I would do such a thing? He was the child of Jo—of the man I eloped with.'

'You eloped? You didn't run away from home to avoid a forced marriage as you told me? So what you told me was a lie?' What a fool he'd been. Respectable ladies did not run away from home like that. Of *course* there had been a man.

Julia pressed her lips together and her gaze dropped from his. 'Yes. I…I thought you would not help me if you knew what I… the truth.' She was stumbling over the words, biting her lip. 'I thought he loved me, would wed me, but it was all a plot between him and my cousins to get rid of me. I lay with him before I realised he never had any intention of marrying me.'

'So you ran away from him soon after you had eloped?'

'Yes, the very first evening. When I realised we were not heading north I confronted him. He admitted he was taking me to London. I waited until he was…asleep and then I ran away.'

There was something wrong with the story, he could sense it. Not all lies, but not

the whole truth either. 'And after one bed-
ding you were with child?' To his own ears
he sounded as sceptical as he felt. 'I do not
think so. You ran off when he refused to provide for a fallen woman with a brat in her
belly. It explains why you were so anxious
to secure a husband.'

Julia flinched at his crudity and Will bit
back the instinctive apology. 'You think
that was why I agreed to your scheme?' She
pulled back against his grip and this time he
let her go, expecting her to retreat. Instead
she stayed where she was, a puzzled frown
on her face, as though she looked back to
that night and was surprised at what she saw
there. 'You may believe what you will, but
strangely enough the possibility that I might
be with child did not occur to me then. I was
ruined and desperate: that was enough.'

No, my lady, I do not believe you, he
thought. There was something she was hiding, he could sense it, almost smell it. How
the devil had he been so deceived that he
had thought her an innocent, a respectable
woman with nothing to hide except a bully-
ing family? The memory of her reluctance
to share his bed on their wedding night, of
that innocent, trusting kiss came back. *In-*

nocent. He had been sick, exhausted, in a fever—he supposed that accounted for his lack of perception.

'Henry and Delia must have been frantic when they realised you were pregnant,' Will observed, finding a certain grim humour in the thought. He would have liked to have been a fly on the wall during that conversation—and yet Julia was on good terms with Delia now. That argued some clever diplomacy. Oh, no, it would not do to underestimate his wife. Not just another man's mistress and a liar, but as intelligent as he had first thought.

'They were as relieved as you obviously are that my child was stillborn, although at least they managed to conceal it decently.'

'And what would you have done if the baby had lived?' How subtly the colour ebbed and flowed under her skin, he thought, studying the curve of cheek that was all he could see of her averted face. She had grown into a kind of understated beauty that he could have sworn she had not possessed before. One tear trembled on the end of her lashes. Very effective, Will told himself, fighting the instinct to pull her into his arms and comfort her. That was what she wanted, hoped—to twist him round her little finger.

'If he had lived, I would have had to admit the truth. I was prepared for that: I could not have cheated Henry out of his rights.'

'No? You expect me to believe that you could deny your own child a title and an inheritance? Keep silent and you would have been the mother of the heir. You would have had another twenty-one years as mistress of King's Acre.'

'It would not have been right,' she said doggedly, as though she really believed what she was saying.

'So you would have bastardised your own son? Forgive me if I do not believe you.'

She swung back, control lost at last, her fury with him plain on her face. 'You think I could live a falsehood like that?' Her voice was low and shaking with vehemence. 'You think I could defraud a decent man of his inheritance and make my own child an innocent party to that for his entire life?'

'I have no idea what you might do, Julia,' Will said, as much to see the fire spark in her eyes—flint struck against steel—as to continue the argument. His body was beginning to remind him that he had been celibate for a very long time. Too long.

'Well, I could not do such a thing. You hardly know me, so you will just have to accept my word.' She caught her full lower lip between her teeth in a way that had him biting his own lip until the pain reminded his body just who was in charge. When he did not speak she turned and went to the dresser, smoothed her hand over the garments that lay inside the open drawer, then pushed it closed.

'Do I?' Will asked her unresponsive back. 'What if I chose not to accept it? What if I decide that you have lied to me, deceived me from the start in order to foist another man's bastard on me? What would the law's opinion of our unconsummated marriage be then, I wonder?'

Julia turned and looked at him steadily as though down the blade of a rapier. 'You think to cast me off? You may try if you are so unkind—and so uncaring of the world knowing you were incapable of making me your wife. But if you think to do it so you may court your pretty Caroline Fletcher, you will be disappointed. She is betrothed to the Earl of Dunstable who appears to be in complete possession of all his faculties and a great deal of money besides.'

Of course she is. Caroline had thought him dying and could not cope with that. Once she believed him dead she would not have gone into mourning. Curiously, he found he did not care in the slightest. Will shrugged. 'She is beautiful, richly dowered. It is a miracle she is not already wed. It is nothing to me.'

Julia turned towards the door. The white-muslin wrapper flounced around her feet as she walked, her steps rapid and jerky as though she really wanted to run and was holding herself in check. The sash was belted tight around her natural waistline and showed the curve of hip and buttock, the elegant line of her back.

His mouth dried and he had to moisten his lips before he said, 'We can hope that the next one is also a boy to put poor Henry out of his misery.'

'The next one?' Julia stammered.

She was going to refuse to sleep with him? 'You want to have it both ways?' Will demanded. 'You want me to acknowledge that I was the father of your stillborn child, you want the rights of marriage and yet you would deny them to me?'

'You would not expose me?' She had gone bone-white, whiter even than when she had told him about the baby. The possibility of scandal seemed to terrify her.

Will shrugged. 'No, of course not. I am not attempting to blackmail you. But if you cannot be truly my wife, then we will have to end this marriage somehow for both our sakes. Coming back from the dead rearranges one's priorities somewhat. You'd be amazed what I find utterly unimportant now. What I *do* find important, what I have always, is that we have the truth between us. I will not be deceived and lied to, Julia. I grew up in a household of lies and deceptions and I'll not stand for it now. I cannot live like that and I certainly cannot bring up children in that atmosphere.'

Chapter Eleven

They stared at each other and gradually Julia found she could focus and move from blind panic to actually listening to what they were saying to each other. Will thought she was going to try to keep him from her bed and that was never what she had intended.

Julia swallowed hard. 'I have no intention of being other than a proper wife to you, if you will have me. I just needed a little time to come to terms with it, that is all. I am sorry if you cannot believe me about the elopement, but it was the truth.'

If only she could understand the roiling mix of emotions inside her. Over all of it was the terror that a public scandal would expose her and that she would be arrested for Jonathan's murder. Below that, like fish swimming in muddy water, were layers of other feelings. There was fear of the intimacy, of being hurt again, physically and mentally. And there was the attraction she felt for Will, due, she supposed, to him being such an attractive man. But if she became pregnant again, what would happen? Could she carry the child safely? If she lost another... Her mind shied away from the thought because it was simply too painful to think about.

But she had her duty to her husband and she owed Will a great deal. If it had not been for him, goodness knows what would have become of her three years ago. The fear and the pain and the doubt she would somehow have to overcome.

He was studying her with those dangerous amber eyes. 'It was a shock,' he said eventually. 'If it had not been for the baby, would you have told me about your lover?'

'I do not know,' Julia confessed. 'Would you have been able to tell?'

'Possibly,' Will said with a wry smile. 'Probably.'

'Shall we...I mean, do you want to...?' How difficult it was! To want something and yet to be so frightened of it.

'Yes, I want to,' he said. 'If you are sure.'

Julia nodded and walked before him, back to her bedchamber. She turned when she reached the bed and watched her husband as he closed the door and came towards her.

Courage. Seduce him. Oh, who do you think you are fooling? You could not seduce anyone to save your life. No, don't think that...

One glance at those skintight breeches told her that her husband did not need much encouragement. Of course, he had been without a woman for a long time, which would explain it. But she wanted him to want *her*, not just any woman to slake his desires with.

What would he expect her to do now? Jonathan had simply ripped off his clothes, then her clothes, tossed her on to the bed and threw himself down beside her.

Will pulled the shirt over his head, dropped it at his feet, flipped back the covers and waited courteously for her to get into bed. 'Now that is a very piquant contrast,' he said as he stood and studied her. 'All that prim white cotton tight around your legs and all that slipping lace up above.'

Julia looked down. Her nervous shifting about had wrapped the nightgown around her legs. Then she looked up at Will. Looked properly and felt dizzy. When she had met him on the bridge that night and had held him in her arms she had felt nothing but skin and bone. Now she was contemplating muscle as defined as that on any classical sculpture of an athlete. Only this was not cold white marble, this was golden tanned skin, a dusting of dark-brown hair, the blue of veins, the nipples so much darker than her own.

Jonathan's body had not made that much impression on her, she realised. When he had first undressed it had all been so fast she had no time to look at him and afterwards… Afterwards she seemed to recall thinking that he was beautiful. But not with the emotions that looking at this man produced. Better not to think about Jonathan.

It was hard to think about any other man clearly at all with this one so close and so nearly naked.

'I am all in favour of piquancy,' she managed, her gaze fixed firmly on his chest and the curls of crisp dark-brown hair.

'Good,' Will murmured, 'because I am intending to leave you nicely wrapped up for a while.' And while she tried to work out what that meant he slipped open the fastening of his breeches, slid them down his legs and kicked them away. Underneath he was quite naked. And quite magnificently aroused.

Will lay down on his side on the sheet, his body touching hot down the length of her. He propped himself up on one elbow so they were eye to eye, reached out, tugged one of the pillows away and followed her down when she fell back with a little gasp of surprise.

A gasp that left her mouth open, Julia realised as Will leant in and kissed her, his mouth warm and moist and tasting of brandy. The move had been assured and predatory and she found both amazingly arousing.

She had learned from that morning's kiss and had learned, too, what she liked. If she tangled her tongue with his then Will thrust more deeply, if she closed her lips a little then he would nip and nibble at them. She tried nibbling in return and felt his mouth curve in response. *He likes that.* She tried a little nip and was rewarded by a growl deep in his throat.

That was encouraging, she thought. He no longer seemed shocked or angry with her. But what now? Jonathan had been fast, and, she was beginning to realise as Will nibbled down the line of her jaw and sucked gently at the base of her throat with leisurely relish, not at all subtle.

She should be doing something seductive, but it was difficult when she was not at all sure what that involved and when her legs were restricted by her twisted nightgown and Will's arm was effectively pinning hers to the bed.

Julia moaned in frustration and arched up to try to free herself, squashing her breasts against Will, who was nuzzling into her cleavage. The effect was startling. He growled, twisted, seized the collar of her nightgown, ripped it clean down to her waist, then spread the two halves open and stared down at her.

Was something wrong? Why was he looking at her like that? It was her figure, that was it. She was no longer fresh and young and virginal… Just when she could not stand the suspense any longer he bent his head and licked, lavishly, slowly, over her right nipple. And then the left. And back. They went hard and tight and he caught first one, then the other in his teeth and Julia sobbed, arching again, wanting more. He increased the pressure until it was a tiny stab of pain that arrowed into her belly and became something else entirely: heat and weight and need. Then he licked again while his hand took hold of the torn edge of her nightgown and yanked down hard and it tore as far as her knees.

Now he would cover her with his body, push her legs apart, take her. She fought a silent battle with the memories and the fear. It had hurt and Jonathan had not been careful. And Will was very aroused, she knew enough to understand that. Julia tried not to let her apprehension show, tried not to freeze.

But Will kept on tormenting her breasts as he stroked down into the brown curls that were embarrassingly damp. *Wet*, she thought, shocked, as his fingers parted her and then she forgot to be self-conscious as the strange deep ache got worse and worse and she twisted, pushing up against the heel of his hand.

Am I supposed to feel like this? It was so much more than when she had lost her virginity. Then she had felt a little of this, but not the all-consuming desperate need for *something*. 'I want you inside me,' she gasped, beyond shame. That must be it, that was what her body was clamouring for.

'Patience,' Will said and blew on her nipples while his fingers played and teased and suddenly found a point of perfect, shocking pleasure.

'*Will.*'

He came to his knees, freed her completely from the nightgown and finally, *finally,* covered her with his body. But his fingers did not stop their torment and everything was tightening into an impossibly tangled knot and she did not know how she could bear it.

'Julia. Look at me.' Will's voice was husky and she dragged open her eyes and stared into the amber heat of his. 'Are you all right?'

'No! No, I'm not...I can't bear it. Please...' She had no idea what she wanted, only that she needed him inside her and his weight on her and his mouth on hers. And by some miracle he understood her incoherent plea. He lowered himself, speared his fingers into her hair, drove with his hips and filled her in one long, hard thrust. Everything unravelled, broke apart as she heard herself scream, felt her body close, tight, on Will as he moved and then he froze, shuddered under her clutching hands and collapsed on to her body.

Selfish bastard, Will thought as his brain stopped spinning. He lay pillowed on Julia's sweet warmth and contemplated her lover, the one she had eloped with, the one who had not, apparently, thought to give her any pleasure at all while he took what he wanted.

She had been as ignorant of what her own body could experience as a virgin. He smiled into the crook of her neck and lipped gently at the warm skin. Her arms were still around him and he became aware of the gentle movement of her fingers. She was stroking his shoulders lightly, as if exploring, like someone blind reaching out to map their world with their fingertips.

Had she any idea how seductive that innocence was? How sensual and responsive he found her? Of course not. Which was a very good thing, he decided, as he reached out a hand and pulled the covers over them. If she had any idea, then she would use it against him, use her feminine power to try to weaken and undermine him. It was bad enough having her fight him for control of every aspect of the estate without her deciding she could seduce him into letting her carry on being master here. Not that it would work.

Still, it was a pleasure how she had reacted to him. And fortunate, because after all those

long months of celibacy he found it a miracle
he had held out against his climax as long
as he had. The next time—which had better
be soon, he thought with a wry grin—would
be even better. He was looking forward to
teaching Julia the arts of love.

His harsh words when he had accused her
of being another man's mistress, of lying
about her lack of experience, came back to
deliver a sharp jab to his conscience. Her
story had obviously been true and he must
make that up to her. If only he did not have
this nagging instinct that she was still not
being completely honest with him.

*God, this is comfortable. I must be squash-
ing her.* He rolled off the soft fragrant body
cushioning his so uncomplainingly and gathered her into his arms. She came with a little
sigh, snuggled up against his chest and went
quite limp. *Asleep.* It was endearingly trust-
ful, the way she simply let go, just as she had
on that strange wedding night so long ago.
He should slide out of bed now, let her rest,
go back to his own chamber. *In a minute...*

Her right arm had gone to sleep and there
was a warm draught in her ear which tick-
led, but was oddly pleasant. And a strange

beat under her ear. In fact, the pillow was rather harder than feathers and was not a pillow at all.

Julia blinked her eyes open and found she was wrapped in Will's arms, her cheek on his chest. He was asleep, breathing into her ear. And neither of them was wearing a stitch.

It was tempting to press her lips to his skin. She could smell the faint muskiness of sex and sleep and warm man and the nipple close to her mouth was puckered and hard, perhaps from her breath.

But if she did kiss him, then he would know how much she wanted him and she would only demonstrate all over again how inexperienced she was. She needed to think and she couldn't do it here with her body distracted by Will's closeness. He had not hurt her even though he had been so strong, so forceful. She could not quite believe it.

Her dreams had been as bad as always, the wisps of them still hung around her mind like dirty fog. The dream where she was running away on feet that were raw with blisters, the dream where she was so mired in guilt she could not move, the dream where they told her that her child was not breathing… But the waking memories were amazing. Would it always be like this?

Julia slid out of bed, held her breath until she could lower his arm to the mattress, and got to her feet. She would just tiptoe into the dressing room, put on her habit…

'Good morning.'

She turned to find Will regarding her with sleepy appreciation. There was nothing to wrap herself in. 'Good morning.' Julia began to back towards the door.

'Where are you going?'

'Riding. I wanted the, er, exercise.'

One eyebrow lifted in mocking disbelief.

'And the fresh air.'

'Open a window wider for the air and come back to bed for the exercise.'

'But I wanted to ride.' *I need to escape before you realise that you only have to touch me and I turn into melted butter. If you don't know that already.*

Will flipped back the sheet and lay back. 'Come here and I'll teach you to ride astride.'

There was absolutely no mistaking his meaning. Julia could feel the blush spreading from her toe-tips to her cheeks. She wanted to flee, she wanted to run to him. She tried to look as though it was actually a rational decision, as though she was in charge of her emotions. Julia held Will's gaze and walked back to the bed, tossing her hair back over her shoulder as she did so. His eyes narrowed and she saw a perceptible reaction in his already aroused body.

I please him. And despite everything, the fears and the dreams and the knowledge that Will still did not trust her, the realisation that this aspect of their marriage might be happy was like a benison. *If it lasts.*

Chapter Twelve

By the time she and Will sat down to luncheon Julia had managed to stop colouring up every time he looked at her. After a prolonged, very instructive and shatteringly pleasurable interlude in bed Julia had managed to take her horseback ride after all.

Nancy had fetched her conventional riding habit without being asked and Julia was glad to be saved the temptation to put on her divided skirt. She didn't want an argument with her husband to spoil the remarkable closeness their lovemaking had created. Will had accompanied her and even listened, without apparent irritation, to her comments on how the fields were being used and what the situation was with the tenants. He had admired the rebuilt cottages that replaced the row he had shown her that first morning and complimented her on the design of the well cover and the pigsties.

Perhaps, after all, things were going to settle down. He would accept her as a partner, her position would be safe and, with shared interests, they could begin to build a marriage.

And yet… She watched him from beneath her lashes. Will had been attentive, had listened and yet somehow she had felt that he was flirting with her, humouring her. He knew, because quite plainly he was a man of very considerable experience in these matters, that she was attracted to him, that she had enjoyed herself in his arms. *The balance of power*, she mused. *My lord and master. In bed and out of it—is that how he sees it?*

'I expect we will be besieged by visitors,' Will remarked now as he cut into a cheese. 'Aunt Delia will have spread the gossip all about the neighbourhood. We were spared all the bride-visits three years ago, but we are in for them now.'

'I suppose we will be.' People would soon sate their curiosity, surely? Then they would leave them in the peace she was used to, with only morning calls from close neighbours and her particular friends.

'We must hold a dinner party as soon as possible.'

'We must?' Will did not mean the informal dinners she enjoyed, with good plain food on the table and casual card or table games, music and gossip afterwards.

'Certainly. A series of small ones, I thought, rather than try to deal with everyone at once. In fact, I have a list of guests drawn up we can use to sort out the invitation list for the first one.'

A series of dinner parties would mean hours of planning. They would be an event in the neighbourhood and people would compare notes, which meant a different menu for each, and different table decorations. 'I will have to buy some new gowns.'

'Is that such a hardship? I never thought to hear a woman say that sentence in such a depressed tone of voice.'

Julia smiled and shrugged. 'It is simply the time, but I can go into Aylesbury tomorrow and order several.' She made no mention of the discomfort she felt walking around the crowded streets full of strangers.

Will had said nothing about pin money

or housekeeping and she had no intention of bringing the subject up until she had to. It was not that she had been extravagant while she had sole control of the money, but she did not relish the thought of having to account for every penny spent on toothpowder or silk stockings. She had been earning the money that she spent so prudently. Now she would be beholden to her husband for everything.

'We will go up to town in the autumn,' Will said. 'Presumably you go fairly frequently.'

'No. I have never been.' Ridiculously it seemed more dangerous than any other place, as though Bow Street Runners would be waiting around every corner for her. Fingers would point, constables would pounce and drag her before magistrates...

'Why not? Is this another foolish scruple, like not wearing the jewellery?' Julia shook her head, unable to think of a convincing explanation, and Will frowned. 'Well, we will go up in a week or so. It will be short of company, but we can both shop, I can make myself known at my clubs again and so forth.'

'Of course. I shall look forward to it.' The irrational panic was building inside, beating at her, and Julia made herself sip her lemonade and nibble at a cheesecake. She needed peace and time to reflect.

The next day after luncheon Will rode off to interview the village blacksmith about the ironwork for the new stables. Julia waited until his long-tailed grey gelding had vanished from sight, then went into the garden to gather a handful of white rosebuds. Ellis the gardener controlled his usual grumbles about anyone picking 'his' flowers and gave her a smile as she passed him. He knew what the little bouquet was for.

The path wound through the shrubbery, past the vicarage and into the churchyard. The ancient village had been moved by some autocratic baron early in the last century when it got in the way of his new parkland. As a result the villagers found themselves with new homes, but a longer walk to the now-isolated church which also served as the chapel for the castle.

Julia made her way round to the south side and pushed open the ancient oak door. Inside the light was dimmed by the stained glass windows and the silence was profound and peaceful. She made her way to the Hadfield family chapel with its view through an ornate stone screen to the chancel.

The table tomb of Will's fourteenth-century ancestor, Sir Ralph Hadfield, stood in the centre. The knight, his nose long since chipped off, lay with a lion under his feet and his hand on his sword hilt. Beside him his lady, resplendent in the fashions of the day, had a lapdog as her footrest.

Between the east end of the tomb and the chapel-altar steps was a slab with a ring in to give access to the Hadfield vault beneath. Delia always said the thought of the vault gave her the horrors, but Julia found the chapel peaceful. The ancestors beneath her feet, lying together in companionable eternity, held no terrors for her. It was quiet, cool, strangely comforting in the chapel as she gathered up the drooping roses from the vase standing on the slab and added the new flowers, then sat and let her tumbling thoughts still and calm.

That morning she and Nancy had folded and packed away all the tiny garments, the shawls, the rattle, the furnishings for the nursery. Now they were in silver paper and lavender, the cot stripped of its hangings, everything put away in the attic.

She had set the door wide open on to the room and left it for Will to find, or not. She did not feel able to talk about it. What if she was already with child again? All that pain to risk. Not the physical pangs, but the mental pain of nine months of anxiety and then...

But she was well and healthy now, she reassured herself, not the nervous girl who had spent those first months jumping at her own shadow, convinced that she would step out of her front door and find the constables waiting for her, her new neighbours pointing, crying, *Imposter! Murder!* Surely that would make a difference? And part of her ached for a child.

She was not sure how long she had sat there before she heard the creak of the outer door being pushed open and footsteps coming down the aisle. The vicar, she supposed. Mr Pendleton was gentle and kindly; she did not mind his company.

The realisation that it was not the elderly scholar came over her with a sort of chill certainty. Julia did not turn, but she was not surprised when Will said, 'He is here, then?'

She should not have risked it, coming to the chapel while there was the slightest chance Will would find out. He would be furious that this was something else she had kept from him. He would insist that the interloper was removed...

'I know it is wrong.' She found she was on her feet, standing on the slab as though she could somehow stop this. Will stood with his hat in his hands, his face serious. 'I know he isn't yours and he has no right here. But he wasn't baptised, so they would have buried him outside the churchyard wall in that horrid patch under the yew trees and Mr Pendleton understood when I was distressed, so we put him here...'

'Does he have a name, even though he was never baptised?' Will said gently.

It was the last question she expected. 'Alexander, after my father,' she stammered.

'Alexander is very welcome here,' Will said and came to her side. 'Do you know who he is lying there with?'

'No.' He was not going to insist the tiny coffin was taken and buried in that dark, dank patch with the suicides and the other tiny tragedies?

'My brother and two sisters,' Will said and she saw his fingers were curled tight over the edge of Sir Ralph's tomb. 'The loss of two children after I was born shattered my parents' marriage.' His mouth twisted in a wry smile. 'Not that it was well founded in the first place. Afterwards things went from bad to worse. They hardly communicated other than by shouting and the third child, a daughter, was not my father's—or so he always maintained. You may imagine the atmosphere.'

'Oh, the poor things!' Julia cried.

'The babies?'

'Well, of course. But for your mother to lose so many and for your father… He lost two children himself and then they were obviously not able to reach out and comfort each other or things would not have gone so wrong between them.'

'You are an expert on marriage now?' Will asked harshly. Was he recalling that she had taken a lover before she had come to him? Might he fear she would do what his own mother had done if she was unhappy?

'No.' Then she saw the pain in his eyes. How hard it must have been to grow up in a household full of grief and anger. 'No, but I can understand a little of what your mother felt. If she had no one to talk to, the loss of the children would have been so much worse.' She hoped she had kept her voice

steady and not revealed how much this cost her to speak of.

Will half-turned away and stood staring down at his long-ago ancestor, then he looked back at her as though he had been translating her words in his head and had just deciphered the meaning. 'And you had no one, had you? Even if Delia behaved decently, you would have known that in her heart she was relieved that Henry had not been displaced.'

'That is true.' She fought to find a smile. 'I managed.' *Somehow.* 'There was not much choice.'

'You should not have had to,' Will said roughly and the anger in his voice undid her in a way that gentleness would never have done. 'Damn it, I didn't mean to make you cry. Julia—' He pulled her into his arms and for the first time since he had returned there was nothing in his touch but the need to give comfort. He cupped her head with one big hand and held her against his shoulder. 'Perhaps it is not a bad thing if you weep now. Were you even able to cry properly after it happened?'

She shook her head, afraid to speak and lose control.

'Then do it now. Mourn for the first child of this marriage.' Julia gave a sob and then simply let the tears flow while Will stroked her hair and held her tightly and murmured comfort.

How long they stood there she had no idea. Eventually the tears ran their course and Julia lifted her head and looked up into Will's face. 'Thank you.' She became aware that her lashes were sticking together and she wanted to sniff and her nose was probably red. The breast of his coat was dark with moisture. 'Have you got a handkerchief?'

'Of course.' Will eased her down on to the pew, produced a large linen square from his pocket and moved away to study the memorials on the walls.

Julia put herself to rights as best she could and found she could express the anxiety that she had thought she could never speak of to him. 'Will, what if it happens again? What if I am not able to give you an heir?'

He came back and sat beside her, his hands clasped between his knees. He seemed to be engrossed in the design of a hassock. After a moment he said, 'I hope that is not the case, because I would hate to see you suffer such a thing. But if it did, then Henry, or his son, inherits. It is not the end of the world and besides, do not anticipate troubles. Now come back into the sunshine or you will get chilled. It is like an ice house in here and it is a lovely day outside.'

Julia took the hand he held out to her and went out, arm in arm with him as fragile hope began to unfurl inside her. Will understood how she had grieved and her need to weep and be comforted. He had been kind about letting her place Alexander in the vault and she had seen, with piercing clarity, just how wounded he must have been as a child by his parents' unhappy marriage.

Perhaps one day he might even come to trust her, even though she knew she would never be able to burden him with her secret. Perhaps, Julia thought optimistically as the sunshine and the relief of the tears did their work, this was the real beginning of their marriage.

'Will, how much did you understand of what was happening? When your brothers and sisters died?'

'Understand? Nothing. They told me nothing other than that I was now the only son because my brother was dead so I must grow up to be the perfect Baron Dereham because there was no other option. They didn't tell me at all about the little girl my father said was not his. I only found out about that when I overheard two maids talking about it afterwards. I would have liked to have had a brother,' he added after a moment, his voice utterly expressionless. 'And little sisters. I asked my tutor what it meant when the maids said one of them was a bastard. So he told me and then I was beaten for eavesdropping.'

'That is outrageous!' Julia forgot her own melancholy in a burst of anger for the unhappy, confused small boy. 'They should have told you the truth, all of it, but kindly so a child could understand.'

He shrugged. 'Water under the bridge now.'

They walked on in silence, but it seemed to Julia that some of the tension between them had lifted a little. The roofs of the Home Farm came into sight to their right and Julia recalled that the workmen had finished building the foundations for the extension to the stables and were beginning on the walls. With the new horses arriving so soon Will had decided on a single-storied wooden building to save time and he had ordered the work without, of course, any reference to her.

Now, as they strolled back from the church, it seemed the time to build on the intimacy of the moment by showing an interest rather than offering suggestions. 'I would like it if you would show me the new stables. They seem to be coming along very well.'

Will changed direction and took the path to the farm. 'You have not been to look at them yet?'

'You made it clear that you did not require my interference.' She tried to say it lightly, but his arm stiffened under her hand.

'I am sorry you see it like that,' Will said. 'But there can only be one master giving orders or it confuses the servants and the workers. And I am the master.'

'I realise that.' Julia bit her lip. If he was prepared to be conciliatory, then she must not be grudging. 'And perhaps I had not taken that into account sufficiently when you came home. But this has been my life and my responsibility for three years. It is what interests me, what has always interested me. I do not want to displace you—I could not do that even if I wanted to—but I cannot bear to be shut out. May I not be involved? Can we not discuss things together?'

He was silent as he opened a gate for her.

'Will, I will go mad if you expect me to retire into the house and become a domestic paragon!'

'You seem to be that already,' he remarked. 'I do not recall the house ever looking better.'

'Thank you. But there is nothing left to do except maintain it, whereas there is always something with the estate.' He raised an eyebrow and she knew she was being too enthusiastic, but she could not help herself. 'I love it! There are always new things to try, experiments to plan, even a crisis or two to enliven the week.' They stopped abruptly, confronted by a six-foot wide patch of mire where the cows had churned up the entrance to the milking yard after an unseasonal cloudburst a few days before. 'See? This needs filling with rubble and tamping down.'

Will stopped, pushed his hat firmly on to his head, took her around the waist and swung her over the mud to a large flat stone in the middle, hopped across to it himself and then swore under his breath. 'I've misjudged this—there isn't enough room to stand securely and swing you across to the hard ground.' They clung together in the middle, swaying dangerously.

'You must let me go or we'll both fall in. We will just have to wade,' Julia said. Will was enjoyably strong and large to cling to, even if it did seem they were both about to land in the mud. *What we must look like...* 'I have old boots on.'

'Well, I have not!' Will protested as he took a firmer grip around her waist. 'These are Hoby's best.'

'They *are* very beautiful boots.' She had noticed. And noticed too how well they set off his muscular legs. 'If I go, then you will have room to get your balance and jump.' An irrepressible desire to laugh was beginning to take hold of her. Where on earth had that come from? Relief, perhaps, after the cathartic tears in the church.

'I am not going to leave my wife to wade through the mud in order to protect my boots,' Will said. Julia managed to tip her head back far enough to see the stubborn set of his jaw. There was a small dark mole under the point of it and the impulse to kiss it warred with the need to giggle. He sounded so very affronted to find himself in this ridiculous position.

'If we shout loudly enough, someone will come and they can fetch planks or a hurdle,' she suggested. 'Or is that beneath your dignity?'

'Yes,' Will agreed and she saw the corner of his mouth turn up. 'It is. I feel enough of an idiot, without an audience of sniggering farmhands. Can you put your arms around my neck?'

Julia wriggled to lift her arms. The stone tipped with a sucking sound. 'I think it is sinking. How deep can this mud hole be?'

'We are not going to find out.' Will put his hands under her bottom. 'Jump up and get your legs around my hips.'

'My skirts—'

'Are wide enough,' he said with a grunt as he boosted her up and then, with a lurch, made a giant stride to the milking-parlour threshold with Julia clinging like a monkey round his neck. She gave a faint scream as he landed off balance, jolting the breath out of her, then, with a ghastly inevitability, they were falling.

Will twisted and came down first into a pile of straw with Julia on top of him. 'Ough!'

They lay there gasping for breath until Will said, 'Would you mind moving your elbow? Otherwise we are endangering the future heir.'

Shaking with laughter, stunned to find she could laugh about it, Julia untangled herself and flopped back beside him. 'At least it is clean straw.'

'You find this funny?' He was grinning with the air of a man caught out by his own amusement. It was the first time she had realised that he had a sense of the ridiculous and it was surprisingly attractive.

'Exceedingly,' she admitted. 'Look at us! You have lost your hat somewhere, you have straw in your hair, your shirt is coming untucked from your breeches and, my lord, despite your exquisite boots, you look the picture of a country swain tumbling his girl in a haystack.'

'And what do you resemble, I wonder?' Will raised himself on one elbow and looked down at her. 'Your bonnet is no doubt with my hat in the mud, those boots are deplorable, your skirts are mired around the hem, your cheeks are pink and I do not blame the country swain for wanting to tumble you in the least.'

He leaned over and slid his hand into her hair, very much the lord of the manor exercising his *droit de seigneur*, she thought, rather than a farmhand. 'Now then, my milkmaid…'

He kissed her, laughing. She kissed him back, as well as she could. Will's weight pressed her down into the straw as his free hand began to creep up her stockinged leg. Julia's giggles turned into a little gasp of arousal. 'Will…'

Chapter Thirteen

'Coom oop, Daisy! Get along there, Molly!'

'What the hell?' Will sat up and Julia scrabbled at her rising hem. 'Oh my lord, the herd is coming in. Up you get.' He hauled her to her feet and began to bat at her skirts as Julia brushed straw off his coat-tails.

'Too late…here they come. For goodness' sake, Will, tuck in your shirt!'

The dairy cows pushed through the wide entrance from the field, bringing the smell of grass and manure as they stared with wide, curious black eyes at the interlopers in their milking parlour. 'Go on, get along with you.' Julia waved her hands and they wandered off placidly, each to its own stall, blinking with their preposterously long eyelashes.

'My lady! Oh, and my lord too. Never realised you was in here.' Bill Trent, the dairyman, stood in the doorway, staring at them with as much surprise, and rather more speculation, than his cattle.

'We came up against the quagmire out there, Trent,' Julia said. 'And we rather misjudged the distance when we tried to get across it. Have you seen our hats? They must have fallen off when we jumped.'

'There they be, my lady.' Bill pointed to the ground behind the straw pile. There was no way the hats would have fallen in that position except from their heads as they sprawled there. On the other hand, she comforted herself as she went to retrieve them, Bill Trent was not perhaps the brightest of the farm workers and might not have the imagination to draw the very obvious conclusion about what the baron and his wife had been doing.

'Come along, my dear.' Will sounded so pompous that she could not decide whether he was perishing with embarrassment, fighting the urge to laugh or was unfairly furious with her for landing him in such a position.

'Of course. Thank you, Trent.' Julia managed as dignified a nod as she could under the circumstances and let Will usher her out of the milking parlour into the main yard. Fortunately there was no one in sight and Will strode across to the drive with Julia in tow. 'Oh dear. I am afraid that was not very decorous.'

'It was, however, exceedingly amusing.' His voice was shaking with laughter.

'Will!'

'And arousing. I assume, my lady, that you will now find it necessary to take all your clothes off in order to remove the lingering traces of the farmyard?'

'Indeed, my lord. And you will doubtless wish to take off your clothing also to assure yourself that no harm has come to those fine boots. Or your breeches. And I fear your shirt may be torn.'

'Quite. This is obviously an emergency. Can you walk any faster?'

'No, but I can run.' Julia took to her heels with Will beside her, burst through the front door and was halfway up the stairs before Gatcombe emerged to see what the commotion was.

'My lady?' He took one look at Will and effaced himself.

'We will have scandalised the entire staff

at this rate.' Julia fell panting on to her bed as Will came in behind her and turned the key in the lock.

'I have no intention of having anyone else as an audience,' he promised as he threw his coat on to a chair and began to untie his crushed neckcloth. 'One yokel and one butler is more than enough.'

Julia watched appreciatively as he dragged his shirt over his head, then bent to unlace her boots. 'I am not a very dignified baroness, am I?' she asked, studying the muddy, battered footwear. A real lady would not have been seen dead in those boots, or in a cow shed, either. She would probably have no idea how milk was extracted from a cow and would faint at the sight of a dung heap.

Julia chided herself for the negative thoughts. *For the first time I feel at ease with him, for the first time this feels like a normal marriage.* They had shared secrets and painful memories and, for the first time, Will had been clear about his feelings over the management of the estate.

If only she did not feel so guilty whenever she thought about the secret she was keeping from him. He was coming to trust her and yet what she was hiding from him was awful beyond anything he might imagine.

'Do you think so?' Will said, jerking her back to the moment. What had she said? Oh, yes, something about not being dignified. He sat down to pull his own boots off. The muscles in his back rippled as he moved and tugged and Julia felt her mouth go dry. 'Rolling about in the straw is not dignified, I will agree, but it is perfectly suitable for a milkmaid and her rustic swain. Why do you want to be dignified, anyway? I don't want you to turn into a sober matron, Julia.'

'My clothes are not very... I suppose I should dress better.' Julia pulled up her skirts and untied her garters, conscious of Will's eyes on her hands.

'That footwear is suitable for walking around the yards or the fields,' Will said, standing his boots by the chair and pulling off his own stockings. 'But do you not want to buy new gowns? Or slippers or hats? Some feminine frivolity?'

'Frivolity,' she said blankly, then hauled her concentration back from the contemplation of Will's bare feet—who would have thought that feet could be so attractive?— and thought about his question. 'I did not like to spend the money on frivolities. It did not seem right.'

He had saved her life, given her hope. It had seemed immoral to indulge in what seemed like luxury with his money into the bargain. And even the fleeting thought of wandering around a large town, visiting shops amidst a crowd of strangers, brought back that feeling of panic and foreboding. She shrugged. 'I do not like shopping much.'

'I cannot believe that I have married the only woman in the country who doesn't enjoy it.' Will stood up to unfasten the fall of his breeches. His eyes narrowed and she realised she had run her tongue along her lips in anticipation. 'We will go shopping together in Aylesbury and then in London and I will teach you to be frivolous.'

'You want me to buy lots of new clothes?' She slid off the bed as he came towards her.

'Oh, yes,' Will murmured, turning her so he could undo the buttons at the back of her gown. 'Then I can enjoy taking them off you. Silks…' he pushed the sensible heavy cotton off her shoulders and it fell to the floor '…and satins.' He began to unlace her stays. Julia shivered despite the warmth. 'And Indian muslins so fine they are transparent.'

The practical, sensible petticoat joined the gown on the floor. 'And when I get down to your skin, like this…' he began to nuzzle along her shoulder and into the crook of her neck '…there will be the scent of edible, warm woman, just as there is now, and perhaps just a hint of something exotic and French.'

Julia reached behind her and found the waist of his unfastened breeches and pushed down, her palms running over the smooth skin of his hips as they fell. Against her bare buttocks she felt the heat of his arousal branding her with its length and pressed back with a little wriggle.

Will groaned, pushed her forwards so that her hands were on the bed, and then entered her from behind with one swift stoke. *'Julia.'*

The blatant carnality of his need, her own excitement, the overwhelming sensations the position produced, all sent her tumbling helplessly over the edge with dizzying speed. She heard Will gasp, his hands tightened on her hips and then they fell on the bed in a panting, uncoordinated tangle of limbs.

Will rolled on to his back and pulled Julia against his side. It was not easy to find words and he was not certain she wanted any just now as she relaxed confidingly in his arms. Something had shattered the pane of glass that had been between them ever since he came home. Was it that shared laughter, or his realisation of how deeply she had been hurt by the loss of her child? Whatever it was, the results felt good. That hollow well of loneliness inside him that had ached ever since he had been given that death sentence by the doctors was being filled with something warm and soothing. He grinned at the whimsical thought. He had not realised just how much the loss of his siblings, the lies and secrecy, had hurt him until he had told Julia about it.

'You are quiet,' Julia said, her breath feathering across his chest.

'Just thinking.' He wasn't ready to share that feeling of loneliness with her yet. It felt like weakness: a man ought to be able to look death squarely in the eye and not fall prey to self-pity.

'I had never heard you laugh like that before.' Julia sat up, curled her arms around her legs and rested her chin on her knees.

'I'm sorry, I hadn't realised I had been so dour.' When he looked back he could not recall laughing about anything since he had fallen ill. Things had amused him occasionally. The discovery that he was recovering and would not die within months had filled him with happiness, but not laughter. Not the healing, playful laugher that they had shared that afternoon. Perhaps today he had finally accepted that he had his life back to live.

'It was the release after the sad things we spoke of earlier, I expect,' she said. 'Sometimes laughter brings healing.'

Will sat up too and tipped his head to one side so he could see her face. 'I am glad you talked about it to me and that you understood about my parents. I am glad that you could trust me. That is important to me.'

'Trust?' She slanted him a look.

'Yes. I suppose it comes from growing up in a household with so little honesty and so many secrets. You must not think it was the fact that you had a lover before that disturbed me when I found out. It was the fact that you had not told me the truth about how you had come to be by the lake that night.' Julia went very still. 'That was all it was, wasn't it? A reluctance to tell a stranger about how you had been led astray and betrayed?'

'Of course,' she said and smiled at him, her eyes clear and limpid. So why did a drop of doubt send ripples to mar his certainty that his marriage was, finally, in calm waters?

'And you have no secrets from me, do you?' she asked, her voice light as though she was merely teasing him.

'Of course not.'

'So you have no regrets that we have consummated the marriage?' She was staring at her toes now. 'There are no possible grounds now to set it aside.'

Something knotted inside him. Did he regret it? No. He did not love Julia. But he liked her, he admired her. He certainly desired her. She would make a good mother.

'Of course I have no regrets,' he said firmly and saw her shoulders drop a little as though she relaxed with relief. Some demon of impulsiveness made him add, 'Are you asking if I still love Caroline? Of course I do not. I never did—it was a suitable marriage, that was all. That is over and done with.'

Julia stiffened slightly, or perhaps it was his imagination. 'I would not dream of prying into your feelings for Miss Fletcher.'

Will opened his mouth and shut it again. *I*

protest too much. I should never have mentioned Caroline.

Julia slid off the bed. 'Look at the time! I must wash and dress.' She seemed perfectly composed and yet something in the relaxed atmosphere had changed.

Will gave himself a shake. Imagination and a slightly guilty conscience at his ineptitude just now, that was all it was.

'Is it this morning that you were going to call on Colonel Makepeace about the pointer puppies?' Julia enquired at breakfast as Will broke the seal on the last of his post. Every month on this day she had been helping Henry with his accounts and it had not occurred to her to write him a note and say that now he should come and ask Will for his counsel instead of her. Henry was not comfortable with his cousin yet and she had no idea how patient Will would be with him.

One more time, she told herself. Henry would turn up this morning as usual, full of his usual mixture of enthusiasms, doubts, hare-brained ideas and, increasingly, thoughtful insights into his responsibilities. Will would be safely out of the way and she could persuade the younger man that her husband would not scorn his efforts to deal with his debts and the needs of his own estate.

Will looked up from the letter. 'Yes, it is. Do you want to come along? Or was there something you need me to do?'

'Oh, no, I was just wondering.' She did not like prevaricating, but if he did not know she was still helping Henry he could not tell her to stop. Which was a very dubious argument, she knew.

An hour later she was profoundly grateful Will had gone out. Henry was pale, distracted and seemed almost on the verge of despair, however hard he tried to cover it up.

Eventually Julia gave up on the accounts, put down her pen and demanded, 'Henry, what on earth is the matter with you?'

For a moment she thought he would deny anything was wrong, or refuse to answer her, but he slammed the ledger closed and said, 'It's Mama. She is matchmaking again, only this time she's invited Mary…this young lady and her mother to stay. She's never done that before and it is so marked an attention when

there are no other guests that I know they
will be expecting a declaration from me!'

'That is somewhat obvious, I agree. Have
you shown any interest in this girl?'

'No!' Henry looked positively flustered.

'Is there someone else? You must tell your
mother if you have formed an attachment
elsewhere.'

Henry got to his feet and went to look out
of the window without answering. The tips
of his ears had gone red.

'So there is someone? Someone unsuitable,' Julia guessed. She got up and went to
sit on the window seat, close, but not crowd-
ing him.

'God, yes.'

'Has it been going on for long?' He turned
his head away so she added, 'I swear I will
not mention a word to a soul. You know I
keep my promises, Henry.' It would not do,
of course, this attachment to an ineligible
woman, but there was no need to add to his
misery by telling him that, he obviously already knew it perfectly well.

'A year.'

Serious, then. 'Is it a courtesan, Henry?'
Perhaps he had sought to deal with his shy-
ness with girls and had become attached to

the professional he had gone to. A vehement shake of the head. 'An older woman?' He shot her an incredulous look. 'Someone not of your station?' He bit his lip. Ah, that was it. 'Someone of the merchant class? A servant?'

He had gone white now. 'A servant. I cannot tell you, Julia. You will be shocked.'

'No I will not, truly I will not, Henry. I have not led a very sheltered life, you know. Tell me about her, do.'

Henry sat down abruptly next to her, his hands fisted on his thighs as if to stop them shaking. He seemed unable to speak and a suspicion began to creep over her. 'Henry, is it a young man?'

'How did you—?' He broke off, his face stark with the realisation that he had given himself away. Julia managed to keep the shock out of her voice. Henry was confessing to something that could, at the worst, see him go to the scaffold.

'I just guessed. Henry, is this serious? Who is he?'

'A valet. I met him at the Walsinghams' house party and then… Well, you don't need the details. But it *is* serious, Julia. I love him and he loves me and I don't know what to do. Mama keeps on about me marrying.' He seemed to run out of words.

Yes, it was serious, she could see that. Lethally serious, if not for him, a gentleman, but certainly perilous for his lover. And Henry looked desperate enough to do something foolish. This was no time to be shocked and uncomprehending—she had to help him.

'How often do you go up to London?' she asked, thinking aloud. 'Quite a lot, don't you?' He nodded, bemused. 'Where do you stay?'

'Hotels, sometimes with friends. But what—?'

'It would be more economical, and an investment, if you bought a small apartment,' she suggested. 'You would need a manservant, of course, to maintain it while you were not there and to look after you while you were in town. Many young men do just that and no one thinks anything of it. A young man trained as a valet would be ideal, don't you think?'

'Julia, that is brilliant!' Henry took her hands and beamed at her. Then his face fell. 'But Mama keeps on trying to pair me off with girls.'

'Learn to flirt,' Julia said with sudden inspiration. 'Cultivate a reputation for being dangerous and the mamas will flee at the sight of you. Become a rake and a ladies' man. Your mother will be furious with you, but it should disarm all suspicion.'

'Will you show me how?'

'Certainly not! You'll have to be observant and work it out for yourself. Oh, Henry, don't—' There were tears in his eyes despite his smiles. 'Just do be careful, my dear. It will be more than just a scandal if you are discovered.'

'Thank you. Oh, thank you, Julia.' The next thing she knew she was in Henry's arms and he was hugging her with desperate affection, his cheek pressed against hers.

The door banged closed. Henry started and clutched her tighter. 'A touching scene,' Will remarked. 'Henry, get your hands off my wife and come here.'

'Will—'

But Henry was already in his feet. He tried to thrust her protectively behind him even as she resisted him. 'Don't you dare look at Julia like that, as if she could do something wrong—as though she would dream of it! You can name your seconds, Cousin!'

'And cause a scandal? I don't think so. And as for my wife's capacity for wrongdoing, well, *Cousin*, you have a far longer and more recent acquaintanceship with her than I have.'

Henry went very still. 'You are just like your father,' he accused. 'I can remember him all too well and you—'

'That is enough, both of you.' Julia stood and put herself between Will with his clenched fists and his hard, angry eyes and Henry's rigid form. 'I have just given Henry some advice with a difficult problem that was worrying him and he was relieved and grateful. If you believe I would be unfaithful to you, and with a young man I regard as a brother, then, my lord, I am sorry for you.'

'What problem?'

Beside her she heard Henry's sharp intake of breath. 'That is a confidential matter. I do not break confidences, my lord. Not yours, not anyone's.'

The dangerous silence stretched until she thought she would faint from holding her breath, then Will said, 'Very well. Keep your hands off my wife in future, Cousin. I do not care how *grateful* you might be feeling.' He turned on his heel.

'I think it might be best if you come here only in company for a week or so,' Julia said as the door closed with exaggerated care behind her husband. 'Will does not like secrets.'

Chapter Fourteen

The evening gown was the most fashionable garment she had ever possessed. Julia regarded the sweep of silken skirts, the elaborate ruffles around the skirt and the tips of her sea-green slippers peeping out below the hem with some satisfaction.

She had shaken off Will's attempts to take her into every shop in Aylesbury—and probably Oxford and Thame, too, if he had his way—by the simple expedient of sending to the best local dressmaker and requesting that she attend her at King's Acre with patterns and samples. When the fabric was chosen she had charged Madame Millicent with taking a sample to her usual shoemaker and with bringing a selection of ribbons and artificial flowers with her to the first fitting.

With the addition of her gauze scarf and silver-spangled fan she was elegantly outfitted from head to toe without the stress of a visit to the crowded shops and was able to contemplate the thought of the first dinner party of their married life with composure.

It had taken some time to arrive at that state. Will had been punctiliously polite since the scene with Henry, although an attempt to discuss it was met by his assurance that he had no intention of prying into her affairs, but that it might be sensible not to be alone with an impressionable young man. This advice was delivered in such a patronising manner that she went from apologetic to thoroughly irritated and made no attempt to raise it again. There were moments when she wondered if that had been his intention. She also wondered uneasily if his insistence on her buying clothes in such a lavish manner was a way of asserting his ownership.

Now she did her best to push such thoughts away and rehearsed the guest list in her head. She knew almost everyone. There was Aunt Delia and Henry, of course. That might be awkward, although Delia would have been affronted not to be invited to the first dinner after Will's return. Then there was the vicar and his wife; Major Frazer, Will's grooms-man and old army comrade and Mrs Frazer; the Marquess of Tranton and Lady Tranton, with whom the archbishop had, so providentially, been staying three years ago, and Caroline Fletcher and her parents, Viscount and Lady Adamson, along with her betrothed, Andrew Fallon, Earl of Dunstable.

Will had combined the highest ranking of their neighbours and those with a special connection to the wedding and she could not fault his reasoning, even if it brought her face to face with not only Henry, but also Miss Fletcher, in Will's presence. But Caroline would be accompanied by Lord Fallon so really, Julia scolded herself, there was absolutely no reason to feel any awkwardness. That betrothal was long over.

Her seating plan had required some thought, and Gatcombe's assistance, but she was pleased with the result. Thanks to a strict adherence to the rules of precedence, Miss Fletcher was almost the length of the table away from Will and separated from Julia by the marquess.

Julia swept downstairs, reminding herself that she really was the Baroness Dereham and not an interloper. Three years of grass widowhood running the estate was no preparation for an evening of entertaining a marquess, an earl and a viscount, but they were all pleasant, civilised people, she assured herself.

Will looked up as she entered the dining room, her seating plan in his hand. 'This looks perfectly all right,' he remarked, scanning it as she made last-minute alterations to the flower arrangements in the epergne in the centre of the table.

'I do hope so.' Julia went to the head of the table and tried to see whether the flowers would obscure Will's view of Miss Fletcher. She rather thought they would. It was not irrational jealousy, she told herself, merely what any wife would do when confronted with an acknowledged beauty in her own dining room.

'What are you looking so smug about?'

Julia wrinkled her nose at him. *Smug* was an unpleasant word. She was merely being tactical. Since that strange day with its tears, laughter and explosion of passion she had been unable to clarify her feelings about her husband. His furious reaction to seeing her in Henry's arms had not helped either. Possessiveness, or genuine jealousy?

He was evasive on the subject of Caroline Fletcher, she had noticed. But whether that was because he still wanted her or whether it was simply that he felt he had let Caroline down by breaking the engagement she could not fathom.

But she had told him she trusted him and that was the important thing, to be true to that. Trust was obviously a sensitive point with Will and she could hardly fret about any lingering feelings he might have for Miss Fletcher and forget the secret she was keeping from him herself, or Henry's worrying revelation.

Comparing her mild unease about Caroline Fletcher to the secrets she was keeping was like comparing the nearby Downs with the Alps, she thought with a sudden, familiar, lurch in mood. A rapid mental calculation and she realised it was, indeed, familiar. Unless she was very much mistaken her courses would start tomorrow, which meant she was not carrying Will's child.

The mixed feelings took her by surprise. Regret she had expected. But relief that she had another month's respite before facing that fear took her by surprise. She wished she could confide all that in Will, but she feared she could not articulate it without breaking down.

Gatcombe was hovering and probably thought she was finding fault with the table. Julia told herself to stop fussing and followed Will to the salon so she could pass the time with an unexceptional piece of embroidery until her guests began to arrive.

Will seemed on edge, but that was doubtless her wretched imagination playing tricks on her, Julia decided, and managed to stab herself in the thumb with her needle. He shook out the pages of *The Times* and began to read, creating an effective barrier between them. *And that is just your foolish fancy,* she told herself, sucking at the tiny wound. *Just as you are imagining that things are different in the bedroom.*

Ever since that afternoon when they had tumbled laughing on to her bed and made frantic, urgent love, it had seemed to her that Will had changed. His lovemaking was polite, restrained, considerate. He always left her satisfied…and yet it was as though he was holding something back from her. Had she revealed too much that afternoon? Was he shocked, on reflection, by her abandoned behaviour? Was he retreating back to a safe emotional distance? Or did he still harbour suspicions about Henry?

The French knot she was working had become tangled. Julia tried to unpick it, but the light was bad, or perhaps her vision was blurred. *Or perhaps I am just weepy because of the time of the month,* she told herself.

'I hear carriages.' Will folded the paper and got to his feet to stand by the hearth, facing the door. Julia rose, too, and went to his side. How very handsome he looked in the severe evening clothes. Her sea-green skirts brushed against his legs as she turned to take up her position and she saw him close his eyes for a moment.

'I feel as though a portrait painter will come through the door at any moment and set up his easel. *Baron Dereham and His Lady* about to be immortalised in oils,' she said.

That provoked a snort of laughter from Will and they were both smiling and relaxed as Gatcombe announced, 'The Earl of Dunstable, Viscount and Lady Adamson, Miss Fletcher.'

Julia fought to keep every iota of that

smile on her face as she realised that four pairs of eyes were trained, not on them as a couple, but on Will. The earl, Lord Fallon, had that focused look she had learned to recognise in men who were on their mettle, even spoiling for a fight. The earl was on tenterhooks to see how Will reacted to Miss Fletcher, and how she behaved in her turn. Lord and Lady Adamson, she saw in an instant, were on edge, no doubt catching the tension emanating from Lord Fallon in the presence of the man who should have been their son-in-law by now.

And Miss Fletcher? Julia had met her several times before Will's return and knew her a little, but not well enough to sense whether her instinctive dislike was simple prejudice because Caroline had not fought to stay with Will when he had thought himself to be dying, or whether she would have found her uncongenial under any circumstances.

There was an infinitesimal pause, then Will stepped forwards to greet their guests and Julia lost the ability to detect anything but conventional social greetings and the exclamations of pleasure at Will's safe return.

Will was not looking at Caroline. Caroline was carefully not looking at Will and

Lord Fallon was watching both of them like a hawk. Julia stepped between the two men. 'I am so pleased you could come, Lord Fallon. Will you be staying long at Heathfield Hall?' She turned a little as she spoke and he had, out of simple politeness, to follow her.

'For several weeks, Lady Dereham. We are making wedding preparations, as you know, and that takes a great deal of planning.'

He began to prose on about the guest list. Julia fixed a smile on her lips. At least she had succeeded in creating space for Caroline's parents to talk to Will and, as she suspected, there was long acquaintance and considerable liking between them.

'Mr and Mrs Pendleton. Mrs Hadfield, Mr Hadfield.'

Delia, unconsciously doing the tactful thing, swooped on Miss Fletcher and began to interrogate her about her trousseau. Henry, who had met Lord Fallon on the hunting field, came up with a question about a horse and, with a sigh of relief at the thought of another awkward confrontation averted, Julia was able to slip away and greet the vicar and his wife.

The big salon filled up quickly and Julia

relaxed. Will had hardly so much as glanced in Caroline's direction and both he and Lord Fallon appeared to have decided there was no need to bristle at each other. Will had even spoken civilly to Henry and the younger man had relaxed from an all-too-obvious tension into his usual cheerful self.

By the time she walked through to the dining room with the Marquess of Tranton, Julia realised that she was actually enjoying herself.

'I hear that you are expecting a positive herd of horses shortly,' the marquess remarked as the soup was served.

'Indeed, yes. Lord Dereham purchased some very fine animals while he was in Spain and North Africa. We have had to extend the stables to accommodate them all. I will let you know when they arrive, if you are interested, my lord.'

'That would be a pleasure, thank you.' He passed her the pepper, then remarked, 'My steward tells me that you have been managing the estate here in Dereham's absence with remarkable success.'

'It is kind of him to say so.' The Tranton

farms were famous—praise from that quarter was praise indeed.

Julia had been having qualms about entertaining a marquess and what topics of conversation might interest him. She had not been expecting him to show so much approving interest in her agricultural endeavours and the meal seemed to fly past in a highly satisfactory sequence of courses and a lively buzz of conversation.

Julia's other big fear had been that she would forget to rise and take the ladies out at the appropriate moment, but even that went smoothly without Delia having to shoot dagger-glances down the table to remind her. Will caught her eye and nodded and she felt the warmth of his approval.

The ladies settled in the salon to gossip and await the tea tray. Julia relaxed, then tensed in surprise as Caroline Fletcher settled beside her.

'I was amazed that Lord Tranton should have chosen to talk so much about farming.' She gave an artistic shudder. 'Why, he hardly spoke of anything else and I am sure he has all the Court gossip at his fingertips. You must have hoped to forget such tiresome things as cows and corn at dinner, Lady Dereham.'

'Not at all, Miss Fletcher. I was flattered by his interest. He is very knowledgeable.'

'I have never understood why you had to be involved with it at all. Could you not have hired a man instead of labouring over something so…unfeminine?'

'If I was both ignorant, and idle,' Julia riposted with a smile, 'I would have done. As it happened I knew what I was doing and I find it of great interest. Beside which, I considered it my duty to look after King's Acre until Lord Dereham returned.'

'You expected this miracle cure, then?' Caroline enquired, making no effort to hide her scepticism.

'I never gave up hope.'

To anyone knowing the history it would seem an implied criticism and Caroline certainly took it as one. Her eyes widened and her lips tightened as the colour slashed across her cheekbones. 'You must be congratulated upon having no imagination, Lady Dereham,' she riposted. 'To marry under the circumstances must have required the most ruthless control of whatever sensibility you possess.' Her smile indicated that she thought Julia had none.

'My sensibility goes with refined taste in all matters, I believe,' Caroline continued with staggering complacency. 'I cannot tell you what a pleasure it was to be in London the past few weeks. One may find the very best shops there.' Her gaze slid over the bodice and sleeves of Julia's gown. 'I could not bear to have to rely on provincial dressmakers. Do let me know if there is anything I may purchase for you when I return, dear Lady Dereham. Skin creams, for example.'

'That is so kind of you,' Julia said warmly. 'I am sure you must have experience of a *very* wide range of cosmetic aids. Do excuse me, there is something I have remembered I need to tell Mrs Frazer.'

If she did not remove herself she was going to say something she would regret. Anyone would think that she was some sort of threat to Caroline's position as reigning local beauty.

The men entered the room as she was crossing it. Mrs Frazer was deep in conversation with Lady Tranton but, having told Caroline she intended to speak with her, she could hardly walk away. Julia sat down beside them and sought some composure for Caroline's little barbs were beginning to get under her skin. Will had married her for her knowledge of estate management—he had never expected to have to live with her or for her to be the mother of his children. Did he now see her as some sort of rural bumpkin he was ashamed to come home to?

Julia swallowed the lump that had suddenly appeared in her throat. Is that why Will had seemed mysteriously remote since the incident in the milking parlour? He had been swept into thoroughly unseemly passion—was he now regretting it and despising her for her enjoyment? Had she seemed like nothing but an ill-bred romp foolish enough not to be able to manage Henry's youthful affections? Was his generosity with clothes and jewels an attempt to make her more *comme il fait*?

Imagination, just foolish imagination, she told herself and looked around for Will. There was no sign of him, or of Caroline Fletcher.

The room was full now and conversation was lively and general. It was doubtful that anyone had noticed who was missing, but that could not last for long. Instinct told her it was not coincidence and that she had to get one or other of them back into the salon as soon as possible.

What were they doing? *No, don't think about it, just find them.* Julia slipped out of the room and began to search. There were servants clearing in the dining room, the breakfast parlour was empty, the hall and billiards room were quiet.

Please not the bedrooms. The thought was so strong in her mind that, when she opened the door into the library, the sight of Will and Caroline, locked together in an embrace, was almost a relief. At least they were not on one of the beds.

They did not hear her open the door and she stood there, her hand on the latch, frozen into silent immobility, while she absorbed the shock that followed the relief. Somehow part of her had not quite believed she would find them like this. Caroline had her arms around Will, her head rested on his chest and he was holding her against his body, his cheek crushing the elaborate curls of her coiffure.

The only sound was of muffled sobs, the only movement, Caroline's shoulders shaking and Will's hand stroking her back. Julia found she could not stir. Certainly she could not speak, even if she had any idea what to say. Then Will opened his eyes and looked straight at her.

Chapter Fifteen

The spell broke as she met Will's gaze. It held nothing but a desperate appeal for help. Julia found her voice. 'I suggest that you go back to the salon as soon as possible, my lord, before someone notices exactly who is missing.'

Caroline went rigid. Will dropped his hands from her and turned. 'Julia.'

'Leave her. Go back now—do you want to make a scandal?' Will did not move and Julia's tenuous hold on her emotions gave way. *'Go,'* she hissed. 'It is quite safe to leave her with me, I am not going to start a cat fight!'

He shot her another harassed look, then strode past her without another word and she was alone with Caroline who stood, head averted, face buried in her hands.

'Do you need a handkerchief or to wash your face?' Julia demanded. 'Or are those crocodile tears?'

The other woman dropped her hands to show dry eyes, an unmarred complexion. 'You have no *feelings*!'

'No, apparently not. But I do have a quantity of common sense. It may be a cliché, but you really cannot have your cake and eat it, Miss Fletcher. However delightful it is to use your powers on Will, you risk a scandal and if that happens you would lose your earl and a great deal of money.' Caroline's big blue eyes filled with furious tears. 'For goodness' sake, do not start crying now! Do you want people to feel sorry for you?'

'*What?*'

'It will seem that you cannot bear to see Will healthy and happily married.' Julia shrugged and turned to the door. 'I was going to say your flounce had snagged and torn and we were pinning it up, but if you want to make an exhibition of yourself—'

With a gasp of outrage Caroline pushed past and swept down the corridor towards the salon. Julia caught up to her and linked her arm into hers as they entered the room.

'Such a pity if that has damaged your lovely gown,' she said clearly as they entered. 'I am not surprised you were upset.'

Caroline glared at her and swept away to her mother's side.

Spoiled little madam, Julia thought, trying to feel sorry for the other woman, shocked to realise that she had been suspicious when she had found them both gone and that she was jealous and upset now.

Ridiculous, she scolded herself. She trusted Will and, if he had been misguided enough himself to offer his ex-fiancée some comfort then who was she to complain? He had hardly protested his love and devotion to her, had he?

Will was standing before the fireplace, staring at her as he might at a bomb with a hissing fuse. He started across the floor as, behind her, salvation arrived.

'The tea, my lady.'

'Thank you, Gatcombe. Over there, if you please.' She turned to Will. 'Have you come to help me with the cups?' Faced with two full teacups, he had little choice but to take them. The surface of the liquid shivered as she handed them to him, and his hands, it seemed, were no steadier, but the vibration was not visible and he, too, kept his poise.

The clock struck twelve before Will could finally make his way upstairs and along the gallery to his room. The last guests had gone. The little crisis with the trace on the vicar's carriage snapping had been dealt with by sending them home in his own vehicle. The servants had been thanked and the house was secure. Now there was nothing between him and the confrontation with his wife and the consequences of his own actions.

Nancy passed him, her arms full of linens. 'Her ladyship's retired for the night, my lord. She's not feeling quite herself, you understand.'

For a hideous moment he thought Julia had confided in her maid, then he saw there was no accusation in Nancy's expression, only mild concern. Julia must have said she was suffering from a headache.

'Thank you. Goodnight.' He went into his own room and endured Jervis's punctilious attentions for twenty minutes until finally, mercifully, alone he went and listened at the jib door between their dressing rooms. Nothing. He opened it, half-surprised to find it unlocked, and went through. The door into her room was unlocked too. Will tapped and entered.

'Julia?'

She was sitting up in bed, her hair in its night-time plait on her shoulder. 'Come in.'

Will had not known what to expect. Reproaches, certainly. Tears, probably. Accusations, of course. Even, although he had never seen Julia lose her temper, things thrown at his head. He deserved the lot, especially after the scene he had created when he found her with Henry. What he had not expected from his wife was calm.

'I am sorry,' he said, knowing it was insufficient but that it had to be said. 'That should never have happened. I had no intention that it should.'

'But Miss Fletcher waylaid you, threw herself on your chest and sobbed?'

That was exactly what had happened. Caroline had followed him when he went out to fetch a book he thought the vicar would be interested in and the next thing he knew he was in the library with the door shut and feeling more confused than he could ever remember. Short of violence he had no idea how to detach her and he had absolutely no experience in dealing with a sobbing woman. He shoved all the explanations away and said, 'I cannot lay the blame on Caroline.'

'It was inevitable, I suppose, given her refined sensibilities,' Julia remarked as though he had not spoken. 'Will, I do not blame you for embracing her, I just wish it had not happened where it would have been so easy for you to have been discovered.'

'You do not mind?' He stared at her, his mind going back, as it so often did, to the day he had found her in the chapel. After that rough, impulsive coupling she had slipped from the bed cool, collected, distant. She had been through an emotional storm in the church and the laughter, the passion afterwards, had been a reaction to that, he supposed. And when she had come to herself she had been disgusted with his crude love-making and his lack of tact in mentioning Caroline minutes later—he had seen it in her reserve, the way she had distanced herself from him emotionally and physically.

He had been very careful with her ever since, even after the scene with Henry when he had wanted to find the comfort and forgiveness in their lovemaking that he could not bring himself to ask for in words.

But this? It seemed as though Julia was not even remotely jealous, simply annoyed that he had risked a scandal. But what did he expect? Their marriage had been a sham from the start, there had not even been acquaintanceship to precede it. He had made no bones about his reasons for marriage, she had been betrayed and discarded by a lover she had given up everything for. So why then, when he could perfectly understand her indifference, was it so painful now?

'I am not in love with Caroline,' he said.

'You do not have to tell me whether you are or not. It is not my business. And I do not believe that you would do anything… dishonourable.' Julia studied her hands as they lay on the lace edge of the sheet. She was twisting her wedding ring round and round her finger.

'But I am glad if you are not breaking your heart over her, because I do not think she is worth it. She is very lovely, but there is far less to her than meets the eye.' She laughed, a small, breathy sound. 'Listen to me! That was a catty remark if ever I heard one.'

'I think you are entitled to be as catty as

you wish, Julia,' Will said. His chest hurt with guilt and tension and something else that he did not recognize, but which was damnably uncomfortable. 'It is unfair that you should be made in any way distressed. I promise that I did not seek a meeting alone with her and that all I did was to try to comfort her.'

He sat on the edge of the bed and reached for her hand—for the reassurance of touch, to still that endlessly turning ring, because he wanted to hold her. Because, surely, he had hurt her.

'I am sorry, Will.' Both hands vanished under the lace. 'I am not... Tonight I cannot...' He stared back, appalled that she should think him so crass as to try to make love to her moments after they had been confronting his indiscretion with another woman. Julia cleared her throat, her cheeks pink, her gaze still firmly fixed on the sheets. 'I mean my courses have started.'

It took him a moment to realise what she was talking about. Then it dawned on him that was what Nancy had hinted when he had passed her just now. Probably, *Not feeling quite herself* was code a husband was expected to understand.

'Of course.' He couldn't even begin to explain why he had reached for her, what he wanted. How could he? He had no idea himself. Will stood up. 'You are tired, I won't keep you awake any longer. That was a fine dinner party, thank you. Goodnight, Julia.'

'Goodnight, Will.'

He closed the dressing-room door and leaned back against it to steady himself. It was as though a gulf had just opened up in front of his feet and he was hanging, dizzy, over it. What the devil had he thought this marriage was about? He had come home intent on seizing back his old life, taking control of King's Acre, putting his convenient marriage firmly into its rightful place. He had been confronted by the evidence of Julia's heartbreak and loss and he had seen everything through the lens of himself and his feelings.

With a muttered curse Will pushed away from the door and went through to his bedchamber. It had all seemed to be going perfectly well. He had acknowledged the child and, by doing so, tied himself to Julia. She had, after some resistance, come to his bed and now she seemed to enjoy his lovemaking. And he had thought that was all there was to it! Marry: tick that off the list. Sire an heir: working on it. But, be happy? Make Julia happy? Were those on the list too?

What did she want? Not, apparently, *him*, or not enough to be distressed when she caught him with his arms around another woman. *Arrogant devil*, he told himself as he threw off his dressing gown and lay down. *You expected her to be jealous, you* wanted *her to be jealous. Why should she be? She isn't in love with you and there isn't one reason why she should be. But your pride is hurt because of it, just as it was hurt when you found her comforting Henry.*

He punched the pillows, snuffed the candles and lay staring up at the underside of the bed canopy, lost in the dark. He had got what he needed: an attractive, intelligent, socially adept and unbelievably forgiving wife. So why, then, did he still feel that pain in his chest?

'The horses are here!' Will burst into the bedchamber like a strong gust of wind. Nancy gave a squeak and dropped the hairbrush. It took Julia a moment to take in what he had said, she was so surprised to see him there. Ten days after the dinner party he had not returned to her bed and it was proving remarkably awkward to find the words to ask why not. Was it guilt keeping him away or did he simply not want her any more? But he wanted an heir and he had never seemed to find her repellent...

'What, with no warning?' He was dressed in breeches and boots, his hair was tousled by the morning breeze and the lines of tiredness she thought she had discerned lately around eyes and mouth had quite gone. It must have been her imagination, for what could have been keeping him up at night? It was certainly not her!

'I heard from my agent in Portsmouth two weeks ago to say they had just landed and he intended to rest them, then start hacking them up in easy stages once he was certain they were all sound. But Phelps's letter saying they had started must have gone astray. Look.'

Julia could feel the excitement running through him as he took her arm and drew her to the window. It was an almost sexual force, that energy, and her body responded, warming, softening. If Nancy had not been there, she would have leaned into him and snatched a kiss. And would then no doubt have regretted it if he had failed to respond.

Instead she looked out at the sweep of parkland and the horses approaching at the trot. Julia narrowed her eyes against the morning sun: five riders, each leading two horses. Even at that distance she could see the quality of the animals in the way they moved.

'They look fresh. They must have spent the night close by.'

'Thank goodness the stables were finished yesterday,' Will said. He released her arm. 'I must go down again.'

'But your breakfast...' The door swung to behind him. Julia managed a rueful smile for Nancy's benefit. 'Men! I shall have to have something sent down to the stables.'

She supposed she should not feel awkward about going down to look at the new arrivals. 'My riding clothes, please, Nancy.'

'Which ones, my lady?'

'My old habit,' Julia said. Since that first time she and Will had never ridden together. Whenever they had travelled around the estate it had been in a gig. He knew she had her own horse, of course, and he had probably not noticed the other saddle hanging beside the side saddle. Would he be angry when he discovered she rode astride around the estate?

Somehow, without any formal agreement, they had arrived at a working compromise over responsibilities. Julia looked after the tenants' welfare, the dairy herd, the chickens, the gardens both decorative and productive, the house and the indoor staff. Will controlled everything else. So far there had not been any discussion about the housekeeping allowance or her own pin money, so Julia just kept on spending at the same level as she had before, maintained her scrupulously accurate accounts and waited to have those removed from her control too.

As with the subject of the bedchamber, and the events of the dinner-party evening, it seemed that they existed most harmoniously without confronting the issues. But it was an uneasy peace. Julia felt she was cramming unwieldy truths into a cupboard and sooner or later the door would burst open and release all of them.

Nancy fastened the divided skirt at the waist and then helped Julia into the coat. Really she was perfectly decent, she thought, bracing herself for the confrontation. Perhaps it was as well to have it while he was distracted by the horses. Perhaps he would not even notice. That was a melancholy thought.

Julia arrived at the new stables with a bite of roll and a mouthful of coffee inside her. Will was standing in the middle of the yard, talking to a wiry individual, while around them four grooms she did not recognise stood holding the horses. She stopped, knew her jaw had dropped and did not care.

'What's wrong?' Will turned at the sound of her gasp.

'Love at first sight,' Julia breathed. 'They are beautiful!'

'They are that, ma'am.' The grizzled man pulled off his hat. 'His lordship's got a fine eye for a horse.'

'Lady Dereham, this is Mr Bevis, who has had charge of the horses since Portsmouth. So you like them, do you?'

The Arabians were elegant, with their fine bones and dished faces. Will had told her he intended to breed them with thoroughbred stallions for speed and endurance as well as looks. The three Andalusians were very different and they drew her as though they called her by name.

They were not big animals. The stallion was about fifteen two hands, she supposed, his three mares a little smaller. They all had deeply arched necks, long, rippling manes and all were a perfect dapple grey in colour with iron-grey manes and tails.

Four pairs of dark, liquid eyes watched her as she approached and held out her hand to the stallion. He snuffled at her fingers, then stood rock-still as she bent and blew lightly into his nostrils. He blew back and butted her gently with his head.

'Do you wish to ride him, my dear? One of the grooms can get your saddle.'

Julia managed not to gape at Will. It never occurred to her for a moment that he would give her the first ride on any of the new animals, let alone allow her on the stallion.

'He's not used to a side saddle,' Bevis warned.

Oh well, it was now or never. Will was not going to create a scene in front of all these men. 'It is quite all right.' She took the reins from the groom and led the stallion over to the mounting block, adjusted the stirrup leathers and swung into the saddle before anyone appeared to realise what she was doing. 'What is his name?'

'He hasn't got one yet, my lady. He's got the manners of a gentleman, that one.' Bevis was carefully not staring at her legs as she adjusted the folds of the divided skirt. The horse stood still and patient, mouthing gently at the bit.

Will walked over and put his hand on the pommel. 'You, my dear, are full of surprises,' he said softly. She could not tell whether he was angry or not.

'I only ride astride on the estate. And my legs are better covered than they would be side saddle.' She tried not to sound defensive. It was not the actual degree of decency or coverage that was the question, she knew that. It was the shock of a woman imitating a man, the unspoken, sexual, connotations of being astride.

'I am not objecting.' He moved his hand to rest on her thigh then, as she was absorbing the surprise of that, raised his voice back to normal conversational levels. 'Would you like to name him?'

'Me? But I thought… He is a stallion, he will be your horse. Do you not want to name him yourself?'

'I realise I have never given you a wedding gift. It is rather late in the day for one, I know, but you seem to like him. He is yours.'

Chapter Sixteen

There did not seem to be any words, none Julia could say without bursting, ridiculously, into tears. What was the matter with her? Her fears over their marriage? Her state of physical frustration or Will's sudden wild generosity? Julia laid her hand over his and squeezed and then, ignoring their audience, bent from the saddle and kissed him on the cheek. 'I shall call him Angelo.'

'A Spanish angel? I hope he proves to be so.' Will grinned at her.

Emboldened, Julia murmured, 'Not many men would give their wives a stallion.'

'Perhaps they do not feel very secure about certain things and feel they have something to prove,' he suggested. 'I intend continuing to ride Ajax.' That was his raking thorough-bred gelding. 'I may be flattering myself, but I do not feel that puts my masculinity at question.' The look in his eyes was decid-edly wicked.

Julia felt herself growing warm. 'I have missed you,' she whispered.

'We need to talk.' His eyes said that he meant with more than words. 'Why not try him in the paddock and then we'll see them all settled in?'

Mr Bevis was right, the powerful stallion had perfect manners and a soft mouth. He curvetted slightly, showing off, as he went past the mares, but answered her hands on the reins and walked past into the paddock.

'You are not to flirt,' Julia scolded and he put one ear back, listening politely. They circled at the walk, then the trot, Julia rising in the saddle as a man would, enjoying the stretch in her leg muscles, wondering if she was shocking Will and rather hoping that she was. When she settled into the saddle and pressed with her heels Angelo went into a perfect canter and then back to the walk as she reached the gate again.

'He is superb,' she called and reluctantly turned back into the yard.

The sun was warm and Julia went to sit on the mounting block, her elbows on her knees, and watched the men taking the horses to their appointed boxes. Everything was a controlled bustle, the sound of hooves on the stone setts, men giving orders, stable boys running back and forth, and yet she felt filled with the kind of peace she had experienced after she had recovered from the loss of the baby. In those months before Will returned she had come to feel she belonged here, that she was in control and understood what she was doing.

And then she saw Will walking towards her. He was hatless, his coat hooked on one finger over his shoulder, his shirtsleeves rolled up. He looked big, physical, intelligent, this man she was married to, had made love with, hardly knew.

'A penny for them. In fact...' Will put one foot on the bottom step and regarded her, head to one side '...I may offer two pence, your thoughts seem so deep.'

'I was thinking that I feel as I did just before you came back,' Julia said without calculation. 'As though I belonged here.'

'And when I came back, you no longer did.'

'Yes. That is exactly how I felt.' She had

said it now, the hurtful, tactless thing. It was out in the open and they could no longer pretend that everything was just fine.

A shadow passed over Will's face. He would turn away now, deal with this in a civilised manner by ignoring it as usual. The loneliness and regret washed through her like the winter sea.

Will stood very still, studying her face, then, to Julia's surprise, came and sat next to her, hip against hip. 'We have not talked, have we?' It was a statement and he sounded reflective, not angry or hurt. Julia shook her head. 'There were the really big things,' Will continued. 'We talked a little about those, of course. The baby, Caroline. We could hardly avoid those subjects, although there is much more that could be said.'

'And we spoke of your love for this place and your parents. As you say, the big things, the difficult things, but not the small things,' Julia agreed. There was no tension. It seemed natural to lean against his shoulder as they sat there. 'I do not know how much housekeeping money I have, or pin money. We simply fell into some kind of division of responsibilities. You were surprised by the timing of…my cycle. We have been married for three years and yet we know nothing about each other. What are your political opinions? What is your favourite meal? Do you read novels or are the ones in your library there because you buy all the latest books?'

'I did not know how to open negotiations again,' Will said, surprising a laugh from her. 'I made such a mull of things with Caroline and Henry. I knew I must have hurt you, if only by my sheer clumsiness. And then I could not come to your bed and somehow I did not like to simply make assumptions and walk in after I thought the timing would be right. Perhaps it was a good thing or I suspect I would have tried to make up by making love and we would have talked even less.'

That was true. Lovemaking was something they could use to avoid confrontation as much as to give and take pleasure. 'You know who you are, don't you?' Julia asked. 'You know you belong here, you are so secure in being a man that you can give me a stallion to ride while you keep your gelding, you can admit when you are wrong and try to solve things by talking.'

'Are you implying that I am perfect?' She shot him a sideways glance from narrowed eyes and saw his mouth was curling into a smile.

'Not at all. You had not given a thought to what you were going to do about me when you came home.' She realised something as she studied his profile, the sensitive, mobile mouth and the stubborn chin. 'You thought that because I love this place, too, there must be a power struggle over it. But that's idio— I mean, there is no need for that. It is yours, I would just like to share it. And you do that typically male thing of ignoring uncomfortable things until they are pushed under your nose.'

'Ah. An idiot and a typical male?' He was still smiling. 'Do you think we can make this work, Julia? If you can overlook my idiocy and kick me when I'm ignoring things?'

'I can do that. But a marriage takes two people. What are my faults that must be addressed?' She was certain he would have a list as long as her arm. Julia braced herself.

'I want you to be honest with me.'

The cold grabbed her stomach as though she had swallowed a lump of ice. She had not expected that. 'What do you mean?'

'Don't hide things and bottle them up because they are difficult to talk about.'

'You think I do that? I cannot break Henry's confidence, you know that.' *I cannot tell you about the weight on my conscience, the dreadful thing I have done.* Julia got down from the mounting block, the urge to twine her arm into his and lay her head on his shoulder vanishing. 'I am starving. Shall we have an early luncheon? You had no breakfast.'

Will fell into step beside her as she walked towards the house. 'Yes. I would like to eat and, yes, I do think you hide things from me. I don't mean my cousin's secrets. You were terrified of what I would do when I discovered where little Alexander was resting. You didn't tell me that your lover was such a selfish lout. No wonder you were reluctant to come to my bed if your previous experience had been so bad.' She must have gasped because he added, 'You didn't need to tell me about it, I could see that from your reactions. But I would rather have known so I could have been more…sensitive.'

Julia found she was speechless. Will opened the front door for her. 'Gatcombe, we'll take an early luncheon if Cook can manage it.' When they reached the landing Will drew her into his chamber and closed the door. 'I am just a man and sometimes we need things holding up in front of our faces. Will you promise to tell me when you are unhappy, when things worry you? Don't have secrets from me, Julia, not about the things that will hurt this marriage.'

'Oh, Will.' She stood on tiptoe and curled her arms around his neck. His honesty, his willingness to admit his own faults, touched her. As their lips met she whispered, without thinking, 'No secrets, I promise.'

Will reached out and turned the key in the door, then simply walked backwards, still kissing, so she followed him until they tipped back on to the bed. 'At the risk of making Cook irritable, I think we should seal our new resolutions, don't you?'

'Oh, yes.' Julia rolled on to her back and lay looking up at him. *New resolutions, a new beginning.* And then as he sat up to work out the complexities of the closures of her divided skirt, the cold realisation gripped her again. *I promised, but—Jonathan. I cannot tell him about what I did to Jonathan.* If she told Will, even if he could accept why she had done it, that it was an accident, it would make him an accessory after the fact. His choice would be to become as guilty in law as she was or to hand her over to the magistrates.

And I have promised to be open with him. Yet there was nothing to be done but break that promise and keep her secret, or hand herself in or run away and disappear. Naked in Will's arms, Julia acknowledged that she did not have the courage to confess and take the consequences and she could not bear to leave King's Acre. *Or Will.*

Her body rose to his, cradled him, her arms and legs curling around him as though they were one and she would not let him go. As he sank into her and she felt him inside, as she gripped him with those internal muscles that made him groan as he stroked, tormenting himself as much as her, she knew she did not have the strength to do anything but stay. And lie to him.

'Do you mind if we go to London in a couple of days?' Will looked up from a large and imposing letter. It crackled expensively as he spread it out on the cloth amongst the breakfast things. 'My lawyer wants me to sign papers and I need to discuss investments with my banker, Jervis tells me that my shirts are a disgrace and he is ashamed to be known as my valet and I need new boots.'

'It sounds as though you hardly require me.' Julia sorted through her own post. Household bills, a letter from a friend in the next village, a note from the vicarage about the Sunday School, an account from an Aylesbury milliner. 'You will be far too busy on your own account.' The county newspaper was at the bottom of the pile and she turned to the inside page and the local news.

'You need a complete new wardrobe— stop putting it off,' Will said. 'I promised myself the fun of taking you shopping and you are not going to wriggle out of it, my lady.'

'But it is August. Nothing will be happening.'

'We can go back in the winter for parties and the theatre. But now it will be quiet and we can explore. You do not know London, do you?'

'No. Not at all.' Julia smiled at him. He was obviously set on going and looking forward to treating her. It was cowardly, and churlish, to refuse. 'Of course I will come with you: I will enjoy it.' She ran her eye down the columns of tightly packed type, skimming the stories. An unseasonable storm of hailstones had flattened just one field of hay at Thame. A small boy had been saved from drowning in a village pond. A calf with two heads had been born at a local farm and was being exhibited for a penny and a woman who had killed her husband had been hanged outside Aylesbury town hall and her body given to the surgeons to be dissected.

The room seemed to be full of buzzing, as though a swarm of bees had filled it. The print blurred before her eyes and Julia realised she felt hot and then cold and sickeningly dizzy.

She gripped the edge of the table as Will said, 'Good. We'll stay at Grillon's in Albemarle Street and look for a house to hire for the Season while we're up there. Is the day after tomorrow all right for you? I'll send to the hotel today.'

'Lovely,' Julia managed as she closed the newspaper and folded it with trembling hands. A woman hanged. Was that where they would hang her if they caught her? In front of the town hall before a mob jeering and shouting and making a holiday of it?

'Julia? Is anything wrong? You have gone

quite pale.' Will was half out of his seat. She waved him back to it and, from somewhere, found a smile.

I killed a man. For one terrified moment she thought she had said it out loud. 'Just the most alarming bill from a milliner! What a good thing we have not yet discussed allowances or I am sure I would be asking for an advance already.'

Will chuckled and sat down again. The room stopped swaying. She made herself open her clenched hand. Her mouth was dry, she felt sick with dread and the temptation to tell him was almost overwhelming. But she could not put him in that terrible position. Julia forced herself to calm. It was just the shock of seeing that gruesome report and the way her conscience was troubling her for breaking her promise to Will. She was in no more, or less, danger than she had ever been.

'I must spend the morning on my accounts,' she managed.

'Mmm?' Will glanced up from his post. 'Don't forget to tell Nancy to start packing.'

'No. Of course not.' *It will be all right. I have nothing to fear after all this time. Forget it and it will just become a bad dream.*

* * *

'You are very pensive, Julia.' Will took her hand as the chaise pulled up at the King's Arms in Berkhamsted for the first change of horses.

He had been as good as his word, those few days since their conversation in the stable yard. They had talked—or rather Will had talked and she had forced herself to respond. The housekeeping was agreed, her generous allowance settled. They discussed who would do what with the estate and what Will felt comfortable with letting out of his control.

If she was only able to sleep without nightmares, Julia knew she would be happy. It was as if she had cursed herself with that resolution to make those dreadful memories only dreams. Now her nights were made hideous by images of blood. Never of Jonathan, but always of blood. On her hands, on her body, curling like seaweed into the water in the wash bowl.

She leaned against Will's wonderfully solid and reassuring shoulder. 'I am just a little tired with all the preparations.'

'And I have been keeping you awake at night,' he teased.

Julia felt herself blushing. Even with the

fear gnawing at the back of her mind of what
would follow when she slept, their lovemaking was perfect. At least, it seemed so to her.
Drowsing in his arms, her body limp and re-
plete, she felt so safe that just for a while she
could believe nothing could hurt her. But in
the cold light of dawn she knew even Will's
strength and courage could not protect her
from the terrors in her own mind.

'It would have been a saving to have taken
the carriage instead of two chaises,' she said
repressively. Across the yard the other vehicle with Nancy and Jervis had just drawn up.

'I wanted to be alone with you,' Will said.

'In the chaise!'

'What a very wicked mind you have, Lady
Dereham.' He chuckled and dipped his head
to give her a fleeting kiss on the lips. 'I meant
so we could talk. There is something I wanted
to know and a journey means we can be un-
interrupted. You have been remarkably quiet
about your life before we met by the lake.'

It was so apposite to her thoughts that his
remark almost struck her dumb. 'What…
what do you want to know?'

'What your home was like, the estate. Tell
me about your parents. Did you have a dog,
a pony?'

'Oh.' The relief was physical and air rushed back into her lungs. 'You want to know about my childhood.'

'I was not intending to interrogate you about your lover,' Will said drily as the chaise left the yard and turned eastwards.

'Thank you, although I do not mind speaking of him…a little.' She did not want to leave Will with the impression that she had anything to hide from him. 'He was a mistake. A terrible mistake.'

'What is his name?'

'He was…*is*…called Jonathan.' She remembered how Will had not believed her story when he had first come home. Suddenly it was important to tell him as much of the truth as possible. 'When you first found out about him, you did not believe that I had only been with him a short while—a day and not quite a night. But that was honestly how it was. Before I ran away he had always treated me with respect, courted me with propriety. I truly thought we were eloping, I believed he would take me to Scotland and marry me. We lay together only the once.'

'I know.' His voice was firm and definite.

'How can you know? Or are you simply trusting me?'

'I would trust you, of course I would.' Was he trying to convince himself as much as her? She could sense a slight reservation. 'I know you now, Julia. Before, when I was so disbelieving, it was simply the shock of coming home, of being alive, of hearing about the baby. I was not thinking straight. But when I made love with you, I realised. It was all very new to you, was it not?' She bit her lip and stared out of the window and tried not to remember. 'It was not simply that he was too selfish to make it good, it was all unfamiliar because you were so inexperienced.' She nodded.

'Then we can forget him. Pretend he doesn't exist,' Will said. 'That's all behind you now unless there is anything it would help to talk about?'

'Yes, I can try to do that,' Julia said. *Pretend he doesn't exist. That is easy, he doesn't, because I killed him. He was a wicked man, but he did not deserve to die for it.* 'But I cannot promise that his ghost is not going to haunt me sometimes.' *Every night.*

'It will have to get past me,' Will said. 'Now, forget him and the past. I'll not stir that up again. Can you read in the chaise without getting sick? Because my London agent has sent me details of a number of eligible houses he thinks would be suitable to rent for the Season. See what you think.'

'How exciting.' Julia took the portfolio he handed her and infused her voice with as much enthusiasm as she could. Will was looking forward to London, to the London Season in the new year, to the sort of married life a man of his station should expect. And she could bring it crashing down around his head at any moment if she did not have the courage to keep her mouth shut and the intelligence to hide the truth. Whatever happened, she must make his happiness last as long as she could, she owed it to him.

'My goodness.' She riffled through the stack of papers. 'The addresses all sound very grand. I like the sound of this one.'

He took the paper. 'Half Moon Street? Why? It might be a trifle small, I thought.'

'I like the name.'

As she guessed it would, that made him laugh. 'Julia, you are a delight of a wife.'

And she laughed, too, as her conscience tore at her.

It was only half an hour later as she laid the stack of house particulars on one side that

Will's actual words came back to her. *A delight of a wife.* Did he truly mean that? She watched him as he studied the work he had brought with him, his dark head bent over the papers, his face remote and intelligent as he studied the pages. She had wanted him to want her as his wife, to build a relationship with him. Certainly things were good in the bedchamber and harmonious in everyday matters. She believed he would be faithful. That was all she had hoped for, surely, so why did her heart beat faster at his affectionate teasing? Did she want him to fall in love with her?

Julia stared out of the carriage window at the passing landscape. *Do I? Am I in love with him?* She was not certain what that meant any more. She had thought herself in love with Jonathan, so much in love that she would trust her entire future to him, and yet that feeling had evaporated the moment she realised his deception.

And what she felt for Will was nothing like that light-headed, romantic dreamy feeling. She liked him, she respected him and she desired him, but she was no longer so naïve that she thought a woman must be in love in order to ache for a man to lie with her.

She felt for Will, in short, all those things that a woman making a marriage of convenience would hope that she would come to feel for her husband.

But it was not love. That was just a romantic dream and a sure way to a broken heart, Julia decided. And why should she want to be in love with her husband in any case? If she was fortunate, there would be children who would be healthy and strong and she would experience all the love she could want with them. Julia closed her eyes for a moment in silent supplication that if she was fortunate enough to become pregnant again then all would be well this time.

But even so, when Will looked up and caught her studying him, and his eyes crinkled with amused affection, her heart made that foolish little leap again. 'Your hair needs cutting,' she said prosaically. 'You must add that to the list of things to do in town.'

Chapter Seventeen

William was as good as his word about the shopping. He gave Julia one day to settle into Grillon's Hotel in Albemarle Street while he had his hair cut, ordered his boots from Hoby's, wrote to summon his tailor and sent messages to his lawyers and bankers, then the next day swept her out to, as he put it, discover the lie of the land. With Nancy in attendance, so she knew where she was going when Julia wanted to shop in future, they explored Bond Street, located Harding, Howell and Company in Piccadilly, scanned the myriad of temptations in the Parthenon Bazaar and came home loaded with band-boxes and armed with the latest guidebooks.

Julia was thrilled to discover that King

Louis XVIII had stayed at Grillon's Hotel in 1812 and even more excited to discover they were opposite the offices of James Murray, the publisher. It was only when Will pointed out that she would not recognise any of her favourite authors if she saw them that she could be persuaded away from the window.

'Would you like to see the City?' he asked over dinner. 'St Paul's Cathedral, the Royal Exchange, the Bank of England? We could even climb up the Monument if you feel really energetic.'

'Yes, please. All of those are on my list and I am hardly a quarter of the way through the guidebook yet.'

'I am not certain we can do all of them in one day. I must call on my bankers in the morning and then my lawyer, who is in Amen Corner.' He grinned at her expression. 'It is by St Paul's, which I suppose accounts for the name. We can decide what to do when we see what the time is, but we can certainly fit in the cathedral.'

Julia had tried to be patient, but an hour sitting in the banker's outer office, even sustained with coffee and ratafia biscuits and the copy of *La Belle Assemblée*, which she had prudently brought with her, was more than enough tedium.

As the hackney carriage made its way along Paternoster Row she asked, 'Is there any reason why I cannot walk around outside with Nancy while you are with the lawyer? The sun is shining, the shops seem to be cheaper than they are in Mayfair...'

Will nodded as they drew up in a narrow lane. 'I do not see why not. You can hardly get lost, not with the dome of St Paul's to act as a landmark. Shall we say you will be back here in an hour?' He helped them both out, making Nancy blush at the attention, then pointed. 'Go down Ave Maria Lane there and turn left and you'll find all the shops around St Paul's Churchyard.' He felt in the breast of his coat and handed her some folded banknotes. 'Do not let anyone see you have that.'

'Thank you.' Julia cast a quick look round, found the lane almost deserted and stood on tiptoe to drop a swift kiss on Will's cheek.

'Cupboard love,' he said with a smile and paid off the cab.

The previous day had been unalloyed pleasure. Julia had not felt at all alarmed in the fashionable streets, despite the numbers of people. On Will's arm, and in such fashionable lounges, her fears seemed foolish. Now she set off with confidence, Nancy at her side. They emerged from Ave Maria Lane to find themselves on a busy street with a pronounced slope. 'Ludgate Hill,' Julia said with the certainty of someone who had studied the map.

'My lord said to go left,' Nancy said as Julia turned downhill.

'I know, but see this silversmith's shop— is that not a delightful ink stand? I think something like that would make an admirable present for Lord Dereham.'

And the next shop down was a print seller with amusing cartoons in the window. And the next a jeweller's, its window stuffed with enticing oddments.

'My lady, it is getting rather crowded.'

Julia looked up. In front of them a press of people were heading into a street parallel to Ave Maria Lane. They were noisy, a motley crowd of working people and tradesmen, men and women. They seemed in good humour, but Julia's old fears came flooding back to cramp her stomach.

'Yes, we must turn back.' As they did so another crowd swept down the hill towards them. 'Nancy!' Julia was jostled, caught up. She struggled to find her feet and fight her way back, but she was carried, like driftwood on a stream, down the hill and round the corner.

Julia tried not to panic, knowing if she struggled she would simply exhaust herself or fall and be trampled. She let herself be borne along and tried to think coherently. Nancy would be all right, she was sure, for she had been further up the hill. If she could just get to the end of this street and turn right, go uphill again, keeping St Paul's in sight and then turn right, surely she'd be back in Ave Maria Lane?

Then the movement began to slow. She was still crushed against unwashed bodies and rough clothing, but at least there was no longer any danger of falling over and being trampled. Julia stared around and found the street had widened into a square shaped like a funnel. The crowd milled about, elbowing for room, but everyone faced the building that towered over them on her right. Wedged in place, she had no option but to turn with them. In front of her was the massive bulk of a grim stone building.

'What is that?' she asked the man at her side, a prosperous shopkeeper, she guessed.

'Why, that is Newgate Prison, ma'am. Aren't you here for the hanging, then?' He pointed and her reluctant gaze followed. High above the heads of the mob, the scaffold and the noose stood waiting for their first victim of the day.

'Let me out!' Julia turned and burrowed through the tight-packed spectators, fear and desperation lending her strength as she used her elbows and pushed, shoved, wriggled through every tiny gap that opened up, like a mouse through long grass with a hawk hovering above. Her bonnet was dragged off, she lost a shoe, but there was a thinning of the crowd ahead of her and she fought her way towards it.

Laughter, improbable in this mayhem, made her glance up to the right. There was an inn and, surrounding the swinging inn sign, its windows were crowded with people laughing and chatting as if they were in the boxes at a play. *Horrible*, she thought. *How could they?* And then a woman turned and nudged her husband and pointed at her and she found herself staring up at Jane and Arthur Prior, her cousins.

Julia gasped, stumbled and when she looked up they had gone. It was imagination, that was all, she told herself as she struggled on, the panic beating in her chest like a trapped bird against a window. With shocking suddenness she was finally out of the press, stumbling on the uneven cobbles. Her unshod foot jarred against a stone and she fell, throwing out her hands in a vain attempt to save herself.

The cobbles were rough, disgustingly dirty and wet. Her hands hurt. Almost winded, Julia lay where she was, felt the blood oozing through the split in her glove and wondered if her heart was going to burst.

'Julia! Sweetheart, it is all right. I'm here. Are you hurt?'

And, miraculously, there Will was, gathering her up in his arms. Julia turned her face to his shoulder and clung on as he lifted her, then carried her to a hackney carriage where Nancy waited, white-faced.

'My lady—oh, your poor hands.'

'Just grazed. I am not hurt otherwise,' she managed to reassure them as Will gently opened her fingers and wrapped them in his handkerchief, still holding her hard against himself. 'Are you all right, Nancy?' Concern for someone else helped, she realised. The panic was ebbing, her breath was calming.

'I am fine, my lady, just all shaken up. I didn't know what to do, I couldn't reach you, or see you, so I ran back to the lawyers and made them get my lord. What was it, my lady? A riot?'

'No, a hanging.' She would not be sick, not if she closed her eyes and thought of nothing but Will's arms around her, keeping her safe.

'It is Newgate Prison,' he said, his voice grim. 'I should have warned you not to go that way, it isn't very salubrious at the best of times, but when there's an execution it is a glimpse into hell.'

'People were watching from the windows, as if it were a play,' she managed. *Jane and Arthur. It couldn't be. It was my imagination, my fear, a couple who looked a little like them. I haven't seen them for almost four years*, she comforted herself. *They will have changed, I wouldn't recognise them now if I really saw them. I am safe with Will, I don't imagine things when he is here.*

'It is disgusting,' Will muttered, his voice rough with anger. 'They moved the hangings from Tyburn because it was supposed to be more *civilised* to do it outside the prison instead of parading the condemned through the streets to the place of execution. It is not my definition of civilised. Just try to relax, sweetheart. I've got you safe.'

'I know,' Julia murmured and closed her eyes so that her entire world became just Will. She inhaled slowly and there was the familiar smell of his skin, of clean linen and the sharp male edge of fresh sweat. He had run, and run hard, to reach her. The feel of him was familiar too, the strength that made her feel so safe, the warmth of that big, desirable body under fine linen and smooth broadcloth. She listened to the sound of his heartbeat against her ear, a little ragged still. *Home. I am home when I am with him.*

Will cared for her, he was angry for her. He shifted a little to hold her more securely and she felt his cheek press against her hair and something happened in her chest as if a bell had tolled silently, reverberating through her whole body.

I love him. She felt herself go still as though to move would shatter the moment, break the spell. This was nothing like her emotions for Jonathan, this was a deeply complex, rich emotion like velvet swirling around her feelings. It was not about desire or liking or respect, although those were all in there somewhere. It was inexplicable and unexplainable and that, she supposed, was how she knew it was love.

She would tell him this evening when they were alone, when they were in bed together: it would be the naked truth, after all. He did not love her, she knew that, but that was all right. Well, no, perhaps not all right exactly. But she could not hope for the moon and the stars. She would explain to him that she did not expect him to feel the same way, that she was not asking him to pretend and to lie to her.

'Better, sweetheart?' Will murmured in her ear.

'Much, thank you, Will. You keep me safe.'

'Always,' he said and his arms tightened around her.

'I will sleep in the dressing room,' Will said from the open door of the bedroom as the clocks in their suite struck nine. 'You should be asleep.' Julia was pale against the heaped pillows. He wished he had her home again where she would feel safer as she recovered from her ordeal and not here, in a strange place.

'I have slept, for hours,' Julia protested. And she did look better, despite the pallor. 'That hot bath was like taking laudanum! Come to bed, Will.'

'You are still nervous? Then of course I will sleep with you.' He closed the door behind him and watched her carefully as he shed coat and waistcoat. No wonder she was so reluctant to go into the neighbouring towns for anything but the most essential shopping if crowds made her so frightened. Some people had a fear of them, he knew. It was like the fear of heights, or spiders—not something that seemed to be rational to anyone else, but very real to the sufferer. And a public hanging was probably, short of a riot, the most frightening mob to find oneself in.

'I wish you had told me how you felt about crowds,' he said as he pulled off his neck cloth.

'It was so irrational, I thought you would think me foolish,' she said, not meeting his eyes. 'I pride myself on common sense and keeping calm and then to experience such panic when no one means me any harm...'

Her voice trailed away and he bit his

tongue on the reproach that she had kept this a secret from him. It was not a rational fear, he reminded himself, so perhaps she found it harder to confide about it.

'We all fear something,' Will said and sat on the edge of the bed to pull off his boots.

'What do *you* fear?' Julia curled round on the pillows and watched him as he tossed his stockings aside. 'I did not think you were afraid of anything.'

'Lies and powerlessness,' he said instantly, then stopped undressing to think about what he had said. 'Not seeing the whole picture when there is something to confront, so all the time you think there is something worse lying in wait. I think that was what was so dreadful with my parents when I was growing up: I did not know what was wrong, no one would tell me the truth and admit that the marriage was a sham. I was expected to act as though we were a happy family and nothing was amiss, yet I sensed the world as I knew it was all falling apart.

'And then at first when I was ill, no one would tell me the truth—or what they thought was the truth. In my heart I believed I was dying and yet I could not face it, deal with it, because the doctors insisted I would be cured in the end. I have no idea why they wouldn't tell me. Perhaps they thought I couldn't cope with it, or perhaps they thought I was a better source of income if I was hoping for a cure! It took three months before they would admit the truth, that they were certain there was no hope.'

'Was it any easier after that?' Julia asked. She reached out a hand and laid it over his on the bedspread. She did nothing except press lightly, but it was curiously comforting. Will curled his fingers into hers and dug deeper into his feelings than he had for a long time.

'It made the dying easier,' he confessed with a grimace. 'Which seems strange, but I suppose I had suspected the worst for so long it was a relief to know what I was dealing with. But then the powerlessness over King's Acre, that was terrifying.'

Julia's fingers closed tighter. 'You are in control of all of it now.'

All of it except my wife, Will thought wryly. He honestly had no idea what Julia would do next or how she would react to what he said or did. Most of the time that was refreshing, but there was still some secret, deep down, he was certain of it and it nagged at the foundation of trust that he thought they were building together. At least he understood her reluctance to leave the estate now if crowds brought on attacks of panic.

She began to stroke the inside of his wrist and Will lost the thread of his thoughts as desire began to build, hot and heavy. He tugged his shirt over his head and let Julia pull him back on to the bed. 'Nothing is going to get you in here,' he protested.

'I am not afraid,' Julia murmured, running her nails lightly down his torso. 'I am…' She blushed.

'Lustful?' Will suggested as he rolled over on his back and began to unfasten his breeches. It was not the easiest thing to do flat on his back, with an erection and with a wanton wife crawling over him.

'Will! Amorous sounds better.'

'Both of them sound good to me,' he growled as he kicked his legs free and sent the breeches flying. Julia gave a soft *huff* of laughter as he rolled over on top of her, but as she lay looking up at him the laughter ebbed away, leaving her serious. It was on the tip of his tongue to ask her what was wrong when she pulled his head down and lifted herself to kiss him.

It was the first time she had ever taken the

initiative in their lovemaking. Before she had been responsive and willing to follow wherever he led, but he sensed that this exploration with soft lips and delicate strokes of her tongue was different.

Her hands drifted down his rib-cage, down his flanks, stroking in fluttering caresses that made him want to purr like a big cat and then to plunge into her to assuage the ache that gripped him. He was almost impossibly hard, aroused, simply by a sweet kiss and gentle hands. This was some enchantment she was weaving, it had to be.

Without freeing his mouth she wriggled, almost tipping him over the edge beyond control, then wrapped her legs around his hips so he was cradled against the hot, wet centre of her. Will tried counting backwards, then doing it in Arabic. He was going to lose his grip any moment and behave like an animal and it was obvious from Julia's gentle, languid movements that was not what she wanted.

It was also obvious she had no idea whatsoever that she was driving him to the brink, he thought in despair as she fastened her teeth on his earlobe with a delicate nip.

Then she wriggled again, and tilted her

pelvis and he realised through the fog of desire that she knew exactly what she was doing. They were positioned perfectly for her to arch up and take him into her in a smooth, seductive glide that had him gasping for mercy until, somehow, he wrenched some self-control back.

And then he found that he could slow down, be as gentle as she was, make this exquisite pleasure last and last until there was nothing in the world except for their ragged breathing and the scent of arousal and the sound of their bodies moving against each other.

'Will.' She shuddered under him, around him, the force of her orgasm caressing him until he was falling with her. He knew he called her name, knew he found her mouth and stifled both their cries with his kisses, and then the world was still again.

'Will.' Seconds later, hours later? He had no idea. All he knew was that was the most perfect physical experience he had ever had in his life and that, somehow, it went beyond the physical into emotion. He opened his eyes and raised his head from the softness of Julia's breast and saw her eyes were wide and dark as her mouth trembled into a smile. 'I love you.'

It took a long moment before her words sank in. 'Julia—' He did not know what to say, what to feel.

'It is all right,' she murmured, lifting one hand to brush his hair back from his face. 'You don't have to say it too. I know you don't love me, but I had to tell you. How could I keep that a secret from you?'

He was squashing her, Will thought distractedly. But if he rolled off her she would think he was avoiding meeting her eyes. Those painfully clear, honest eyes. Will took more weight on his elbows and sought for the truth. 'I don't know about love,' he said at last. 'I was not in love with Caroline, I know that. Just dazzled and charmed and rather a lot in lust.'

That made her laugh, a soft gurgle of amusement. 'I know you were not. That is why I was not more angry with you after the dinner party. And I want you to be honest. I would hate to think you were telling me you love me and lying to be kind.' She hesitated. 'That would *not* be...kind.'

'I know.' How did he feel? 'I desire you more every time I lie with you, every time I kiss you. I like you. I miss you when we are not together. I admire your intelligence and your strength of will and I like that you need me to protect you sometimes despite it. I do not know what that adds up to, sweetheart.'

'Enough for any woman,' Julia said. 'I can live with that and be happy, believe me.'

'I believe you,' Will said, knowing in his heart that it was not enough but that he could not give her what he did not possess or understand. He pulled her with him as he rolled over, then gathered her against his chest. 'Go to sleep now, Julia.'

So that was what the secret was that she had been keeping from him, he thought as he began to drift off to sleep. She had needed the shock of that day's events to give her the courage to tell him how she felt. Perhaps he did love her. If only he knew what it felt like so he could recognise it. But whatever this was, he decided as Julia's breathing became slow and her body relaxed against his in complete trust, it was the start of happiness. A more complete happiness than he had dared hope he would ever find.

Chapter Eighteen

Will looked content, Julia decided, watching him over the breakfast table the next morning. She felt wonderful, strong enough to keep the key turned in the lock of that dark little cupboard buried deep inside her, the one where the memory of Jonathan's death lurked along with the new acceptance that she loved a man who, however fond he was, did not love her.

We are content, that is enough.

'Excuse me, my lord, only there's a message from the desk downstairs: there are visitors asking for you.' Nancy closed the door on the uniformed page who waited on the landing.

'What name?' Will folded his paper with

a sigh and slapped it down beside his plate. 'This is very early to be calling. I suppose it might be about an investment I was particularly concerned about. Hapgood must have thought I was impatient for news of it after our discussion yesterday. I will come down.'

'No, don't do that.' Julia laid her napkin aside. 'We have finished our breakfast. If it is Mr Hapgood and he wishes to talk business you can give him a cup of coffee and I will go into the bedroom. I have lots of things to sort out.'

'Very well.' Will looked resigned to business. 'I will not take long, I promise, then we can resume our interrupted sightseeing. Ask them to come up, if you please, Nancy.'

It would be the banker, or perhaps the lawyer, Julia thought, finding a clean cup and saucer from the tray for the visitor. After all, they knew no one else in town.

The door opened as she bent over the coffee jug to make sure there was enough. 'Mr and Mrs Prior,' Nancy announced.

For a moment she thought she was imagining things. Julia looked up and found herself staring into the face of Cousin Arthur and, beside him, smiling smugly, Cousin Jane.

She was going mad, seeing visions. Julia

clutched the edge of the table and was dimly aware of the sound of falling china.

'Good morning, Cousin Julia,' Arthur said. 'What a relief to find you well and safe. You can imagine the worry we have been in, you wicked girl. What a terrible, terrible thing to have done! And now what are we to do?'

'And who the blazes are you?' Will demanded as Julia's knees gave way and she fell back onto her chair.

It had not been an hallucination yesterday. She had seen them and they had seen her and somehow discovered where she was.

'Lord Dereham, I presume?' Arthur advanced with an outstretched hand that Will completely ignored. 'I must make allowances for your natural agitation, I can tell. I am Arthur Prior, Julia's cousin, and this is my wife, Mrs Prior. I cannot begin to describe to you the anguish we have experienced since Julia ran away three years ago! To see her yesterday from the window of our lodgings was such a shock I hardly know how we had the presence of mind to send the lad to follow the hackney carriage and establish where she had gone.'

Will turned on his heel to face her. 'Is this

the cousin who inherited your father's estate? The one who laid violent hands upon you?'

'Yes, he is my father's heir. But he never—'

'Violence! Is that what the wicked girl is saying?' Jane reeled back into the nearest chair and fanned herself with a napkin. 'Nothing but kindness she received from our hands. And how did she repay us? By running off with my uncle's stepson, despite being told what a wicked rake he was. The poor, poor boy.' She glowered at Julia who stared back, unable to form a coherent sentence.

'But it seems as though she's fallen on her feet here, has she not, Mrs Prior?' Arthur demanded with a rhetorical flourish.

'Before you go any further,' Will said in a voice that somehow managed to convey a threat of violence under a coating of ice, 'I should tell you that I am perfectly aware of my wife's elopement and of the reasons behind it. I can see no purpose in this call—she most certainly does not wish to receive you, now or in the future. Good day to you.'

'Not so fast, my lord.' To do him credit, Cousin Arthur was standing his ground against a man who Julia hardly recognised. Will looked bigger, angrier and more frightening than she had ever imagined he might. She struggled to find words, but she had no idea what to say, what to do in the face of this utter disaster. 'We have been to a lot of trouble and expense trying to find Julia and I consider you would be doing only the right thing if you were to recompense us for that. And our silence of course.'

'Your silence?' Will enquired dangerously. 'About what, exactly?'

'I cannot imagine you would want the truth about Lady Dereham to become common knowledge, would you? You might be able to gloss over the elopement, I suppose. But the violence?' He smiled slyly. 'I'll not pretend Jonathan Dalfield was anything but a sinner, but did he deserve such treatment? His poor head...'

Julia found her voice and the strength to stand. 'I never meant to kill him,' she said. 'Never. He was trying to rape me. It was an accident. I did not realise the poker was in my hand.'

The room went utterly quiet. Will turned slowly to face her, his eyes wide and dark with shock. 'You *killed* a man?'

'You did not know, my lord?' Arthur interjected. He was white and flustered, but he gabbled on. 'Of course, I should have re-alised you'd never keep such a thing quiet, not a gentleman like you. But it won't look good for you if it all comes out, now will it, my lord? Many will not believe you. And it puts us at great risk, always has. But you could be assured of our silence, my lord. We would be very reasonable. Five thousand pounds and no one would ever know and you would never hear from us again.'

Without taking his eyes from her face, Will said, 'You despicable, blackmailing worm.'

'Hard words don't break my bones, my lord.' Arthur had recovered some of his poise. 'But a hempen noose will snap your wife's neck if we aren't all very careful. And it wouldn't look good for you, would it? Accessory after the fact, they call it. I'm no lawyer, but I think that's a capital offence as well, my lord.'

'Julia, go to the other room,' Will said, his voice as soft as if he invited her to sleep with him. Beneath it she could hear the anger beating like a tocsin, his eyes blazed gold, and the skin was tight over his cheekbones as though he was a wolf with its hackles laid back.

Without a word she got up and went into the bedchamber. Now the worst had happened she felt strangely calm. It was shock—she recognised it from when she had killed Jonathan and it was strange to be able to diagnose it now as though she was an observer examining herself at arm's length.

What would Will do? Pay what Arthur demanded? But they would never be safe either from betrayal or from more and more bloodsucking demands. Will was a law-abiding English gentleman: his duty was to hand her over to the authorities, whatever the damage to himself. It was not even as though he loved her, she thought bleakly, sinking on to the edge of the bed to await his judgement. She should not put him in this position, make him decide what to do. She should walk out of here, surrender herself.

There was a door in the far corner of the dressing room concealed by a screen. It gave on to the service stairs and Nancy used it to bring hot water and to take away the slops. She could use that route, ask at the desk for the nearest magistrates' court and be there before Will realised what she was doing.

It all seemed very simple and easy now there was no choice. The important thing was not to think about what would happen afterwards.

The sound of voices from next door ceased. The outer door closed. Silence. Julia got to her feet and found her reticule. Her cloak and bonnet were on the chair. She should just—

The bedchamber door opened and Will stood there, framed in the opening. He looked, she realised with a twisting pang of guilt and shame, as though someone had dealt him a mortal blow and he had not yet realised it. 'I knew you were keeping a secret from me,' he said, his voice as steady as a judge. 'I should have listened to my instincts.'

'I could not tell you.' She found she was on her feet. 'It would have put you in an impossible position.'

'Not unlike the one I am in now?' he enquired and walked into the room, pulling the door to behind him with a savage slam that was like a gunshot, terrifying in contrast to his utter calm. 'I was happy last night, this morning. Pathetic, is it not? I thought we could be content together, I believed my wife loved me.'

'I do!'

'But instead,' he went on as though she had not spoken, 'she tells me of her love, so sweetly, so innocently, because she has seen her relatives and knows what will happen when they find her. Did you really think that telling me you loved me would stop me doing the right thing?'

'No,' Julia protested. 'Of course not! That is not why I told you. I said it because it was true. I saw them yesterday, I admit it, but I thought I was seeing things in my panic, that they were not real. I always expect to see people accusing me, pointing me out, calling the constables. That is why I am so afraid of crowds.' The tears welled up and she fought them back with savage resolve. She had to make him believe that she would not use those words to him so cynically. 'I would not lie to you, Will. Not about that.'

'No? Just about the important things, then? The fact you killed a man?'

'Love is the important thing! Will, I had discovered Jonathan had deceived me. I was in shock, he tried to drag me back to the bed. I refused, but he did not care, he was going to rape me. He dragged me by my wrist and I fell into the hearth amongst all the fire irons. He bent to pull me to my feet and I hit out to stop him. I did not realise the poker was in my hand until it struck him.

'There was so much blood. So much. On my hands, on my body. I screamed. Then I had to wash it off. All that blood. There was a screen half-hidden in the corner concealing the wash stand and water, my clothes. I washed my hands and dressed. I could not bear to be dragged away like that.

'They all came pouring in—the inn guests from the bedchambers, the maids, the innkeeper, everyone. I heard them, but they didn't seem to notice the screen, or if they did, to realise someone was behind it. And then…'

'Then?' Will demanded as she faltered to a halt. 'You tell me no-one saw you at all?'

'They were all crowded round the…body. And a woman had fainted and it was chaos. I came out in my cloak and bonnet and no one looked at me. I moved into the room and became just one of the crowd. Then I slipped downstairs and hid in a cart and escaped. It is the truth,' she added flatly.

Will did not comment on that. She noticed and it cut like a knife through her shocked numbness. He did not believe her at all. He thought she had meant to kill Jonathan, perhaps in revenge at his betrayal.

'There was no identification?' he said. She realised he had been analysing her story.

'I took it all. I burned his cards.'

'Very cool and calm. One could almost say professional. You were certainly composed enough when I found you. I must have seemed like a godsend. I have never considered myself a flat before, an easy mark. It seems I was wrong.'

'If taking pity on someone who needed help and offering them food and shelter makes you a flat, then that is what you were. All I knew was that I was exhausted, frightened, utterly adrift. You offered me respite, a chance to regain a little strength and calm. And then you made me that offer...'

Will sat down on the nearest chair as though standing was no longer an option. He passed one hand over his face, rubbed his eyes and answered with the weariness of a man who had fought to a standstill but must keep battling on. 'I made you an offer you could not have dreamt of. You must have been beside yourself with delight.'

'Yes,' Julia agreed. 'I was so relieved. I saw some hope. And I knew I could do what you needed in return. Do not pretend I did not,' she threw at him, some spirit flaring deep inside her. 'I looked after King's Acre with devotion. I did my best to help Henry become a worthy heir for you.'

'It would hardly have been safe if you'd been arrested for murder.' Will pronounced *murder* as if the word hurt him to utter.

'I considered the odds as best I could. My first name is one no one even thinks of me by. My surname is commonplace. I was hundreds of miles from home. Because of your situation the marriage was not reported outside the neighbourhood. I thought it safe and, if it were not, the authorities would believe I had deceived you.'

'The poor dying man deceived by the wicked murderess?' Will's mouth twisted into an ugly smile. 'And when I returned you were terrified that I might seek an annulment. Of course—that would have made a scandal indeed and it was not my good name you were worried about. How you must have quaked until I consummated the marriage and you were safe. And to think that the worst I considered was that I had been cuckolded in my absence.'

'Yes, I was fearful of a scandal. I will not

lie to you. I knew I could not tell you.' His face darkened. 'Will, if I had not married you then you would be dead now. Henry, with no guidance, would be ruining King's Acre.'

'So dragging my name and honour in the gutter was actually a favour to me?' He looked down at his clasped hands. 'Finding that the woman I was becoming…attached to had killed and lied and deceived me was not supposed to hurt?'

'You never truly trusted me, did you? Julia said. He had become *attached* to her. 'Thank God you never grew to love me.'

'Thank God, indeed.' He stood up and went to the door. 'You will stay here.'

She would not beg him to save her. How could he, even if he wanted to? And besides, she had deceived him and, perhaps, brought him to ruin. 'I did not think it would come to this. I thought that if I was discovered it would be by the authorities and I would have some warning to be able to vanish before they could catch me and hurt you. What are you going to do?'

Will looked back at her and suddenly she saw him as he had been when she first met him, when she had thought him an old man. The skin was tight over those strong

bones, the colour had left his face, his eyes
were stark and full of anger. 'I have no idea.
Think, I suppose. I have promised those
bloodsucking relatives of yours that I will
write to them by the end of tomorrow with
my decision.'

This time he closed the door slowly, qui-
etly, behind him. The key turned. He thought
he had imprisoned her.

Think. She must think, too, and not give
way to the tears or the paralysis of fear.
Jonathan was dead. Nothing she could do
would bring him back. He had no family
in need to whom she could make some res-
titution. She would be hanged, of course,
but the person who would have to live with
this was Will.

The only question that mattered was how
to inflict the least damage and pain on Will.
Once she put it like that, then the answer
seemed clear: not to drag his name through
a public trial, an even more public hanging.
She must vanish. But to do that she must silence the Priors and the only way she could
think of was to hold over them the threat
that they, too, would appear as accessories.

She would tell them that, rather than let
Will pay blackmail money for the rest of his

days she would surrender herself and then she would have killed their golden goose for them. If they did not believe her, called her bluff, then she would have to decide what to do—give up and surrender or run and try to hide. But she would deal with that if she had to.

Will would go to the authorities himself, of course, but then he would be seen as someone deceived, someone doing the right thing as soon as he found out the truth. His pride would be hurt, but that was better than the alternatives.

But she needed time to compose herself and think this through, to make certain Will did not try to find her. There was one certain way of doing that, she supposed. If she could make Will believe that she had taken her own life he would not search for her. But she would not lie to him. Never again, even in this.

Julia went to the desk, pulled a sheet of paper towards her and dipped the pen in the inkwell. She wrote:

Dearest Will,
When you read this I will be beyond
the reach of the law and beyond the ca-

pacity to cause you any more pain or scandal. I am too much of a coward to take poison. I have heard that the river is the last resort for many of London's despairing souls.

There is nothing to say except that I am sorry and that I never meant to hurt you. You will go to the authorities with this letter—I know that you are too honourable to break the law over such a matter. I will not write anything to embarrass you more, except that I love you. Believe that if you believe nothing else.
Julia.

There was a small portmanteau that she had pushed into the bottom of a larger one, anticipating having to pack more clothing on their return than she had when they arrived. He would not notice that it had gone. Julia changed from the smart morning gown into a plain walking dress, put on strong half-boots and packed a change of undergarments that hopefully Nancy would not notice were missing. A handkerchief, a comb, her reticule. She must take nothing that would be missed or, if it was, be unlikely that a woman going to drown herself might take out of habit.

Money she would need. She doubted Will had counted the notes he had given her the day before, or, after all that had passed, even recalled doing so. Julia unfolded it: twenty-five pounds, a year's wages for many people. She put it in the reticule, then checked every pocket, all her other bags, and found another two pounds in small coin and a crumpled five-pound note. She had enough to get a long way away.

'I love you,' she murmured, one hand flat on the door panels, as close to him as she would ever be again. 'Goodbye, Will.' Halfway to the service door she turned back and took another two handkerchiefs from the drawer. She would need them.

Then, feeling as shocked and desperate as she had when she had stepped out from behind the screen in that inn room, she slipped into the dressing room, went behind the screen in the corner, eased the door open and tiptoed down the back stairs.

Chapter Nineteen

Will splashed brandy into a glass and tossed it back in one swallow, poured another and stood gripping the glass as he stared down into the busy street below.

His mind could not seem to get past the fact that Julia had killed her lover. It seemed utterly out of character—everything about her spoke of the need to nurture. He had obviously not understood her at all and it was no wonder he had sensed that she was keeping something from him: any other secret he could conceive of paled into insignificance beside this horror.

Nancy came in and he snarled at her so that she fled, white-faced. He could not bring himself to explain. Not yet. Outside the traffic built as the morning progressed and his mind became as tangled as the mass of hackney carriages and carts, pedestrians and riders down below.

His name would be ruined. King's Acre would always carry the stain of this scandal. And his heart... Well, thank heavens his heart was not engaged, that was the only mercy in all this. What if he had loved his wife as she, the deceitful witch, had said she loved him? The pain in his chest was anger and betrayal, nothing more.

The glass was empty. He filled it. And again. It did not help, all it did was to fire his memory. The pale ghost on the bridge over the lake who had run to his aid. The desperate, grieving mother who had been so afraid he would evict that pathetic little coffin from the vaults. The intelligent farmer arguing for some improvement to the farm, the mistress that the staff, indoor and out, loved and supported with devotion.

Julia in those scandalous divided skirts riding the stallion with such skill and teasing him about his manhood as she did so. Julia, passionate and sensual in his arms.

Julia. And all he had been thinking about was how this was going to affect him. The

empty glass dropped from his hand and he
stared at it as it rolled on the carpet, wondering at his own selfishness. He believed her
when she said she had not meant to kill. You
could not live with a woman as closely as he
had with her and not know whether she had
a capacity for violence or not. *He dragged
me by the wrist.* He had seen the bruises,
savagely black and blue, that first evening.
He meant to rape me. He knew from her
responses in bed that the man had been a
selfish lout. Of course she had tried to fight
back.

And the story of her escape was probable.
He could imagine the scene, the chaos, the
gawping crowd avid for sensation. The body
would have been the focus of all attention.
Julia, almost sleepwalking with shock, could
well have dressed in that simple grey cloak
and plain bonnet and merged into the crowd
until she vanished.

He believed everything she said, he realised. And that meant he must believe her
when she said she loved him. The knife that
was carving its way through his chest gave
a sharp stab.

Julia had been abused, ravished and then
threatened with more violence by the man

she thought loved her. What had happened to him had been an accident and, if anyone was to blame it was Jonathan Dalfield. And now, with every excuse never to trust a man again, never to allow herself to love, she had given him, Will Hadfield, her heart.

And in return he had accepted the worst of her without question, verbally attacked her, locked her in her room, left her in fear of the worst kind of justice. Will was across the room, unlocked the door, flung it open, all before the thought was even finished.

The bedchamber was empty. He found the service door and then the note lying on the pillow. *Dearest Will.* His hand was shaking so much he had to sit on the edge of the bed and steady himself before he could read on.

He was halfway down the stairs before any kind of rational thought hit him. He sent the hall porter sprawling as he barrelled his way through the crowded lobby, down the steps and into the road under the nose of a startled cab horse.

'Westminster Bridge, at the gallop and there's five pounds in it for you,' he yelled at the cab driver, who shut his mouth on the stream of invective and whipped the horse up before Will could get the door closed.

He clung by on instinct as the cab swayed and swerved across Piccadilly, down St James's Street, across Pall Mall and into St James's Park. Westminster was the closest bridge and she would need a bridge to be certain of falling into the deep, lethal water. The banks were too uncertain, the water slower, there were too many people to stop her, to pull her out again.

Will was not conscious of any plan at all in that wild ride, only the knowledge that he must be in time, that if he lost her he would not be able to bear it. The cab pulled up in the middle of the bridge and he leapt out, stared along the length of it. And saw nothing. No hubbub as there surely would have been if a woman had jumped off in broad daylight. No sign of anyone resembling Julia.

'Well, guv'nor? What about my fare, then?'

Will pulled out his pocket book and handed up a note without looking at the driver, his eyes scanning the northern approaches of the bridge. 'Wait.'

'For that money, guv'nor, I'll sit here all day.'

Will gripped the parapet and tried to assess what was best to do when all he wanted was to rush on to Blackfriars Bridge. She did not know London, but she had read the guidebooks, would know that Westminster was the nearest bridge to Mayfair. And she could expect to get here before he found the note. But she should have arrived by now, even at the normal pace of a cab horse.

He would have to risk leaving his post here. 'Blackfriars. As fast as you can make it.'

Up Whitehall, along Strand, down the hill to the foot of Ludgate Hill and then down to the river and the bridge. Again, only the bustle of everyday life greeted him. Will stood looking down at the dark water rushing beneath and thought about his first sight of Julia, a pale grey ghost in the moonlight, leaning on the bridge over the lake. And he had feared she would jump and drown herself, of all the ironies.

It was as though he could hear the nightingale again, feel her arms around him, holding him against her warm body. And as if she spoke in his ear he heard her voice.

I cannot imagine ever being desperate enough to do that, she had replied when he told her he had thought she was about to jump. *Drowning must be such terror. Besides, there is always some hope.*

Will dragged the note from his pocket and smoothed it flat on the worn Portland stone. The threat to kill herself was a feint, a clever bluff, all implication. And no lies. And he had fallen for it. The hope that surged back into him made him dizzy for a moment until he realised he still had no idea where to find Julia.

'You all right, guv'nor?' When Will looked up at him the driver scratched his stubbled chin and frowned back. 'Not choosing the best bridge to jump off, are you?'

'No. I have lost someone,' Will said. He needed help. Rushing about like a headless chicken was not going to answer in a city the size of London. 'Take me to the Bow Street offices.'

A busy coaching inn was the ideal hiding place, Julia realised as she closed the door of the cramped chamber and listened to the bustle and racket from the yard below. It was the one place where a woman alone was not conspicuous, for it was full of them, some modestly bonneted and cloaked, clutching their battered portmanteaux—servants and

governesses, she supposed. Some were fine
ladybirds, dressed to the nines and out to attract attention, others were harassed wives
and mothers with a baby in their arms or
fractious children at their heels.

The coaches came and went, the tide of
passengers ebbed and flowed and she felt
safe from detection for the first time in
hours. Desolate, lonely, heartbroken and
frightened. But at least no one would find
her here.

What was Will thinking now? How was
he feeling? Betrayed, of course. He believed
she had deceived him and she had. He believed she had lied about loving him and that,
Julia realised, hurt more than anything. And
he loved King's Acre and he was having to
face the fact that the woman he had thought
would help him save it would smear it with
the stain of blood and disgrace.

She wanted to write to him, to justify herself, to try to convince him that she truly
loved him. But that would not help him, all
it would be was a small, selfish, balm to her
smarting conscience. Now she had to plan
for where she would go to if she could silence Arthur and Jane and what she should
do if she could not.

* * *

Bow Street was home to the Runners, and they would be a danger, but it also attracted a motley crowd of thief-takers and informants who hung around in the hope of commissions, legal and semi-legal. They would think nothing of being sent to every coaching inn in search of a carefully described woman who had bought a ticket and left town that day.

Will had paid twenty of them better than they asked and promised more for results, then went to the hotel to wait. The inaction was hellish. Worse was the nagging fear that he might be wrong, that Julia might even now be floating in the muddy waters of the Thames.

No, he told himself for the tenth time. She would not give up, she was a fighter. But man after man came to him and reported nothing. Women answering her description had been seen, but not buying stage or mail-coach tickets. Nor had any of the carriers sold places on their slow, heavy wagons. She was still in London and that, he was all too aware, would make her far harder to track.

Will paid them, then sent them back out to check again in the morning, pushed his dinner around the plate, left it away uneaten and tried to rest. He could not let her hang, he knew. Whatever the cost, whatever the consequences, he would find her and get her out of the country.

Why? he wondered, suddenly shaken out of his circle of dark thoughts. Why risk everything, his good name, King's Acre? The answer came with shocking clarity. *Because I love her and nothing else matters.*

He needed to rest because Julia needed him. Will took off his boots and his coat, lay down on the bed, tried to come to terms with that shattering piece of self-knowledge and attempted to sleep through nightmares of Newgate and the gallows, the look of stunned misery on Julia's face as he had hurled those bitter words at her that morning, the smug, blackmailing faces of her cousins.

There was something there, something his mind fretted at and yet could not quite grasp. In the floating state somewhere between sleep and waking Will lay still and let his thoughts chase the puzzle. Something had not been right, something had been out of kilter. But when? The answer flicked out of sight whenever he seemed close, like a

shadow vanishing from the corner of his eye
when he turned to confront it.

Surprise. It had something to do with surprise. Shock. No, that was not quite right, he
was missing the point somehow. Frustrated,
Will thumped the pillow, turned over and,
somehow, managed to sleep.

The sun was bright on the gilded cross
atop St Paul's as the Mail clattered on to
the yard of the General Receiving Office.
Julia joined the crowd of travellers emerg-
ing from the numerous inns all around making their way towards the Receiving Office
to take the morning coaches out, or to continue their journey by hackney carriage or
on foot. A restless night had left her aching
and weary, but Julia set off towards the great
dome, thankful at least for a landmark. Once
she found the cathedral then she only had to
go down Ludgate Hill and turn into the Old
Bailey and there would be the inn where she
had seen her cousins watching the execution.

Her tired brain went over and over the ar-
guments she had worked out during the long
night. Firstly she would appeal to their good
nature, then to the threat of scandal to themselves, tarred by association with her. If nei-

ther of those worked, well, then she would threaten to hand herself in at Bow Street and to implicate them as accessories.

And if that failed? She still did not know whether, if that happened she would have the courage to surrender herself and trust to a jury to believe she had acted in self-defence. But if she did not, could she spend her whole life running?

Whatever happened, she thought as she trod across the cobbled path through St Paul's churchyard, Will could not be implicated. It was bad enough that he would be seen as a man deceived, but she would not allow him to become implicated as the scandalous baron who knew of his wife's crime, but who did nothing.

There were the shops she had stared into so light-heartedly only a few days ago. There, busy now with the passage of lawyers, servants with their marketing baskets, bankers and tradesmen, was the opening into the Old Bailey. There were no hangings today and if it were not for the ominous bulk of the prison at the end of the street, and the stench in the air when the wind changed to blow from that direction, she would think it a pleasant enough district.

Opposite her was the King's Head and Oak, its sign of the crowned oak tree that had sheltered Charles II swinging in the light breeze. No baying onlookers hung from the windows. It looked respectable and well kept, a suitable lodging for minor gentry come to the city.

There was a bay tree in a pot by the front door, she saw as she hesitated there. Perhaps this was the last time she would walk outside as a free woman. Julia reached out and broke off a twig, crushed the aromatic leaf between her fingers as she entered and summoned up the dregs of her courage.

'Mr and Mrs Prior, if you please,' she said to the man who came out of the taproom as she entered. 'Tell them Lady...tell them Miss Prior is here.'

They kept her waiting only a few minutes, which was a mercy for she was not certain which would go first: her nerve, to send her fleeing down towards the Fleet, or her legs, to leave her huddled on the floor.

The man came back before either happened. 'You're to follow me, if you please, miss.'

The old wooden stairs were well waxed, she noted as she climbed. Every trivial detail was imprinted on her senses. The man's apron was clean, but his shoes were dusty and he had been eating onions. That picture hanging on the wall at the head of the stairs, so dirty it was impossible to tell the subject, was crooked. They were boiling cabbage below in the kitchens. Her guide tapped on a door, opened it and she stepped into a small parlour. Her relatives regarded her with identical expressions of supercilious amusement as she tried to control both her breathing and her face.

'I'll not pretend I am not surprised to see *you*,' Cousin Jane said, her over-plucked eyebrows lifting as she took in the sight in front of her. 'Where's his lordship?'

'I am here on my own account.' Julia looked at Arthur, who lounged in a carved chair before the empty hearth. He had not troubled to get to his feet as she entered and the deliberate insult somehow steadied both her nerve and voice. For three years she had been Lady Dereham, used to receiving respect and courtesy—she was no longer the poor, subservient, relation.

'I am sure that, having thought this over, you cannot wish to betray me to the law, not when you know full well I was deceived and forced by Jonathan Dalfield.' That was her first suggestion, the one she knew they would ignore.

'There's no evidence of force. No one else was in the room, were they? No witnesses.' Arthur folded his hands over his small paunch and smiled benignly. 'You're all alone, Cousin. Left you, has he? The baron, I mean. Can't stomach what you did, or just doesn't like being tricked into marrying used goods?'

Julia ignored him. Jane, after all, was the one who always wanted to keep up appearances. She tried her next bargaining chip. 'Do you want the scandal to attach to your name, Cousin Jane?' she demanded.

'We will appear as the poor, deceived relatives who took you into our home and were grossly imposed upon,' Mrs Prior said, perfectly composed. 'How were we to know that you were a vicious, immoral little slut who was capable of such things?'

Well, that seemed to dispose of both appeals to their good nature. Time for threats. 'If you hand me over to the law, then my husband will not pay you a penny and I will tell the magistrates that you were accessories.'

Arthur shrugged. 'Your husband will pay

up, never fear. That sort will do anything to safeguard their honour and good name.'

That seemed to dispose of the one feeble threat she could make. Julia realised she was not surprised. Her stomach felt entirely hollow and yet she had passed beyond fear. 'Very well. I shall go to Bow Street and surrender myself. And while I am at it I will report you both for extortion.' *Would I?* She realised she simply did not know.

Then, as Arthur still smirked, Julia's fragile hold on her nerves snapped into temper. 'I mean it. I will not have you threatening and impoverishing the man I love and as the only way to avoid that seems to be to expose this whole dreadful situation I will do my damnedest to see you are dragged down with me. And I promise you, Lord Dereham will make your life hell on earth from now onwards.'

That got through. 'Wait.' Arthur rose to his feet. 'Now there's no need to be hasty.' With a glimmer of hope she saw there was sweat beading his brow now.

'You want to negotiate, do you?' Julia said. 'Unfortunately I do not deal with—'

The inner door opened and a man strolled out from the bedchamber beyond. *Will*, an irrational voice in her head said and her heart leapt. Then he stepped fully into the room and she saw his eyes were cold, unreadable blue, not hot amber fire. This was a tall, dark ghost with a streak of pure white slashing through the forelock that fell on to his brow.

'Perhaps you would like to deal with me instead, Julia,' Jonathan Dalfield said and smiled as the room swirled around her.

Chapter Twenty

I will not faint, Julia thought grimly and spun round to the door. Jonathan reached her before she could lift the latch, his strong hands turning her, dragging her up against him. He smelled as she remembered, of lime cologne and the Spanish snuff he favoured and the oil he used on his hair. It was a scent that had once made her head spin with desire.

'You are alive.' It was foolishly obvious, but it was hard to believe that this was a flesh-and-blood man. Not so hard to believe was the remembered pain of his grip on her wrist. So close she could see that the line of his jaw had softened, that there were pouches under his eyes. He looked more than three years older, more dissipated. If he had approached her now, she would have seen him for what he was.

'Alive, but no thanks to you, my dear.' His smile was feral, bitter with all semblance of charm vanished. Once she had thought herself in love with this man. She must have been desperate indeed.

How had he survived that blow to the head? There had been all that blood. But she did not believe in ghosts—her wrist hurt with an exquisite pain that told her she was not dreaming, so it must be true. 'Then let me go. You'll have no money for blackmail now, Jonathan. My husband knows I was no virgin when I came to him, he'll give you not a penny for whatever feeble scandal you think you can stir up.'

'So I will have to get my recompense for *this* some other way, Julia my dear.' He pushed back the hair from his forehead and she saw the scar, a red, puckered dent two inches long. 'Pretty, isn't it? And the headaches are not pretty either.'

'It is your fault, Jonathan Dalfield,' Julia threw at him. She felt giddy with relief that she had not killed him, but she could feel no regrets now for having hurt him—the man was even worse than she had thought. 'You deceived me, ravished me, tried to rape me. Do you believe I had no right to fight back?'

'Women don't fight back, they do as they're told,' he said and smiled as cold ice trickled down her spine. Her anger was congealing into fear and she struggled not to let that show on her face. Bullies fed on fear, she knew that. 'I didn't get much fun for my pains last time. Now, I can only hope you've learned a trick or two from your baron.'

Julia saw it in his eyes, the truth that he was more than capable of dragging her into that bedchamber and ravishing her all over again. No one who cared for her knew she was there, Will thought she was dead, she had walked into this trap of her own volition. No one was going to get her out of it if she could not.

Julia curled her free fingers into talons and lashed out even as she realised that Jonathan had been expecting just that. He caught her arm and pulled her in close, so tight she could hardly struggle, then freed his grip on her wrist so he could hold her with one arm while he forced her chin up. She bared her teeth at him.

'You'll smile for me nicely, my dear, unless you want gaps in those pretty teeth,' he said. 'And if you bite, I can promise you a whipping.'

He bent his head and took her mouth with his, the same mouth she had sought to place shy, loving kisses on when they were courting. Julia tightened her lips, resisted the thrust of his tongue. She was going to survive this and she would see him brought to justice for what he had done. Now she could only endure.

At her back the door slammed open like the crack of doom. 'Jonathan Dalfield, I presume? Take your hands off my wife or I will break your neck,' said a voice she scarcely recognised.

Jonathan freed her with a shove that sent her reeling across the room hard against Will's chest. She grasped his forearms, looked up into burning amber eyes and saw nothing but murder there. 'Will, thank God—'

Will glanced down at her, one searching, scorching stare. 'Thank God I've found you. I did not expect to find you here.' He touched one finger to her cheek. 'He had his hands on you. His mouth.' Then he pushed her gently into the arms of the man who had followed him into the room and took a step forward.

'Will!'

'Never fear, Lady Dereham, you are safe now,' the man holding her said. He tried to bundle her out of the door but she stuck in her heels.

'Major Frazer?' How on earth had he got here? 'No, please stop pushing me, I must stay with Will.'

'There will be violence, ma'am,' the major said pedantically. 'It is no fit place for a lady.'

She simply ignored him. The Priors were standing together close to the bedchamber door, their faces white. Jonathan had backed up as far as the table and stood at bay, his hand at his side as though trying to grip the sword that was not there.

'You think that even if we had weapons I would duel with you as though you were a gentleman, a man of honour?' Will's voice dripped contempt.

'Julia ran back to me of her own free will,' Jonathan said. 'Why do you think she is here? Your quarrel is with her.'

'You seem to have a death wish,' Will observed. He pulled off his gloves, finger by finger, tossed them on to a chair, shrugged out of his greatcoat, laid that on top and added his hat, for all the world as though he was settling down for a comfortable chat. But

Julia could read him now and what she saw was cold, focused fury.

'Don't kill him,' she gasped.

'You see?' Jonathan's sneering voice was at odds with his white face. There was a nerve twitching in his cheek and he did not seem to know what to do with his hands. 'She would protect me.'

'Lady Dereham appears to think that you are not worth hanging for. She is probably correct.' Will took a step forwards. 'So I will just have to deal with you some other way. Frazer, get her out of here.'

'No!'

'I am very sorry, Lady Dereham.' Major Frazer picked Julia up bodily and marched out of the door, pushed it shut with his shoulder, then leaned against it when she lunged for the door handle. 'I apologise for the liberty, but that is no place for a lady.'

'There are three of them in there and Jonathan Dalfield will not fight fairly,' she panted, trying to reach the door handle, but the major was almost as solid as Will. There was a crash from inside the room.

'Will won't be fighting fairly either,' Major Frazer said with a grin that faded as he took in her distress. 'You forget I knew him in his army days. He duels like a gentleman, but he fights scum like a gutter rat. There is no cause for alarm, I promise you. Ah, landlord.'

Julia turned as the man came running up the stairs. 'What is going on, sir? I'll not stand for fighting and my rooms being smashed up! I'll call the constables, I warn you.'

'Excellent idea,' the major said. 'Send for them at once. Your guests have set on this lady's husband in an unprovoked manner— I can only hope they have sufficient money to pay for the damages.'

'But if the constables come they might arrest Will,' Julia protested, as the man turned and ran downstairs, shouting for the pot boy. The door at the major's back was hit with a massive crash that had him rocking on his feet.

'When they come, if we are still here, they will be met by me, in my capacity as a London magistrate, investigating a case of extortion and the forcible imprisonment of a lady. With any luck, we'll be away before it comes to that.'

'You are a magistrate?'

He nodded, his head half-turned as though listening. It had gone very quiet. 'Will knew I was at my town house. Ah, here we are.'

He stepped away from the door and Will came out. One eye was half-closed, there was a cut on his right cheekbone and his lip was split. 'Right, come on.' He clapped his hat on his head, shrugged into his greatcoat and took Julia's arm. 'My thanks to you for your support, Frazer. I owe you a good dinner, but you'll forgive me if we leave at once.'

'Will, your face—'

'Not here.' He took her arm and went briskly down the stairs and out onto the forecourt.

The major tipped his hat to Julia. 'Obedient servant, ma'am. Dereham.'

Will hailed a passing cab, bundled Julia into it without ceremony and called up, 'Grillon's Hotel', before climbing in beside her.

The vehicle rattled away down Ludgate Hill and Julia, speechless, simply stared at her husband. He was here, she was safe. She had killed no one. Julia dug her handkerchief out of her reticule and sat with it clenched in her hand, waiting for the tears of sheer relief to come. Strangely, they did not, nor did the rush of relief she experienced when she dreamed that everything was all right.

Will tossed his hat on to the seat beside him and took the handkerchief when she held it out to him. He dabbed at his cheek with some caution. 'Are you all right, Julia?'

'Am *I* all right!' She found her voice in a flood of anger that encompassed fear, anguish, anxiety and shocked relief all in one muddle of feeling. 'Yes, of course I am. Will, you might have been seriously injured, even killed.'

He raised one eyebrow, gave a wince at the unwary gesture and grinned, somewhat lop-sidedly. 'That is not very flattering, my dear. Your Mr Dalfield is licking his wounds and contemplating the warning I gave him and your cousins: go back to where they came from and never speak of this or approach you in any manner. If they do not comply, they will have a respected magistrate to vouch for their attempts at extortion.'

'Then it is really all over.' It did not seem possible that the nightmare that had haunted her waking and sleeping for over three years had simply dissolved into thin air.

Will nodded. 'I am hoping this is the last of your deep dark secrets, my love.' His face was serious, but his eyes smiled at her.

'I promise.' Had he really said *my love*? Most likely it was a careless endearment, or wishful thinking on her part. She was certainly feeling very strange. Light-headed, in fact, although with that came a certain clarity of thought. 'You were not surprised when you came into the room just now, were you? You said Jonathan's name without even having to think about it. How did you know?'

'I realised he was not dead in the early hours of this morning.' Will got up and changed seats so he could put his arm around her. Julia tried not to lean into him, anxious about cracked ribs, but the warmth of his body was like a balm to her own aching one.

'It was all about surprise, that was what had been niggling at the back of my mind ever since your cousins came to Grillon's. Their purpose was to blackmail us, of course. But all they threatened us with at first was scandal about your elopement and the fact that you had struck Dalfield. *Violence*, they said. Not murder, not killing. No one said anything about death or murder until you blurted out your confession. They mentioned Jonathan's *poor head*, not his dead body.

'They had come all prepared with a shocking tale of a woman who had lost her virtue and assaulted, and probably scarred, a man. They threatened to paint you as a woman who had run away from home, one whom society would be appalled to find as a baroness. They expected me to pay up simply to preserve our good name from unpleasant slurs.

'And then you said what you did. I was stunned. But so were they and that must have registered with me without my grasping the significance, fool that I am.'

'You could hardly be expected to notice nuances when you had just been told your wife had killed a man,' Julia said.

'I suppose not,' Will agreed. 'But Mrs Prior gasped and Prior was struck silent. It only took him a moment to recover his wits and for her to at least regain some composure, but it obviously registered somewhere in my brain.'

'I was not looking at them,' Julia murmured, and turned so she could see his profile. Will was miles away, looking back on that appalling scene, she could tell. 'I heard them but I was watching you.' *Only you, while my heart broke.*

'They had thought I would pay them a few hundred pounds to shut their mouths and go away, I'll wager that was the sum of their ambition. And then they found that you believed you had killed your lover. I have to give Arthur Prior credit, the man can think on his feet. With a brain like that he should be a lawyer. It was a gift to him and he knew what to do with it at once: tell the big lie, ask enough money, and it all becomes that much more convincing. And you, my darling, could not but help them because you believed it and I, knowing you were still hiding a secret, had believed the very worst of you.'

'How could I have been so mistaken?' Julia felt her mind clearing, her strength returning. Perhaps, like Will, she was having to come to terms with the fact that she had a future. The certainty she had lived with so long like a leech on her conscience had been disproved. It was hard to believe she was free. 'Jonathan looked so…dead.'

'All head wounds bleed dreadfully. You saw an unconscious man lying face down, his head laid open by an iron poker. He must have sprawled as still as death amidst scattered fire irons on the hearth. There was blood everywhere. You had experienced betrayal, fear, violence, all within minutes and you had done something utterly alien to you—struck another person. The room was suddenly full of cries of *Murder!* from an ignorant, excited crowd. I can see it as plainly as if I had been there.'

'If I had not assumed the worst and fled—'

'You might have been taken up for assault, for it would have been his word against yours and he was the one with the cut head. And besides, I would never have met you,' Will said as the carriage came to a halt. 'Of course, you may well say that all these years of anxiety and guilt were not worth it, but selfishly I hope you will come to think they were.'

Julia looked at him sharply, but Will was already on the pavement handing up money to the driver. 'Now, to get ourselves back up to our room without setting the entire place on its ear. If the manager gets sight of me, we will find ourselves and our bags out on the pavement, I have no doubt!' he added as he tried to cover the worst damage on his face with the linen square.

'I do not think I look much better,' Julia confessed as a page, trying hard not to stare, came to take her small valise. Mercifully, although there were hotel staff a-plenty to negotiate, they did not encounter the manager or any guests on their way up to the room.

'Oh, my lady! My lord. I was that worried, I didn't know what to do!' Nancy, started to her feet as they entered their sitting room.

She had a basket of mending at her feet, but it did not seem she had been doing much to it.

Julia did her best to calm her down, although for the life of her she could not think of a convincing explanation to offer the maid other than a rather garbled story of family emergency and footpads.

Her head spun with suppositions and hopes and fears, but she allowed Nancy to lead her away to bathe and to change, leaving Will to deal with his own *toilette* in the minuscule dressing room. She suspected they both needed time before the full meaning of these revelations could be faced and she sensed that her husband did not want wifely fussing over what he was trying to dismiss as minor injuries.

'You are a pearl amongst wives,' Will said. He laid down his knife and fork after what she supposed was a cross between breakfast and luncheon and lifted his wine glass in a silent toast to her.

'I am?'

'You do not prattle and cling when the sensible thing to do is wash and change and eat.'

'Now I may do more than prattle,' Julia said. 'I do not know where to start.'

'At the beginning,' Will suggested. 'We have our lives back, both of us. Do you want to live the remainder of yours with me?'

'Of course.' That was the last question she had expected him to ask. 'I love you—do you not believe me?'

'I was just getting used to the idea when you ran away from me.' But he was teasing her, she could see. All the darkness was gone from his eyes and his mouth curved in a smile despite its bruising.

'I could not let you suffer for what I thought was my crime,' she said.

'I know. I am not sure what I have done to deserve that you should put me first, before your own safety, your own life.'

How do I explain to a man why I love him when I cannot even analyse it myself? 'Will, you do not even seem angry with me after all I have put you through.'

Will stood up, took her hand and led her through to the bedchamber. 'That must be because I am in love with you,' he remarked as he closed the door.

'What?' Julia spun round so fast she lost her balance and sat down on the end of the bed. 'Did you say—'

'I said I was in love with you.' Will sounded

thoughtful. 'Actually, I should have said *I love you* because I believe there is a difference. I have never felt like this for any other woman. Nor will I,' he added. 'I suspect I have been lamentably slow in realising it, my love.'

'When did you? Realise it, I mean.' *After he realised I was innocent—or before?*

Will turned the key in the lock. 'The sooner we are back in our own home and our own bed, the better,' he grumbled as he began to undress. 'When did I realise? I will tell you in a minute, but let me try to recount this as it happened. None of it was a blinding revelation, more a piecing together of pieces. After I had left you in this room, after I had said those things to you that I hope you have it in you to forgive, I sat and drank brandy and realised that you could never have killed a man in cold blood, or even intended to kill him in hot blood either. I realised that it must have been an accident and once I saw that I could understand how it all followed on— your flight, why you had kept it a secret.'

He trusted her. He had trusted her even when he believed she could bring his world crashing down around his ears. How could she not love him?

'When I found that note I believed it, at

first. You frightened me half to death with that tarradidle about suicide and the Thames.' He heeled his boots off with scant regard for scratches on their glossy finish and tossed them across the room. 'Hell, woman, I was on Blackfriars bridge before I started to think straight and remembered what you said about throwing yourself in the lake when we first met. And then I looked at the letter and saw it was so very carefully constructed not to tell any lies.

'I did not think you would risk trying to hide in London, so the next thing was to see if you had taken a stagecoach out of town. I had men checking every ticket office. They drew a blank so I knew you must still be in town, but I didn't understand why.' Will sat on the bed beside her to roll down his stockings.

'I knew then that if I lost you nothing would ever matter again. Not my own life, not an estate, however much I loved it. Even a block-headed male can put two and two together faced with that realisation. I went to sleep despite the shock of realising that I loved my own wife and woke to the realisation that the Priors knew Dalfield was alive.'

He rubbed one big hand over his face, betraying in that gesture the hours of anxiety, the lack of rest. 'I still had no idea where you were, but I thought I had best deal with the Priors first, so I told Neil Frazer all about it and enlisted his help as a magistrate in case I needed more than brute force. And there, thank God, you were.'

Julia stroked her hand down his cheek, gently over the bruises, feeling the morning stubble prickling under her palm. *He loves me and he would love me even if the worst had been true.* She supposed it was possible to feel this happy and for it not to be a dream. 'You found me. I think you would always find me.'

Will pulled off his shirt and stood to unfasten his breeches. Julia scrambled out of her own clothes, careless of pulled buttons, and looked up from unlacing her stays to find him naked, bruised all over his torso and flagrantly aroused. 'Those bruises! Will, they must hurt so—'

'Then take my mind off them and do not try to test your theory that I can always find you by running away again. It ruins my sleep,' he added as he joined her on the wide bed.

Julia gave a little snort of laughter and

kissed his collarbone, the nearest part of him she could reach. *Ah, the smell of his skin...*

'That is good—I was wondering if I would ever hear you laugh again.'

'I like this, having you naked and at a disadvantage,' she murmured, pursuing the line of the bone to the point of his shoulder and biting gently. 'Tired and battered, my poor love. I can have my wicked way with you.'

'Disadvantage?' He rolled her over with a mock growl and pounced, wrestling with the squirming, laughing, woman and the loose tapes of the corset. 'It would take more than a few bruises and a disturbed night to weaken me.'

Julia lay back with a contented sigh of agreement as Will began to kiss his way down her body. He paused to twirl his tongue in her navel, which always made her giggle, then raised his head. 'Talking of disturbed nights, do you feel any more comfortable with the idea of children?' He spoke lightly, but she could sense his underlying hesitation in case he hurt her.

'I feel very comfortable with that idea, my lord,' she said. 'In fact, I think we may have already begun the process. I am not certain, but I have hopes.'

Will moved so fast she hardly had time to blink. One moment she had been sprawled in sensual abandon, the next she was under the covers in Will's arms and he was holding her as cautiously as he might a basket of eggs. 'Will! I am not fragile.' Julia twisted to try to caress him, show him that she wanted, above everything, to make love.

'Are you sure you are all right?' His forehead was furrowed with worry lines she had never seen before. 'It must have been bad enough, these past days, but to have gone through all you have if you are carrying a child—'

'I am fine,' Julia said. 'And I might not be expecting, we need to wait a day or two more in case it is simply stress disrupting my system. But I do not want to wait to make love to my husband.'

Will's face relaxed. 'I suppose we could. Just in the interests of securing the succession, you understand, now we cannot rely on Henry.'

The words *You know?* were on the tip of her tongue. Julia bit them back just in time, but Will smiled. 'That was another thing that I thought about yesterday. It helped distract me when I was going insane worrying about you. I realised, when I was thinking with my heart, instead of…other parts of my anatomy, that I trusted you. I also thought about Henry dispassionately and not as simply my rather irritating heir and put two and two together. I may have made six, of course.'

'No, you have not.' Julia snuggled close against Will's flank and inched her fingers across his flat stomach. 'It will not be easy for him, but I have encouraged him to take chambers in London, where the presence of just one close servant would not be remarked upon. Are you shocked? I am sorry if you do not approve.'

'I am not shocked, so much as anxious for him. But you have given him good advice. And now, having settled Henry's love life to your satisfaction, might we resume our own?'

'I thought I was,' Julia murmured, closing her fingers around the evidence of her husband's desire.

Will laughed and rolled on to his back, taking her with him. 'Ravish me, then.'

His eyes were golden, laughing, clear of any shadow. She had never seen them like that, Julia realised as she knelt astride the slim hips and took him into her body with a sigh of pure happiness. 'I cannot remember when I felt so content, so free of anxiety. So *joyous.* I love you very much, Will. I thought I would never be able to make love with you again.'

He pulled her down so he could raise his head to meet her lips and smiled up at her. At the look she melted, yielding and as boneless as a swathe of velvet. 'We've been though hell to get here, my love. I think we are owed our little piece of paradise on earth. We will kiss and we will love and then we will sleep and then we will go home and be happy.'

'For ever?'

'I am prepared to devote the next eighty years to it,' Will said. 'We can review things after that.'

'Very well, my lord,' Julia agreed and sank into his arms and his kiss and delicious contentment.

Author's Note

My grateful thanks go to Dr Joanna Cannon for her explanations of how the symptoms of severe post-viral syndrome would have been interpreted by Regency doctors. With no concept of the condition they would have confused it with *Phthisis*, the normal term at the time for consumption, or tuberculosis, which was fatal throughout the nineteenth-century. Will's recovery would have been greatly hastened by the treatment he received—rest in a warm, dry climate, a good diet and skilled medical attention.

Julia was right to fear the consequences of the law if she had killed Jonathan Dalfield, however unintentionally. The reference to the woman hanged, whose body was then handed over to the anatomists in Aylesbury, is to the real case of the sister-in-law of one of my Regency ancestors who appears to have snapped after years of abuse. Society's horror of such 'unfeminine' violence is reflected in the severity of the sentence.

* * * * *

A sneaky peek at next month...

HISTORICAL

IGNITE YOUR IMAGINATION, STEP INTO THE PAST...

My wish list for next month's titles...

In stores from 7th February 2014:

❏ Portrait of a Scandal — Annie Burrows

❏ Drawn to Lord Ravenscar — Anne Herries

❏ Lady Beneath the Veil — Sarah Mallory

❏ To Tempt a Viking — Michelle Willingham

❏ Mistress Masquerade — Juliet Landon

❏ The Major's Wife — Lauri Robinson

Available at WHSmith, Tesco, Asda, Eason, Amazon and Apple

Just can't wait?

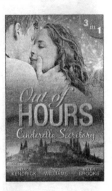

The Regency Ballroom Collection

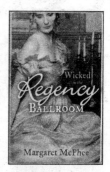

A twelve-book collection led by Louise Allen
and written by the top authors and rising
stars of historical romance!

Classic tales of scandal and seduction in
the Regency ballroom

**Take your place on the ballroom floor now, at:
www.millsandboon.co.uk**

Discover more romance at

www.millsandboon.co.uk